MATT'S MURDER

MATT'S MURDER

Patricia A. Guthrie

Fresh Ink Group
Guntersville

Matt's Murder

Copyright © 2025
by Patricia A. Guthrie
All rights reserved

Fresh Ink Group
An Imprint of:
The Fresh Ink Group, LLC
1021 Blount Avenue #931
Guntersville, AL 35976
Email: info@FreshInkGroup.com
FreshInkGroup.com

Edition 1.0 2024

Cover design by Stephen Geez / FIG
Book design by Amit Dey / FIG
Associate publisher Beem Weeks / FIG

Cataloging-in-Publication Recommendations:
FIC031010 FICTION / Thrillers / Crime
FIC030000 FICTION / Thrillers / Suspense
FIC050000 FICTION / Crime

Library of Congress Control Number: 2024922201

ISBN-13: 978-1-964998-27-5 Softcover
ISBN-13: 978-1-964998-28-2 Hardcover
ISBN-13: 978-1-964998-29-9 Ebooks

CHAPTER 1

Tony Richardson sat at his computer desk, alternately working on his monthly accounts and looking at his vast pastureland. He'd put the desk in the corner of his study, flanked on two sides by windows so he could stare at his horses all day if he wished. It was his business, but it was also his heart. He never wanted to be out of touch with his horses, the barn, land, and friends. The view helped.

It was a bitter April day in Central Illinois, and the mounds of snow had already accumulated from the year's worst storm. Freezing air penetrated aging windows, and he shivered as he watched dark clouds rolling in from the horizon bloated with new precipitation. Feeling disconcerted, he glanced at the picture perched on his computer monitor—the woman's smiling face made his sad, dark eyes brood all the more. Lost in thoughts of broken dreams, he might have moped for hours, but the doorbell buzz shattered the silence.

"Mr. Richardson?"

Two men in dark blue suits stood on the porch as Tony opened his farmhouse door. They both wore grim faces and held DEA identification badges.

"Yeah? What can I do for you?"

"We have a warrant for your arrest."

"You have what? What do you mean?"

"We want to come in." The darker-skinned gentleman took a small step over the threshold. "Now."

Tony stepped back and let them in, the color draining from his face.

They followed Tony into his living room and made tracks on Navaho area rugs, not even bothering to look down at the damage.

"You had two horses shipped to Texas this morning?" The taller one with blond hair, who looked like he might fit in with the Wall Street stock exchange crowd, pulled out a DEA badge and held it up for Tony.

The other one, a darker-skinned gentleman, looked like he was giving directions.

"Yeah, what of it?"

"Mr. Richardson, your driver, Eddie Meeks, was stopped at the Kentucky border and arrested for possession of cocaine. This truck and trailer were registered to you, and Mr. Meeks confirmed it. You'd better come with us."

"Come where?" Tony shook, then dropped his head. "Me? Cocaine? What the...?" His mind flew in a flurry of activity—but nothing could come out of his mouth. Fear gripped him, causing a punching sensation in the pit of his stomach. "Dear God, protect me."

They led him out of his house toward the long white stable where they'd left their car.

As a black van roared up the driveway, all three men turned in unison. A sable and white collie head stuck out the window like a wall trophy. The officers waved the van away, but a young woman with red hair and huge green eyes jumped out.

"Tony, I'm here to see my horse." She smiled at him but looked wary at the other two agents. They stared back, not returning her smile.

"Who are you?" Mr. Wall Street lifted his badge directed toward her.

The other one, who had a grasp on Tony, took a step behind her.

"What?" Her face didn't move, but the shift of her gaze followed the agent as he moved toward her back.

"I'm Julie Bishop. I don't understand. I was…"

Tony wriggled out of the second agent's grasp. "Look, she has nothing to do with this. She's just here to see her horse, nothing more. Julie, you can go ahead and get him… the first stall in the barn."

Concern gripped Julie's face. "Tony, what's wrong? Are you in trouble?"

"No, nothing I can't handle. Just a slight misunderstanding. I must go with them. I'll call my lawyer. Don't worry, Julie. I'll be all right."

Tony got into the agent's car as his cousin and newest client stood staring after him. This had not been a good day.

"What am I going to do? I didn't do it, Arthur. How the hell can I prove it? I'm not a drug dealer. I've never so much as smoked a joint. Someone's framed me. I don't know who, and I don't know why."

Tony paced back and forth across his living room, stopping periodically to catch his breath. Tony's lawyer, Arthur Ashford, sat in respectful silence, letting him vent. The last twenty-four hours had been a long series of downward spiraling events descending into Hell. He wasn't sure he could withstand it anymore.

"Arthur, I'm a horseman, not a drug dealer."

"I know you wouldn't deal in drugs. I believe you, but you need to quiet down. Nothing was ever settled by letting your emotions get out of control. You have to think straight, Tony."

Arthur always managed to maintain composure. That, combined with salt and pepper hair and a face graced with wrinkles, gave him character. If anyone could save him, it was Arthur Ashford. For many years, he'd been like a second father to Tony and his brother, Greg.

Damn, my brother, I'm glad he's out of town. Tony ran his hands through his thick dark hair, mussed it up, fingered it back in place, and continued to pace.

"Tony, think back. Is there anyone who might have it in for you? Someone that has a grudge against you?"

"No, or, well, I can't think of any." He hesitated for a minute.

"Are you sure? Is there something you're not telling me?" Arthur looked at him with a piercing stare.

It made Tony uncomfortable.

"Let's go back over this again. You say you picked up those horses from the Carters. When?"

"Again? I've been through this a hundred times." He took a deep breath, then sighed. "Okay. I picked them up on Monday. I have a client in Kentucky who wanted two well-trained horses for their kids. Paul Carter hauled the three animals over here on Monday morning."

"Three?"

"Oh, yeah. They only wanted two mares. Brenda found a good horse for my cousin. She came to see him this morning just as they hauled me away. Awful." He shrugged his shoulders. "Eddie Meeks, you know my ranch hand, Eddie…"

Arthur nodded.

"Anyway, I loaded the other two, and Eddie drove out early yesterday morning. The police pulled me over at the border. That's all I know." He dropped onto a leather couch facing his lawyer and stared as if in a stupor.

Arthur went over to a Victorian sidebar where Tony kept a fine gun collection and a relatively sparse stock of liquor. He poured a glass of scotch and handed it to Tony.

"Drink!"

With shaking hands, Tony took the glass and gulped it down. He coughed.

"You shouldn't drink that stuff so fast, Tony."

"I don't drink." Tony chuckled, frowned, and then went back to brooding. "But I'm drinking now. I'll spend the night praying. I think they'll throw the damn key away if they convict me," Tony said. "They've got evidence." He shifted, unable to get comfortable, and continued. "Even though it was planted."

"Could it have been Eddie? He certainly had the opportunity. The police were grilling him harder than they were grilling you."

Tony raised his head and blinked. "They did?" He slammed his hand on the coffee table. "And implicated me. Why would he do that?" He winced and held his bruised hand. "It must have been him. He could be working for someone else. I don't think he has the brains to pull off something like this alone."

Arthur flinched when Tony struck the table. "You could be right about Eddie working for someone."

"Eddie? Man, I can't believe he would do this."

"No, of course not. You wouldn't."

"What?" Tony looked at Arthur blankly, then shook his head as if he didn't understand Arthur's remark. "I need to talk to him. Do you have the number over at Forest View Station?"

Tony picked up the phone, glanced at Arthur, and slowly replaced the receiver in its cradle. "Arthur, what's wrong?"

Arthur hesitated. "I didn't want to worry you. Detective Swanson called me after I returned from dropping you off last night. Eddie got bailed out and left about an hour after we did. He was supposed to go to his lawyer. He never showed up and disappeared. They're still looking for him."

Tony looked startled, then said, "He hasn't come back here."

"You sure?"

"Not today. He stays in the apartment Dad built over the stable. I'd know for sure if he'd come back here… I think." He picked up the phone again and dialed the intercom. "No answer." Tony put the phone down. "Arthur, I'm really in trouble." He slunk miserably back down onto the chair.

"Here's what I want you to do, Tony. Please make me a list of all the people you know and what they do. Include everyone you've had contact with this month—all of them. Then, think about all the people who might have some grudge against you, as remote as it might be. Also, think about Eddie. Who does he know? Who are his friends? Then, we'll go through it and see what crops up. Okay?"

"Okay… okay. I didn't know Eddie had any friends." He shrugged and scrunched his eyebrows together.

Arthur left, leaving Tony alone to deal with his thoughts. The old farmhouse seemed so empty—now filled only with memories. It had been a happy home—a home to bring a new wife and raise future generations. Although he had someone in mind, he thought he might make new memories from a prison cell. He returned to his study and started sorting out all the people in his life, making lists and notes.

He looked out the window over his pastures in his study, watching his horses playing in the snow. His life. His love. His girlfriend. Now—what?

A silhouetted figure hid in the doorway of the stable, focusing on Tony Richardson's study--observing. The window was large, and no blinds disturbed the view. Tony's profile shaded the window, revealing his movements. It was risky at best.

The individual strolled along the path leading from the barn to the white farmhouse, taking care not to be seen and feeling cocky and confident in the success of the plan. Taking off cold-weather gloves and switching to a pair of tight, black ones, that person cautiously tried the front door and, finding it unlocked, stepped inside.

The intruder silently crossed the living room to the gun cabinet and selected one of Tony's prized guns—perfect for the job.

With grim determination, he followed Tony noiselessly across the soft carpet.

"Hi, Tony!"

Startled, Tony whirled around, and just as his head turned, the assassin pulled the trigger.

Tony's head crashed onto the desk.

With a sense of satisfaction, the killer placed the gun in Tony's right hand and leaned over the body, taking care to avoid blood splatters on the cross above his desk.

'Sorry, Greg. I cannot live with this drug conviction on my conscience. God bless. You've been a great brother. Tony.'

"Ha!" The killer grinned at the pseudo-confession, looked around the room, noticed the picture of Tony's ex, snatched it, sauntered out of the room, and ambled out of the house.

CHAPTER 2

Julie Bishop sat astride Socks, her sixteen-hand, gray gelding, observing her surroundings and trying to manipulate a cup of hot coffee and reins simultaneously. She wasn't succeeding. The coffee splattered as the horse shifted his weight, and she burned her mouth as a sip turned into a gulp. To make matters worse, her nerves were beginning to get to her. The annual Forest View Quarter Horse Show was about to start, and she was having a tough time breathing naturally and not turning all prickly at the thought of competing against the best horses the Midwest had to offer.

A cool breeze blew in from Lake Michigan over the historic Fairgrounds, a brief sabbatical from the sweltering morning. It was only seven-thirty, and the temperature read 80 degrees. Local weather reports expected another scorcher in an already long string of torrid June days.

Horses loped past, glistening with sweat. Their coats provided an interesting backdrop for expensive saddles loaded with silver trim. Julie knew many of these animals cost more than she made all year as a teacher and above-average mystery writer.

Trailers and horse vans filled the crowded parking area. The logos on their sides displayed names of ranches and horse farms famous in show circles—Fireside Farms, Windemere Acres, Eagle Ranch…Eagle Ranch? Could it be her cousin, Greg Richardson, was here? A year had passed with little word about how Greg was doing since the death of his brother, Tony. A cloud passed over the sun, and Julie suddenly shivered. *Someone just walked over my grave.*

Suddenly, seemingly out of nowhere, a horse and rider charged at her, sliding to a stop within inches. Her horse kicked out, forcing Julie to spill the remainder of her coffee, partly on her leg and partly on her horse. He laid his ears back and snorted.

Matthew Carter reined in a bay gelding and laughed. "Hi, Red."

"Damn it, Matt, that was stupid." She tried to pat the coffee off her horse and her leg.

"Oops." Matt's cheekbones raised into a grin. "Sorry if I startled you. I just came over to see how you were doing. It's your first big show. Brenda's got you in the amateur division, huh?"

"Yes, of course, she does, and don't call me Red. I hate that." *What an idiot. He seems to know just how to yank someone's chain—the wrong way.* She became increasingly uncomfortable when she realized Matt's attention wasn't focused on her hair but on her black tank top. He was grinning, flirting, and not caring who might be watching.

"Socks looks pretty good. What did you put on his coat to make him shine like that? "

"Just an old ladies' shampoo I picked up at Walgreens."

Matt continued to talk, but Julie's thoughts switched back to the show ring. Another breeze fluttered over the grounds and brought the fragrance of wet grass from the previous night's rains, mingling with smells of horse feed, hay, and sawdust from the nearby horse barns. Julie was in love with it all. It was what horses were all about—that and riding.

She turned her attention toward the judge's stand and did a double take. Her cousin was there making entries. She drew an intake of breath, and Matt took notice, swerving sharply around for a look.

"So, Greg's here, is he?"

Julie reacted so fast to Matt's seemingly misplaced hostility that shooting spasms blasted up her neck, causing her to wince in pain.

Greg Richardson looked just like his older brother did a year ago. He was good-looking, dark—almost olive skin with brooding, dark eyes—and his face taut as though strained with memories of his dead brother. Suddenly, Julie felt a premonition of overwhelming disaster and wanted to cry.

A voice startled her from behind, and the moment passed as quickly as it had come. "Hi, Julie." Matt's wife, Brenda, had ridden up behind them.

"Gotta go," Matt said, whirling his horse around and loping to the other side of the ring.

"What in the world was that all about?" Julie said, intrigued by Matt's sudden flight.

"We had another fight, and…" she pointed in the direction of the horse barns, "that," she added, pointing at a woman coming up to the arena gate.

"Lynette," Julie said.

"Lynette," Brenda repeated. "Julie, she's having an affair with him."

Julie didn't know what to say. It had been the gossip around the barn for months, probably starting when Julie and Lynette had been forced to move away from Eagle Ranch when it closed.

"God, what a fool."

"Maybe. I've offered to give him a divorce, but he refused. She wants him to divorce me so she can marry him. I wish the hell he would, Julie. Why does he want me hanging around? If he's not happy, then call it quits."

"Who else would train his horses? And Matt flirts with everyone. He was flirting with me—actually, with my *boobs*—when you rode up."

"I noticed," Brenda said, making a face.

"I didn't encourage him."

"No. No. I didn't mean to imply that you did," Brenda said. "I'd never think that about you."

"I just mean, Matt seems to have a way with women, and he's good-looking. He's not going to leave you for her. He can't. You're his bread and butter. He'll have his fling, then dump her."

After a short pause, Brenda's tone softened. "Poor Lynette."

Julie looked at her friend, surprised.

"I mean, she's as much his possession as I am. That's all we are to Matt. Possessions. So's his brother. Look at Paul over there. He's doing his job, and Matt is doing it as well. Who's hauling all that equipment? Paul is."

Julie turned toward the parking area to see a slightly shorter version of Matt, with slightly blonder hair and bluer eyes, removing equipment from their van.

Brenda continued. "The only one that escaped was Tom. If I had a drink, I'd raise my glass to him."

"Tom?"

"The middle brother. The black sheep who left his horses to become an actor."

"Okay… right." Julie tried to remember the stories about the middle brother but couldn't. "Why did he leave?"

"Long story, Julie. Remind me to tell you sometime. For now, just bad blood between him and Matt, and a blowout with his father."

They continued to watch Matt talking to Lynette by the gate.

"Meanwhile, she stays at the barn and causes trouble. I hate her, Julie." Brenda was biting her lip, wiping her eyes with her sleeve. "And I hate *hating* anyone."

"No, it's Matt's fault. I wish he'd go away or… just die. I wish he were dead, Julie. Then, I could… Oh damn." Brenda suddenly choked and nudged her bay horse into a jog.

Dear Lord, what a mess. What can I do to help these people? She wished she could help and knew she couldn't—didn't know how. She sighed and started to lope her horse around the arena.

"Get that horse moving over that cross-pole, Melissa," a surly-looking riding instructor commanded her ten-year-old student, who popped her crop on the rump of a recalcitrant bay horse in the corner of the arena. The horse's ears lay flat back, and they had a power struggle. Julie narrowly avoided an incident as the horse swerved away from the jump and nearly collided with Socks.

Julie maneuvered her way back to the rail, where she watched Brenda intently bringing her horse into a slow jog and marveled at how her friend could make everything look so easy. She was an artist. Her horses flowed under her hands. She wondered if Brenda even knew how great she was.

As Julie rode past the gate, Matt was still talking to Lynette. She disliked Lynette Williams, although she tried not to feel that way about anyone. Her attitude didn't work on Lynette. She was, in Julie's estimation, a silver-haired little slut with an angelic face and big, intense, baby-blue eyes, the magnitude of a predator. The *angel* was now leaning close to the neck of the horse, alternately petting him and looking up adoringly at Matt. Lynette didn't notice that Matt had one eye on Lynette and the other on Brenda. He's doing this on purpose. Why? she wondered. Then, Lynette, for a split second, looked over and caught Julie's eye before turning and leaving the arena. Her expression was hateful, and for a second time, Julie felt a wave of nausea arise in the pit of her stomach.

Matt kicked Irishman into a lope when suddenly, the horse spooked as a loose dog ran under the rail in front of him. Like a flash, Matt dug his spurs into his mount's side and spun him around, nearly causing the horse to fall. In a rage, he slammed Irishman's rump with his reins, and as the horse tried to rear, he twisted him around the other way. The faces of many bystanders

reflected adverse reactions and total disapproval of Matt's behavior, that didn't go unnoticed by Brenda. She had pulled her horse to a halt and glared at her husband. Matt returned her scowl with a grin, but his expression turned sour when he pulled his horse around.

Julie rode as far away from them as she could and became distracted by a commotion near the parked trailers. A man came flying down the road, running over to the announcer's stand, where the show committee was trying to organize their paperwork. Following a brief conversation, two committee officials rushed down the road, and a third frantically picked up a phone in the stand and dialed.

About fifteen minutes later, sirens shattered the scene as two police cars, followed by an ambulance, pulled into the parking area. Horses and riders crowded over to the rail. Julie dismounted and, walking over to the gate, cornered the out-of-breath ring steward.

"What's happening over by the trailers?"

"A body…" he said, gasping for air. "They found the body of a man in one of the trailers."

CHAPTER 3

Tom Carter maneuvered his red truck into a vertical parking space in front of Forest View's municipal courthouse. Wearing dark blue jeans and a light blue polo shirt with a horse's head embossed on the front pocket and the words "America's Quarter Horse" underneath, Tom made a stunning figure. Good-looking, like his older brother Matthew, he had the same sandy blond hair and deep blue eyes. There, the similarity ended. Tom's eyes were soft and smiling, while Matt's were hard as nails.

Two young women walking down the street turned their heads to look at him. He grinned, and they waved and kept walking.

He looked around at the small-town square—*his* small-town square, where he had grown up and played as a kid. Not much had changed. The police station was still on the opposite side of the courthouse. Across the street were the same small stores and boutiques that had cornered the local trade for a hundred years. Though still in business, the facades showed the financial strains affecting most small shops since the intrusion of the large Walmart and Target stores.

The paint on the old bank building flaked off like autumn leaves. Once the architectural highlight of the entire county, the Forest View Bank paled compared to the new Avant guard structures located on the edge of the mall. Buzz's Hardware Store still maintained a minimal customer base but could afford only the very basics of repair expenses. The massive storefront, once displaying an expensive pane glass window that shattered during the storm of ninety-two, now bore cheaper flat, plate glass like a symbol of a fading American small town.

As he looked around, he remembered his childhood and the times when he and his friends would run around the square after an afternoon at the movies. Nostalgia took hold and he had to bury a lump in his throat. He noticed a small dog dart out in front of a car, causing him to recall when Matt pushed him into the ongoing traffic in the middle of a game of tag. A car had to stop short, swerving into the oncoming lane and narrowly missing another car. His father rushed from the store in a panic, screaming at him while Matt stood off to the side smirking. He suddenly felt pain in his knuckles and realized he was clenching his fists so tight his fingernails were tearing into the skin. He sighed, came back to reality, then walked into the police station and asked for Phil Swanson.

"Yes, sir," the receptionist said, looking at Tom with interest. She batted her brown eyes as she picked up the phone. "By the way, I'm Teisha."

Tom smiled at her. "Hi, Teisha."

"Hi yourself. Uh… Phil, there's someone here to see you." She hung up the phone and tried to hide her grin.

Tom didn't have to wait long. A slightly overweight man in his late thirties, with brown hair and almost matching brown eyes, walked out of his office eating a jelly donut.

"My God, It's Tom Carter." He choked down the doughnut and hugged his friend, almost knocking the wind out of Tom. "I didn't think you were ever coming back. Damn, it's good to see you. Come into my office. We can have some privacy. Teisha, hold my calls, will you? Er… except for emergencies."

Teisha nodded and gave Tom another flirtatious grin as they walked down the hall.

Phil ushered Tom into his fifties-style executive office, encompassing an eclectic mixture of old and new. Cast iron bars covered the two windows, that overlooked the side of the square that housed the movie theater. A computer looked out of place on a huge grainy wooden desk, while its printer sat close by on a modern oak printer stand. The light, almost grey-beige walls mixed well with comfortable wine-colored modern office furniture. On the wall behind the desk, a photograph of the President of the United States was surrounded by local officials and pictures of family and friends. He noticed a photo of himself, Matt, Paul, and Phil riding horses at a local horse show. It brought back memories, and the lump came back in his throat.

Phil shoved a pile of papers off to the side of his desk, making space for two cups of coffee and the box of donuts.

"Grab a seat and sit."

Tom pulled an armchair from a nearby round table, placing it on the opposite side of the desk.

"Let's see. Milk?" Phil asked as he poured from a coffee maker on top of a gray metal filing cabinet.

Tom nodded. "You remembered." Tom smiled at his friend and accepted a Rottweiler mug. "You still have those Rotties?"

"Yeah, they still run our house. They think we are their sole, exclusive property… especially the kids. The mugs commemorated the arrival of our third Rottweiler puppy." He looked at the mugs, then looked at Tom.

"I've missed you, Tom. Why haven't you called?"

"Lots of reasons. I've tried to put things out of my mind. This town was one of those things."

"Your mom? Oh, sorry."

"Yeah. I'll never get over it, but…"

"Tom," Phil said, handing him the donut box. Are you back here to make peace with your family? You look like you have a reason for being here. I'm glad you came to see me, but…"

"I'm here for a couple of reasons." He helped himself to a chocolate donut with frosting, glanced at Phil's nameplate, and grinned. "Chief of Police? Who the hell did you have to bribe to get that title?"

Phil put his feet on his desk and leaned back in his chair, his hands behind his head, giving the impression of pure contentment. "Man. You haven't changed a bit. What's it been, four, five years?"

"Too long to remember…since my mom's death."

"Yeah," Phil said. "You left shortly after that."

"Too depressed to stick around…totally lost it. Had a blowout with my father, too." Tom held his coffee mug with both hands and stared down into it as though it held all the unhappy past events. He shook away the morbid memories and forced a change of subject. "But let's talk about you. How did you get to be the boss?"

"Tony Richardson." Phil removed his feet from his desk and sat forward. "Tom, Tony was always a pretty good friend. I've always felt that this promotion was like thirty pieces of silver…you know… like Judas."

Tom frowned. "You were just doing your job."

"Well, I'm not sure how much you know."

Tom shook his head and shrugged. "Just what I read in the papers. It has something to do with transporting drugs across state lines. Seems hard to believe that about Tony."

"Tom, it was a big drug bust…biggest in the area. Cocaine was found in Tony's horse trailer. You should have stayed for a while after his funeral." Phil's voice had almost an accusatory tone, and Tom suddenly felt uncomfortable. He shifted in his chair.

"I nearly did. But it seemed pointless. I would have had to face Matt and my father. If Tony had lived, I would have returned for his trial." He swirled the coffee in his cup, remembering Tony and Paul and him hopping off the hay loft onto their pony's backs as kids. Stupid idea, he thought, but fun at the time. Worst that happened, they missed or got bucked off and fell into the mud. No one had ever been seriously hurt.

"Anyway, I got an anonymous tip the morning he got arrested. I didn't know who it was, and the informant never came forward. Anyhow, I talked to my boss, and we called in the Drug Enforcement Agency from Chicago. They brought the driver downtown for questioning. You may remember him, Eddie Meeks? Eddie led us straight to Tony.

"They stopped the trailer at the Kentucky border. They brought in Eddie and arrested Tony. The bureau apparently had a close watch over this area for years. They knew something was moving in and out of here but could never prove anything." It was Phil's turn to stare down at his mug. "Anyway, when the Chief retired, I got bumped into his position. So, here I am." He didn't look happy.

"And you're beating yourself up over it, too."

"Yeah, I feel bad about it, but I'm not sorry that the trafficking stopped."

"Anyway, I remember the scuttlebutt at the funeral and stuff I read in the papers. My brother was pissed because the horses came from our ranch." Tom caught himself as he said, 'our.'

"That's right. We questioned Matt, but he said he didn't know where the horses were going, just that Tony had a buyer for them. Eddie swore that he didn't know the drugs were in the trailer, and we never got anything out of Tony. Nothing. They questioned him for six hours. The buyers in Kentucky were questioned but then released—no evidence against them, either. Anyway, the next morning, Tony went home on bail and committed suicide." Phil stared at the ceiling.

"God, what's happening to our families here? One tragedy after another. When will it end?" Tom stared at the ceiling, fighting off a sob of frustration.

"I know. I'm sorry, Tom."

"It hurt bad when Mom died." Tom averted his eyes, blinking away tears that invariably welled up in his eyes when he thought about the loss of his mother. "First Mom, then Tony. Wonder who might be next."

Phil blew through his lips. "Yeah, I know, Tom. It's traumatic for all of you. I hope against hope there won't be another."

Tom thought that Phil was thinking there just might be a next. And could there have been a connection between his mom and Tony? No. That didn't feel right. Then, thinking about his mother, he said, "Yeah, strange about that accident, Phil."

Phil looked up at Tom sharply. "What do you mean strange? The strap broke on her saddle. It happens, Tom."

"Yeah. I know. It's happened to all of us at one time or another, even me. Phil, Mom was an expert rider. I don't think her strap breaking would cause her horse to lose control and fall backward on top of her."

"Horse got scared, Tom. That happens, too."

"You don't understand. Blaze wasn't like that. He never reacted to things."

"So, what do you think happened? You really think someone did something deliberately?"

"I don't know, but it's strange all the same." He didn't want to say what had crossed his mind all those years back. Sabotage… against his mother? It seemed impossible. He sipped some coffee to regain composure. "But, about you, so you got promoted."

"Yeah, I got promoted. I would have preferred to have gotten it another way."

"You know, Phil, what I can't understand is, well, Tony…himself."

Phil nodded, and Tom continued. "This was just not like Tony. Suicide was entirely out of character. Tony was a fighter. It would have been more in character to fight the charges. But even forgetting that, why would he risk dealing drugs? His folks left Tony and Greg well-provided for when they died."

"The big why. I'm not sure they were as well off as you might have thought, and drugs are everywhere… easy money. We're not talking chump change. That cocaine he was carrying was worth a quarter of a million dollars on the market. What a temptation that must have been."

Tom whistled. "But where would Tony have gotten those kinds of contacts? He didn't hang out with those kinds of people."

Phil shook his head. "You can go to your local high school and find out how to get your hands on drugs. This industry's so well organized that it makes some of the largest corporations look like a… I don't know. Oh, you know what I mean. The old Mafia looks like Kiddie Land by comparison. They're hitting society from all sides, especially Chicago. How they get this stuff transported is truly amazing."

"So, was he living high on the hog? Turned his little farmhouse into a mansion and his barn into…"

"No."

Tom noted that his sarcasm had not been lost on Phil.

"Whatever happened to Eddie? I read in a paper that he was released on bail."

"Yeah. Another loose end in this case. He disappeared. I mean, he just walked out and vanished."

"Who put up the money for him?"

"As far as we know, he did. He transferred money directly from his own account."

"How much are we talking about here?"

"About a thousand bucks… or more."

"Whew… where did Eddie get that kind of money?"

As he chomped on a piece of his donut, Tom remarked, "I heard Greg had to sell his ranch. If Tony had so much money, why would he have had problems getting repairs done on his barn? Why did his brother have to sell when his boarders left? Why hadn't he waited for everything to blow over?" He paused, then asked what he really wanted to know. "How long had this been going on? The drug dealing around here, I mean. "

Phil frowned as he replied, "The Feds were watching this area for some time. A couple of years. It wasn't the first time. Damn it, Tom, if Tony was innocent, why did he kill himself?"

"Maybe he killed himself because he didn't do it, and he felt trapped? No way out?" Tom said, unsure of his last remark.

"I thought Tony wasn't the type to kill himself, Tom."

"He wasn't. That's what surprises me. Look, he took over the running of the ranch and took a full load at school right after losing both parents. I can't see him leaving his brother to face all that alone." Frowning and uneasy, Tom continued, "Phil, what if Tony didn't kill himself?"

"What do you mean?" Phil's eyes opened wide. He sat forward in his seat.

"Supposing he had help?"

"Why the hell would anyone want to go do it for him?"

"Maybe he had friends who didn't want to be implicated? Maybe Eddie? Could he have killed Tony before he disappeared?" Phil remained silent for a few minutes, taking time to gulp down some coffee.

"Maybe. He left before Tony got killed. There was one other thing. There was a girlfriend. Did you know Tony's girlfriend, Tom?"

Tom shook his head.

"We tried to find out, but no one, including his brother, seemed to know. I asked Matt, but he didn't know either. Tony kept it a closely guarded secret. There was nothing among his things. No pictures, nothing. She called the school, and nobody could shed any light on her identity. She never came forward. We may never know. It's probably not even important. All that happened long before this came up." Phil got up and went over to refill his mug. "Want some more?"

Tom shook his head.

Both men fell silent for a moment, with the only sound coming from a cuckoo clock on the wall. "Nothing happens here. You live in Chicago. Why wouldn't you choose someone closer?" He looked at Tom curiously.

"This detective happens to be from a small town." He swirled in his chair. "There is another reason."

"Thought so."

"I want to become reacquainted with my family. I miss them, and I miss the horses."

"Oh. Well, why don't we set up something? You could spend the day and come home for dinner. Marsha would love to see you."

"Marsha. How is she?" Tom flushed, thinking about his school-age crush on the older and beautiful Marsha Mayfield. She burst his bubble when she told him about her feelings for Phil, Tom's godfather. Tom stepped aside and helped make the match that set all tongues in Forest View wagging.

"Man, she's great." Phil beamed with pleasure. "She's got a job teaching high school and trying to raise those teens to be solid citizens. We both got our hands full. When are you gonna settle down?"

"Who knows?" Tom replied. "Who'd put up with a poor starving actor, black sheep of his family, and known eccentric?"

"Yeah… right." Phil laughed.

Tom looked at the large round wall clock and said, "I gotta go. Promised Paul I'd stop by their horse show today. It's the biggie . . . the one we always showed at."

"Yep. A big one. Everyone going?"

"I guess. Paul said they were taking a couple of training horses and their own. They're eyeing the big shows this fall."

"Well, see you later, Phil. I'll call you, and we can set up something." As he started to get up, the phone rang.

"Hell. What?" Phil's face turned grey.

"What is it?" Tom asked.

Phil continued the phone. "When… you sure?"

"What?" Tom was on the edge of his seat.

"Know who it was?" Phil paused and looked up at the ceiling for a moment.

"Okay, I'll be right over." Phil hung up and fixed his eyes on Tom. "You still want to come to a crime scene?"

Tom nodded slowly.

"You may as well follow. You were going there anyway. Someone's been killed at the horse show."

CHAPTER 4

The sunny, hot, and carefree morning exploded into pandemonium as show officials scurried around, frantically trying to decide what to do about the horse show. Finding bodies in campers wasn't part of their job description and wasn't listed in the rule book. They decided to go ahead with the show and delay the start until the paramedics had taken the body off the show grounds. Surprisingly, the opening delay met with mixed reactions from the crowd. Most of the participants maintained a stoic attitude, sticking to the business of showing their horses.

Curiosity overwhelmed Julie as she led Socks down the tree-lined gravel road to where the police and ambulance personnel parked their vehicles. As she walked past the clusters of horses, riders, and spectators huddled together in stunned astonishment, she overheard bits and snatches of their conversations.

"Inconvenient. Who'd want to kill anyone at a horse show? Why couldn't they have done it somewhere else?"

"Hope they don't cancel this show. We came all the way down from Wisconsin. We need the points for 'The World Show' in Oklahoma."

"Ooh, wait 'til my mom hears what happened at the horse show today." Julie stared at two young riders in English riding breeches and highly polished, black boots braiding the tail of a tall sorrel gelding. He seemed to enjoy the attention, and the girls enjoyed the odd turn of events.

"My mom is going to s…"

Julie passed out of earshot. The trailer belonged to Eagle Ranch. Julie wondered what connection Greg could have had with the dead man. Then, two things happened. First, a tall, rugged-looking man wearing a tailored western jacket, Stetson cowboy hat, and beige trousers that radiated 'Judge' got out of a Chevy Silverado. As she stared at the newcomer, the second thing occurred. Julie bumped headlong into a man with blond hair, wearing blue jeans and a blue polo shirt. The sudden impact knocked her into her horse and onto the ground, and for an instant, she saw stars.

"Are you okay?" he asked.

She sat on the ground for a minute, trying to decide, then allowed the man to help her to her feet. As she rose, she was surprised to see a combination of Matt and Paul staring at her. She blinked, then realized that this man must be Brenda's outcast brother-in-law, Tom.

She didn't know exactly what to say; the only words that came out were "ouch" and "uh…"

"Whew." He looked at her head. "That's quite a bump. Why don't you sit down for a minute?"

"I just wanted to see what happened." Julie quivered from the shock of the collision and was still a bit dazed as Tom helped her to sit back down on the grass.

"I noticed. I pulled in right behind the cops. Right now, they're dusting for fingerprints and taking pictures. The trailer belongs to an old friend, Greg Richardson. Do you know him?"

"Yes, I do. Do you?" She didn't wait for him to answer. "I just have to know," Julie said, passing over Tom's question. "Are you related to Matt and Paul Carter? You look just like them."

"Well, I'm not sure if that's a compliment. Is being related a good thing or a bad thing? If it's good, yes. If not, who's Matt and Paul Carter?" Tom stooped by her side. He caught her arm as she lost her balance when her horse started nibbling her hair.

"Ouch, Socks, quit." She pushed his nose back with her knuckles. "I think I can get up now."

"Okay." He took her hand and helped her to her feet.

Brushing off leaves and pine needles, she said, "Greg and Tony are my cousins." She turned her head and looked down. "At least Tony was my cousin when he was alive."

He looked at her. "They're your cousins?"

"I'm Julie Bishop. Tony, Greg, and I are distant cousins. Tony got Socks… that's him, from the Carter Ranch in Texas." She pointed to her gelding, who had transferred his affection for red hair to the greener, more nutritious grass. She offered her hand by way of an introductory hand-shake. He took it.

"Julie. Pleased to meet you, ma'am." Tom grinned at her and held her hand just a bit longer than needed.

"I hadn't known Tony long, unfortunately. He died the day after I bought my horse."

She was telling him more than she intended and didn't know why. She stopped to take a breath. Blowing a loose strand of hair out of her eyes, she looked at him a little closer. She realized she felt nervous and didn't like it one little bit.

"I thought it might have been a bad omen for me at the time." She paused, not wanting to say too much, groping for more comfortable conversational ground. "I went to his funeral. Your father was there. I remember meeting him."

Tom frowned, and Julie thought she'd hit an uncomfortable nerve.

"I wasn't there." His tone made Julie look at him sharply, waiting for him to say more. It didn't come.

"Your dad…" Julie stopped and looked at Socks. "Socks came from his ranch. As it turned out, he was the best thing that ever happened to me."

Tom took a step back and appraised him by raising an eyebrow and squinting his eyes. Then, he nodded his head. "Pretty nice horse. He looks like Dad's old grey stallion. He called him 'The Grey Ghost.'" Tom stood and patted the dapple-grey neck. The animal stopped grazing momentarily to put an affectionate, velvety nostril on Tom's face. Tom blew in it, and Socks snorted. He went back to graze, and Tom stood staring at him—almost through him—his attention seemed far away. Then he broke his silence. "Julie, I was just going up to the barns to see if I could find Brenda and Paul. Are you headed back there anytime soon?"

"As a matter of fact, I am."

Tom and Julie maneuvered toward the horse barns, dodging exhibitors, horses, curiosity seekers, and lines of people waiting to get a Cinnabon at a nearby concession stand. Julie's classes weren't scheduled until the afternoon, and with the show starting late, she had plenty of time to observe the surroundings.

People huddled in small groups, discussing the events of the past hour. Everyone wondered aloud, "Who was he?" and "Why was he in Greg Richardson's trailer?"

As they entered the horse barn, Julie spotted Brenda, Matt, and Paul talking to a tall, thin, serious-looking man in his mid-twenties. It was a little over a year after his brother's death, and it appeared as if the shock had not entirely left Greg Richardson.

"Yeah, I know who it was," he said as Julie and Tom approached.

"It was Eddie Meeks. Damn! I found him early this morning when I got to the trailer. He disappeared when Tony got arrested. They had a national search going on for him. He just fell off the face of the earth. The police should have never should have let him go." Greg paused for a moment as if gathering his composure. "He just reappeared in my trailer—dead. Blood all over the floor. Throat slashed. Weird. Really, weird."

"Hey, Greg," Tom said.

Greg spun in his direction.

"Tom. I haven't seen you forever. How the hell are you?"

For the first time that Julie had stood there, Greg grinned—broadly.

"This your wife?"

Julie blushed. "No."

"Oh, sorry. So, you're married to someone else, then?"

"No, I'm not married to anyone." Julie noticed Greg had the same intense dark eyes as his deceased brother. Now, they were smiling—at *her*. Julie's face reddened, and Brenda smiled at her.

Matt turned his attention to Julie and Tom. "Tom, you sure turn up at the most unexpected times." Then he turned his attention to Julie. "I see you've met our star performer… that is, except Brenda."

"Wait a minute," he continued. "No, I've met you before. You were at…" Greg's expression turned serious.

Julie said, "I met you at your brother's funeral. We're cousins." Julie took the burden off him.

"Yeah. That's right, and you're family."

Turning his attention to Tom, Matt said, "What are you doing here? I didn't think you liked horse shows anymore." Two horses brushed past them, forcing Julie and Tom to press together against a stall door to avoid being trampled. "I thought that the country was too small-time for a famous actor who's too busy associating with the rich and famous to have anything to do with us."

Tom maneuvered back into the aisle. "It isn't like that, and you know it." He narrowed his eyes and visibly tried not to ball his hand into a fist.

Julie realized how strongly Matt could irritate people.

"Let's not start in, okay?" Tom said, changing his tone and the subject. "Looks like you've had some excitement around here. I followed Phil into the fairgrounds. They just took away the body."

Matt cocked his head. "That was some timing. What were you doing behind Phil Swanson?"

"Came down here to see him."

"In some trouble, are we?"

"No."

Matt persisted. "So, what were you doing with him?"

"Well, if it's any of your business…" Tom hesitated. It was more than apparent he was trying to control his temper. He was about to turn nasty, and Julie didn't think Tom liked to play that part.

"I'm working on a play and wanted to talk to him about police work. The show committee called about the murder while I was in his office, that's all. I was coming out here to see you, anyhow."

"Really?" Then Matt shrugged. "Why do you want to see us?"

Tom rolled his eyes. "I just told you." Julie wondered just how much of what Tom was professing was an act. If so, he was probably outstanding on the stage. She wondered what else he might be good at.

"I was just getting out of my van when I literally ran into this lady. I felt she needed some assistance getting back here. Otherwise, I'd still be over there."

"I could have made it back on my own," Julie said, getting defensive and wondering why she felt she had to say that.

"My pleasure. Wanted to see my family, anyway."

"Crap," Matt said. "Well, we all have work to do." He turned to his brother. "Don't get in the way."

"I'd better get back down to my trailer. I think they want to question me," Greg said. "You want to come?" Tom nodded and motioned for Paul to come with them.

"Yeah, I'm sure they do." Matt jerked Brenda by the arm and walked her toward their stalls.

"Same old brother." Tom shook his head as the three men left the barn.

Wait a minute. What just happened here? Julie was suddenly alone with her horse, surrounded by throngs of people carrying equipment and leading horses. Shrugging off a feeling of sudden abandonment, she followed Matt and Brenda down the aisle to their stalls.

Julie immersed herself in grooming her horse, polishing his coat so that every speck of dust and dirt was now on her. She was so absorbed in her job that she hadn't noticed the conversation in the next stall.

"And just where were you last night, Matt? You didn't get back until this morning. Where were you?"

Julie suddenly came alive.

"Damn it, Brenda, keep your voice down. Do you think I killed that little bastard? Why should I? He worked for Tony. If you want his killer, no one had more reason than Greg."

Julie suddenly felt the need to hold her breath.

Matt whispered. "Where was Eddie this year, anyhow? Un uh…Greg knew he was coming and set him up… killed him."

"Where were you?" Brenda asked again.

"That's none of your business."

"Yes, it is. Matt, please, I don't want any surprises. If anyone questions us, I want to be able to cover for you, but I can't unless I know."

"*Cover* for me? Why should you have to cover for *me*? Besides," he added, "you know where I was. Lynette can cover for me if I need her. I don't need any help from you. Just ride the damn horses."

"You bastard."

Julie heard the slap and someone falling over against the stall's partition. She gasped.

Matt reacted to the sound, discovering Julie in the next stall.

"Son of a bitch," he shouted and stormed out of the barn."

Julie rushed to her friend. "Brenda?"

"No, Julie. Leave it alone. I'll be all right." Brenda slowly closed the stall door and walked away, letting out a suppressed sob.

Julie came out of Socks's stall shaken up. She hadn't known Matt abused his wife. Her mind continued to spin. What caused Brenda's suspicion? Why the need to cover for him? Matt was more likely to be with Lynette than out killing Eddie Meeks. What reason would he have? Her cousin had a bigger motive. She picked the brush off the floor. Or would he? Eddie was the one person who could clear his brother's name and restore his reputation if Tony were innocent. Suddenly, Julie felt that nothing was making any sense. None of this should have anything to do with the Carters. What was even worse, she cared. The letdown was enormous, and all the excitement of showing her horse suddenly turned sour.

The day passed quickly. Everybody showed their horses and, despite circumstances, did quite well. One moment, when Julie was showing Socks, she looked at Tom standing on the rail watching her, and she lost concentration. Just then, another rider cut in front of Socks, nearly forcing him to break stride to avoid a collision. Julie side-passed her horse out of the situation in front of the judge. He smiled at her and frowned at the rider, who cut her off. Making a note on his pad, the judge placed Julie first in the class, and the Carter Ranch cheered.

Julie sat on her horse next to Brenda, watching Matt spurring his horse in front of the judge.

"He thinks he can do that and get away with it. Unbelievable…" Brenda said.

Brenda motioned for Julie to look at the bleachers, where Lynette sat, whispering and giggling with some other Carter Ranch boarders.

"She looks like a *teeny bopper*, Julie. It's disgusting." Julie noticed an expression in her eye that sent chills down her spine.

"Maybe," she continued, "it's not because I hurt so much, but because I don't care. Maybe I feel nothing." A tear rolled down her face, and she bit her lip. "Pray for me, Julie. Please."

After showering and changing, Julie went next door to Matt and Brenda's motel room. The room was already crowded with Carter family members lounging where they could find room. She settled on the edge of one of the two double beds that occupied most of the area. They almost had to jump from bed to bed to get to the tiny bathroom across the room to avoid bumping into the dressers, suitcases, boots, dirty bridles, and each other.

She had changed into a blue turtleneck jersey and blue jeans, set off by a green vest that complimented her green eyes. Her hair was pulled back with a blue velvet band. Tom sat casually in an armchair with one leg draped over the arm, his eyes focused on Julie. Now and again, he'd try to look elsewhere, but he wasn't succeeding.

Brenda sat across the room, playing with her silver cross, which she always wore around her neck. Her pink scoop-necked cotton blouse accentuated the paleness of her skin and the golden highlights in her hair that hung loosely over her shoulders. She appeared tired and perhaps not feeling well.

It was the first time Julie had seen Paul Carter sitting down since their arrival at the show.

"Well," Paul said. "We all need to go out and celebrate our wins today. Where's Greg? I thought he was coming with us."

They all turned to the door as Phil Swanson pushed in the opened door.

"Hi, all," he greeted them. "Greg won't be joining you this evening. He's just been arrested for the murder of Eddie Meeks."

CHAPTER 5

Phil Swanson blocked the doorway. The light from the early evening sun caused a shadow to spill into the room, creating its own special tension, and the visionary theatrics camouflaged a highly disturbed state of mind. A grim smile masked the anger and sadness he felt. Lynette bumped into him on the way in the door, but he felt nothing. With a pantomime of a gesture, he let her pass. The cast of characters all started talking at once.

He stood silent for a moment, watching lifelong friends look at him like he was the enemy. Lynette plunked herself down on the nearest of two double beds next to Matt. He thought she behaved like she was marking her territory. He noticed Brenda sitting on the other bed, glancing at Matt, then Lynette, and back at Matt, then shook her head and shrugged. So, those rumors he'd been hearing about Matt were true.

I wonder how Marsha would react if she ever caught me cheating on her.

For a moment, Phil's family ties gnawed at his imagination. *I probably wouldn't live long enough to find out. How the hell could Matt ever pick a Lynette over Brenda?*

For a moment, everyone got quiet, unsure what to say. Phil jolted out his thoughts about domesticity and focused back on the room.

Paul broke the silence. "So, you've arrested Greg. Why? I thought he was staying with friends last night."

Phil hesitated, wording what he would say—carefully.

"It appears that he wasn't there the whole night. He went back to the fairgrounds to check on his horses. It puts him at the murder scene. It was his trailer, and…" he said, "his knife."

Phil cleared his throat. "One of the officers found it by the body in the trailer. It was his hunting knife."

"So, you think that just because it was Greg's knife, he had to have killed him?" Tom fingered the ashtray on the cocktail table next to his chair. One leg had crept over the edge, and he dangled his boot over the side.

"The killer probably took it and caught him off guard… Eddie, that is," Brenda said, who seemed to be lost in her own thoughts. Phil watched her take shallow breaths and didn't think she looked very well. Her pale face had turned a full degree whiter than when he'd walked into the room.

"Oh, you don't think it was him?" Phil asked her.

She shook her head. "No, I don't."

"You know, the closest thing we've had to a murder in this town was in 1982 when an old lady took a hatchet to her husband. Unless we call in the FBI, I'm the only detective we've got here."

Phil sat silent for a few minutes. The FBI was well aware of Eddie's murder. He needed to calm his voice—stop appearing defensive. He'd felt for quite a while there was an evilness hovering over Forest View, waiting to rear its ugly head again, as it had been a year ago. A strange feeling overcame him—like prickles moving slowly down the back of his neck and into his spine. He didn't want to admit his fear, and if Greg wasn't the killer, well, who was? And was this just the beginning?

Everyone caught their breath, waiting for him to continue. He noticed that, although facing him, Tom hadn't taken the corner of his eye off the redhead. What was her name? Julie, something or other. He'd noticed her today at the horse show when he'd had the chance to watch one of the classes. She was a good rider. She was also very pretty, and, he thought, she probably didn't know it. He liked that about her.

"Look," Phil said, "Eddie could have been killed for a number of reasons, but right now, the evidence points to Greg. He was killed with Greg's hunting knife in his trailer at about one in the morning when Greg was seen at the fairgrounds."

Tom exploded.

"Oh, brother! Right. He invites Eddie over to knife him at a public horse show with campers and trailers all around so that you can find the body and arrest him the next morning. Yeah right… Greg's not that stupid, Phil."

"I can't believe no one heard him cry out," Julie said. "He was knifed from behind. The killer let him fall backward."

"Oh God," Tom said, grimacing. "Where's Greg now?"

"He's been taken into custody. I don't think they can arrange bail until sometime tomorrow. He has friends who will help raise the money."

"We can keep his horses over at our place if he wants," Paul suggested.

"Yeah, tell him that it's okay with us." Brenda looked at Matt, and Matt looked back with a steely stare. He didn't say anything.

"I'm going back to my room unless you want to question *me*," Lynette said, emphasizing *me*. "I'll be going out to dinner if anyone wants to come along." Although referring to everyone, her glance pointed straight at Matt, who looked at Brenda and smirked. Lynette walked out the door, brushing past Phil. There echoed the sounds of footsteps moving down the corridor and the faint slam of a door. He chuckled to himself. That Lynette was a corker. He'd known women like her, gorgeous on the outside, ugly as sin on the inside. They were trouble—breaking up perfectly good marriages and then making their husbands miserable for the rest of their lives.

"Matt, why don't you and Paul go with them? I have a headache. I think I'll stay here," Brenda said, causing Phil to change his focus.

"Brenda, you need to eat something," Paul said.

"No, I don't think so," she said. "I'm feeling sick." The color on her face cast a greenish hue as she ran for the bathroom.

Tom raised an eyebrow, grinned, watched her go, and said, "Is there something you want to tell us, Matt?"

"Like what?" Matt's vocal pitch bordered on shrill.

"Is she…?"

"No! It's just nerves. She gets that way when there's lots of stress. She doesn't handle it well." Matt followed everyone's gaze toward the closed bathroom door. He turned a boyish grin toward Julie and said, "I don't think Brenda needs anyone right now. Let's find a place to eat."

Paul gave his brother an irritating glance. "Go ahead, I'll stay here and make sure she's okay."

"Look, I don't feel very well. I'd appreciate it if you'd all clear out and let me go to bed."

Brenda was standing in the doorway, her face a pasty chalk-like color shadowed by strands of matted blond hair.

Phil stood motionless, watching the interaction. He thought that, contrary to Matt's opinion, Brenda handled stress exceptionally well. He wondered how Brenda felt having all those men listening to her being sick in the bathroom. He motioned to Tom, and the two walked out of the room and into the outside corridor, which looked over acres of cornfields. A dark silhouette of the show grounds was visible in the distance, and the sun was starting to cast a hazy red glow on newly budding ears of corn.

"Look. I'm going to get a bite to eat," Phil said. "Would you like to tag along? I want the company, but more importantly, I want to talk to you. I want to get some impressions from that redhead, too. She knows the people around here." He wasn't sure why he was getting her involved, but he thought it might have something to do with Tom—pure instinct.

Phil, Julie, and Tom piled into Phil's police car and found an all-nighter truck stop—a restaurant off the interstate. A small convenience store was loaded with souvenirs of Chicago and Illinois, mugs, and freezers full of ice cream, sandwiches, juice, and pop. Bathrooms were in the corridor attached to a restaurant on the other side. Even though the place was in the middle of cornfields, it was busy day and night.

They found a booth next to some truckers who were discussing world affairs, the current administration, their various wives and girlfriends, and how their bosses sucked.

"All right. Tom, you said you wanted to play detective. We have a real live mystery on our hands. You still want to help?"

Tom nodded, and Julie said, "You want to what?"

They made an interesting contrast: Julie with red hair and green eyes and Tom with blond hair and blue eyes, both pretending not to notice but unable to keep their eyes off each other. Yes, this was interesting. Phil thought he might help the kids along. Grinning, he made formal introductions, bringing up Tom's acting career.

"He came to me for advice and some hands-on experience. He's going to get more than he bargained for."

Julie laughed, then turned to Phil and asked him, "But I thought you'd already decided who killed that man."

"No, not at all." Phil lowered his voice. "Greg had every reason to do it. But he didn't."

"What? But then what was that all about, back there?"

"Look, it was Greg's knife. If he had done it, he would have had plenty of opportunity to get rid of it. Whoever did it found it there. A convenience. The killer might... might probably have brought a weapon with him but decided that using Greg's knife would make him a convenient scapegoat."

"A setup?" Tom asked, looking over the menu.

Phil nodded.

"Hell, Tom, Greg is no killer. Like you said, he isn't that stupid. If he set his mind to kill someone, he'd be too smart to leave a trail that pointed directly to himself. No, damn it, I don't want another murder-look-like suicide on my hands."

"Another... wait," Julie said, "You mean that you think Tony was *murdered?*"

"He means that he has an open mind," Tom said.

"You interested in helping?"

"Yes."

"Okay." Phil looked at his godson and grinned. "Since your family is somewhat involved, you'd better help."

"My family? I don't see how they could be. So, they were at the same horse show and were friends with the Richardsons. So what? So was Julie, along with a hundred others." Tom went back to perusing the menu.

Phil sat back, placing his menu on the table. He was trying to decide between the cheeseburger deluxe and spaghetti. With his increasing weight problem, he thought a tuna salad would be best, but he didn't want one. He wanted the cheeseburger.

"Yes, and that Matt's horses were in Tony's horse trailer." He sat back and watched Tom's reaction. He wasn't disappointed.

"Come on, Phil, that doesn't make Matt a murderer, or a drug dealer for that matter."

"What makes you think I meant Matt?"

"Well, who else? Brenda? Paul? Who else is there?"

"Nobody, just forget it," Phil said with a sigh. "No, of course not. I'm pointing out that it will be like finding a needle in a haystack, trying to sort all this out."

"So, you really believe that Tony didn't kill himself," Julie said again as though she was trying to sort out the details in her mind.

"Personally, no. That's what's on the official report. The death of Eddie Meeks might be directly linked to that of Tony. I'm going to look at it that way. Julie, I asked you along because I'd like your help, too."

"Mine? How?"

"You know the horse people around here, don't you?"

"Some, not all."

"People will say things to you that they won't say to me. I was hoping you could talk to everyone at that show, people you know and people you don't know. Get into conversations. Butt in if you must. Find out what people know about Eddie. Has anyone seen him in the last year? Where and in what connection? Has anyone heard from anyone else about where he's been? Notice facial expressions and body language. You can tell when people are lying. They get evasive."

He added, "Unless they're pros." He stopped for a few minutes to take a sip of the black liquid the waitress had brought for coffee and continued.

"Eddie came to that horse show last night to meet someone. That someone killed him. Nothing was found on the body, and there were no fingerprints on the weapon except for Greg's.

"Is Greg going to be released?" Tom asked. "How come you're not there asking questions."

"I have been. Also, I have a friend from the DEA helping. I'm trying to find out where Eddie has been… I thought it better not to question Greg at the same time. We're working together but separately if that makes sense. We'll compare notes, then decide what direction we'll take."

"The DEA?" Julie asked. "Why are they involved? This isn't a drug case, is it?"

"They were involved with the Richardson case. I don't think they were particularly satisfied with the results of that investigation either. I asked them to help with this unofficially."

"This is getting bigger and bigger," Tom said. Phil shook his head and suddenly felt very tired, bone tired. It was going to be a long and dangerous grind.

"Phil, what do you think will happen because of this?" Tom asked. "Something is on your mind."

"Yeah, especially when a killer is on the loose."

"No, I mean, you think something else is going to happen, don't you?"

"I think," Phil said, "that this is just the beginning. I think we've just hit the tip of the iceberg. The Titanic is about to go down, and sharp icicles will shoot around us." Phil was on a roll.

"That may bring out the killer," Julie said.

"It'll bring out more than just a killer. No, if the two deaths are related, a major scandal is starting to brew here. Yeah, I'm worried. If Tony's death was murder, then there is a killer who's got two murders to his credit, and he won't stop there if anyone gets in his way. Damn! I'm having second thoughts about having you involved. You, be very careful."

"We will," Julie said as the waitress came over to take their order.

CHAPTER 6

Socks's squeaky-clean gray coat now seemed to match Julie's tank top, the same one that had been a solid hunter green earlier that morning. She undid the braid in his tail. Its coarse yet silky hairs combed out with a wave, flowing like a bridal train when it reached the ground. Julie figured all it needed was orange blossoms, then wondered why she was thinking about weddings.

Tom sauntered down the corridor, holding two cups of coffee, dodging horses, handlers, and other personnel carrying buckets of water and bales of hay. It was barely seven o'clock in the morning, and the barn was already abuzz with activity. Julie tried brushing off the hair from her shirt as he approached, but she didn't totally succeed.

"Thought you might like a cup of coffee," he said. "The light one's for you."

"Thanks." She took the coffee and opened the Styrofoam container.

"So, how did you sleep last night?" Tom asked, looking like he hadn't had much himself.

"Oh, I guess all right. I kept dreaming about horse shows and dead bodies. It was a real adventure."

"You like to dream, do you?" Tom sat on a hay bale, sipping coffee and watching Julie put Vaseline on Socks's nose.

"Yes, pretty much always. I've even had a few dreams come true. I hope last night's doesn't. I've had funny feelings about stuff all week. Yesterday morning, I suddenly felt like someone had stepped on my grave." Julie stopped abruptly, afraid that Tom might think her superstitions were just plain weird. "Have you ever heard that expression?" Julie was surprised when Tom nodded.

He said, "It was something that periodically happened to my mother. She'd suddenly shiver, and a premonition would flash into her head. Usually, they did too... I mean, come true. The strangest one happened on the day she died. I was sitting with her at breakfast when Matt walked in. Something came over her. Some people sense things. She did..." he stopped and sighed. "Anyway, she died in a riding accident that morning."

"I'm so sorry, Tom."

"Julie, maybe you have that gift, too. Gift or curse, I don't think you're nuts or anything."

She laughed. "I'm glad you don't think I'm crazy." Changing the subject, she said, "I also missed Annie. I usually wake up to a collie alarm clock. This morning, the radio was talking about Eddie. That's all I've been hearing about."

"What did they say?"

"Just that he was killed, and that Greg was arrested. Nothing new that's been offered or leaked," she added.

"Leaked?" he said, grinning.

"Well, of course. Doesn't someone always have inside information that is conveniently leaked to the press?" Julie pushed back a stray strand of hair from her ponytail, and two others popped out, tickling her face like a feather. Absently, she let her hair loose and shook her head.

"You mentioned that you have collies," he said. "How many do you have?"

"Just the one. Annie was supposed to come, but Matt put his foot down, too much trouble."

"Bummer. You should have brought them anyway. He'd have loved that."

Julie laughed. "Well... it wasn't exactly my decision. Maybe, if I had made my own arrangements and came alone... but I didn't. Brenda asked me to come with them."

"You'll have to excuse Matt, I guess. He doesn't like dogs much. Sometimes, Matt seems mean, but it's not entirely his fault."

"How so?"

"Matt was always Dad's favorite. He got away with a lot from the time he was little. Things that we'd get punished for, he didn't. One time, he wanted a dog in the worst way. Dad bought him a Golden Retriever. Wonderful dog. He took to Paul and me. He hated Matt. Matt never let on, but it hurt him. He'd kick and scream at the dog whenever he didn't come. Hell of a way to get a dog to come to you." Tom shook his head and looked at the floor as though reliving the event. "Dad never did anything about it. Never. It was Matt's dog to do as he wished. That wasn't like my father with his animals. Julie, if we'd ever treated an animal like Matt, we'd have been standing for a week." He looked at her and shrugged his shoulders as he bit his lower lip. Julie knew he was struggling. She wanted to hold him, comfort him. Why?

"Eventually, the dog ran away. I saw him a couple of months later at a barn down the road. I never told anyone. The dog was better off. Matt never could get in touch with his feelings and work them out like the rest of us. He'd lash out in frustration. It's not an excuse for him, Julie. It's just the way he is."

Maybe, Julie thought, but is he capable of killing someone? It was a thought she'd been suppressing, and she considered it better not to mention it to his brother. Instead, she just said, "You said you have a dog. What kind do you have?"

"Golden Retriever. The first chance I got, I guess, I got the same kind of dog. His name is Jinx. He's staying with my landlady until I get back."

Julie threw her empty cup in a trash bin and started to comb her horse's mane.

"Jinx is an interesting name." Socks shook his head as she ran the comb through the heavy strands of hair.

"He was a street dog when I found him. He met with several encounters of various kinds. My landlady wasn't too pleased. She named him Jinx for his ability to get into trouble."

Julie mustered up an innocent smile. "Is she your girlfriend?"

"I don't think her husband would like that much," Tom grinned. "By the way, they're in their seventies."

"Oh." Julie blushed.

"Are you involved with anyone?" Tom blurted out his question.

"Who me? No... No, I'm not. I don't want to get involved with anyone right now." Julie deliberately turned away, not knowing exactly what to say. A wave of dizziness grabbed her as she tried to think of a way to steer him in a different direction.

"Sorry. I didn't mean to pry," Tom pitched his empty cup into the same trash can. "I'd better let you finish grooming your horse. Do you need help with the saddle?"

Julie recovered, took a deep breath, and gave him a big smile. She nodded affirmatively.

The horses entered in the morning halter classes were being led out of the barn, gleaming from head to toe with tails touching the ground. They were wearing halters with so much silver that the sun reflected off them, causing Julie to squint from the glare.

Lynette stood holding her horse by the arena gate as Matt swung his foot into the stirrup and lifted his body into the saddle. She stood close to her horse and his rider as though she was an appendage coming out of a sculpture.

Tom stopped and put his hand on Irishman's sweating neck. Julie guessed the sweat was not coming from work but from nerves.

"Hello. So, Matt, I hear you've got quite a horse here," Tom focused on Lynette as he spoke to his brother. I hope he's worth all the trouble."

Lynette flushed and looked uncomfortable.

"What do you mean?" Matt asked sharply, glaring down at his brother.

"Nothing much. It's amazing what we can do to make ourselves feel important."

Lynette's eyes grew wide, and her face flushed a bright red.

Matt glowered. "What are you talking about?"

"You know very well what I'm talking about."

Turning to Lynette, Tom continued, "I wouldn't get my hopes up if I were you, though. This is all business with Matt. I know my brother quite well. I hope it's all business with you, too." Tom spun on his heels and turned to where Julie and Paul stood by the arena gate with their mouths open. It looked like his brother would run him down with the horse, but the horse had more sense and sidestepped out of Tom's way. The animal got a slap on the rump for his trouble.

Lynette turned toward them and asked, "Why do you people hate me so much?" She didn't wait for an answer but turned and headed toward the bleachers.

"Why indeed?" Julie asked softly, so even the nearby men could barely hear her.

"That won't go over big," Paul said. "Watch out, Tom. Matt will get even with you."

"Maybe."

"They make a pair, don't they?" Julie's remark was rhetorical, and she got on Socks and rode him into the arena.

A wave of homesickness hit Tom—hard. While he was occupied with acting, he had swept the love of horses and family out of his mind and his heart—or so he thought. Now, it was coming back again, in spades. Had he allowed Matt to drive him away—or had it been his father who didn't live here anymore? What about the death of his mother? A combination of all three? Sadness overwhelmed him as he watched Julie and Brenda riding their horses. He shook it off. He engrossed himself in local gossip while listening to spectators on the rail.

"Can you imagine someone being killed at a horse show, Sarah?"

"No. Nothing exciting ever happens except someone falling off their horse occasionally," the lady named Sarah replied.

"Was he from around here?" the other woman asked.

"Yeah, I knew him when he worked for Tony Richardson. He drove the trailer that had all those drugs under the floorboards, or spare tires, or something. Do you remember that? Ha… I think half the folks wondered why they hadn't thought of it first."

The other woman nodded her head. "Everything seems to happen at the same time, doesn't it? Don't you remember all those barns being robbed around the same time?"

"Yeah. I sure do. We got a pair of Dobermans to protect our place."

"By the way, did you know that Tom Rogers's barn was robbed last week? I've been worried sick. Anyone could pull up…" They turned their conversation into local thievery.

So, there's been barn robberies in the area, Tom thought. Maybe that's how Eddie existed while he's been hiding. But wouldn't someone have seen him?

He focused on Brenda and Julie loping their horses around the ring. Julie's dark green shirt and blue jeans made her hair look redder, shimmering like copper in the sunlight. The movement of her horse and the gentle June breeze caused it to fly around her face.

It had been a long time since he had been on horseback, and he was thinking about how much he'd like to ride again. Western pleasure riders worked their horses, trying for the slow, steady, and graceful paces they would need during their performance. The reining horses practiced spins, turns, and sliding stops as the English riders waited to take their horses over a small bar in the corner of the arena. They looked like a jumping assembly line.

Tom returned to the main arena, where Paul stood, watching their handlers lead the halter horses into the ring.

"You miss this?" Paul asked.

"A little, I guess. How couldn't you help but miss it?" Tom couldn't conceal his bitterness.

"You really riled up Matt before, you know."

"I know. I meant to. What a trashy way to treat his wife. She's what's keeping their business together."

"I know she is. She's very unhappy. We're both coping as best we can."

"I know." Tom suddenly felt a kindred spirit with his younger brother. It wasn't only Brenda that was unhappy. He wondered why Paul didn't venture out on his own. What was holding Paul there?

"Paul, do you know if Eddie Meeks had been seen in the area?" he asked, changing the subject.

"No. I have no idea. No one's seen him that I know of... Why?"

"Just wondering... overheard some ladies talking. They mentioned some barns being robbed. I was wondering if there was any connection. Phil asked me to keep my eyes open. If you hear anything, let me know, okay?"

"Yeah, sure, if you want."

"Who's that in the ring?" Tom pointed to a big sorrel mare being shown in a halter class. The judge moved her in front of a long line of horses.

"That's one of Greg's horses," Paul said. "She's a beauty, isn't she?"

"Who's showing her?" Tom asked.

"Greg's girlfriend. He's keeping his horses there until he can establish himself."

"Good. I want to talk to her after this class is over."

Tom cornered the woman on her way back to the barn. "Hi, you don't know me. I'm Tom Carter."

The woman stopped short, gave him a terse look, and kept going. Tom followed. "Look, I don't mean to be rude, but I really don't want anything to do with the Carters. Okay? This is a really bad time for you to be talking to me."

"Why?" Tom replied. I just want to ask you some questions. I'm trying to help Greg, really."

"Why should you want to do that?"

"Look. I grew up with the Richardsons. They were my friends, and I knew them." He thought of Tony and his mother and father, all dead. Then he thought of the one living member. Greg. "I know them well. I want to help."

The woman turned to Tom and said, "I'm sorry for being so rude. My name is Laurie Fielding. I'm engaged to Greg. I'm really worried about him."

"So am I," Tom said.

"You're nothing like your brother, are you?"

"Which brother? Oh, you mean Matt? No, I guess we're not very similar."

"Walk with me," Laurie said. "I need to put Greg's horse away."

Laurie Fielding was a woman of average height and medium build. Although a bit heavy around the hips, she carried herself well, and her presence radiated kindness. Her pale face showed agelessness. She could have been between twenty and forty; in reality, she was twenty-six. Her thick, dark brown hair started falling out of her bun, and a bobby pin dropped. Tom stooped to pick it up and handed it to her.

"She's beautiful," Tom said, admiring the horse walking by her side.

"Yes, isn't she? She's a Richardson homegrown special. When Greg left Illinois, he took five horses with him. Esmerelda is one of them. She's already a champion three-year-old halter mare."

They returned to the stalls and found themselves alone. They continued to talk about the horses, and then Laurie said, "What did you want to talk to me about anyway?"

"Well, about the other night."

"Greg went over all that with the police."

"Yeah, Phil told me."

"Okay." She looked at him as though determining how much to trust him and said, "We got here around three o'clock in the afternoon, unloaded the horses and equipment, and then parked in the parking area where the camper is now. Our, my boarders, bless their hearts; they're wonderful. They helped bed and feed the horses. We all went to dinner, and Greg and I stayed with my aunt and uncle, who live about five miles from here. We talked until eleven, mostly about family and a little about Tony. Greg still misses him terribly."

"I can imagine. Please go on," Tom said softly.

"Well, this is delicate. We didn't stay in the same room. My family is not the kind who approves of that arrangement. Greg told me he would check on the horses and come back. I woke up at about one, and his truck was gone. He said that he didn't go near the camper... drove directly to the barn, checked the horses, and then came back here."

"Did you hear him pull in?"

"About one thirty. I saw the headlights outside. My room overlooks the driveway."

"Anyone see him?"

"Yes, the security guard on duty in the barn. But what difference does that make? He was there only for a minute. That man was killed—when?"

"Between twelve and two, they believe. I think they've narrowed it down to around one o'clock."

"Greg must have gotten here when it happened. It's just awful. He could have killed him. He was here at the right time. But he didn't..." she said softly and started to cry.

Tom put his arm around her. "Laurie, it'll be okay." A few minutes later, Tom asked, "Did Greg see anyone else?"

"He said he didn't." Laurie started crying again. "I'm sorry. I'm so worried about him.

"Don't sell police short. Laurie, what will you do now? I mean, will you stay through the show?"

"I think so. I mean... yes. I can't leave until Greg is released."

"Brenda and Paul suggested you bring your horses to our place if you want to stay here afterward."

"I'm grateful for the offer. I think we'll stay here until after the show tomorrow. I might take the horses over to my aunt and uncle's farm. Or I may stay up here and let someone else drive the horses home. That's probably the best solution."

"It would be better if you went with them, Laurie. There's a killer on the loose who wants to frame Greg. They already set up Tony and probably killed him."

"Oh. Then you think that Tony didn't commit suicide, either?"

"Either?"

"Greg thinks that Tony was murdered."

"If it's any consolation, so do I." Tom looked at her, realizing he cared a great deal about who did it and why. "Laurie, be careful."

The show continued for the rest of the day without any major incidents. Tom kept his eyes and ears open and watched as Julie showed her horse, placing first in one class and second in another. Brenda beat the top contenders for the open professional classes, and Matt spurred Lynette's horse into the ring for the Junior Pleasure Class. Lynette hung over the rail.

"Watch it, Lynette, you'll spook your horse like that," Julie said, getting off and handing the reins to Tom as she readjusted her black leather chaps.

"You all really hate me, don't you?" Lynette said, continuing the morning's conversation.

"That has nothing to do with spooking your horse, Lynette."

"You know I love Matt, don't you?"

Julie was stunned as Lynette confronted her.

"Julie, he doesn't love her anymore."

"He told you that?" Julie asked.

"Uh, yes."

"Look around you, Lynette. Who's representing this barn? Who's winning all those ribbons? Who's training all those horses? And..." she paused, "who's making a name for the Carter Ranch? Can you do that, Lynette? This is not about an affair. This is about a horse business and a family. Families stick together. He cannot let Brenda go no matter what Matt does or says. Can't you see that?"

Her intensity hit her. Embarrassed, she shot Tom a look and took the reins back. She wondered why this attack was coming toward her and not Brenda.

And she heard Lynette mutter, "Bitch. You think you're so great, honey. I'll get you good. You just see if I don't."

CHAPTER 7

Early morning sunlight illuminated tables of bacon, eggs, and cinnamon rolls and streamed toward the end of the room, resting on a massive pot of freshly brewed coffee. The show committee was holding a breakfast for exhibitors.

The inviting aromas and spirited breezes from the open windows created false illusions of cheerfulness and offered a shameless contrast to the general mood. Few were smiling.

Julie sat at a table talking with Tom and Laurie, while Brenda and Paul stood nearby talking with friends from out of state. Matt periodically floated in and out. She didn't notice Lynette anywhere.

"Have you made plans for this evening?" Tom asked Laurie.

"Your Chief of Police suggested I take the horses back to Kentucky. For some reason, they think I might be safer away from here. It is getting a little spooky. They won't let me into the camper yet but say I can take it home this evening."

Julie's mind wandered, knowing this was not her conversation. She wondered if she should be jealous and why that even entered her mind.

She put her hand on Tom's arm and excused herself. Bumping her way through the crowded hall towards the buffet table, she spoke with several people she knew, and all the conversations were the same—what the hell's happening here to our community? Her general depressed state started to take an additional plunge with the morose attitudes filtering through the room. Not paying attention, she nearly spilled her coffee when someone jostled her arm.

"Excuse me." A man in his early thirties with dark curly hair and deep blue eyes caught her arm and saved the hot cup from disaster.

"Sorry. I got bumped from behind."

"That's okay. It's a bit tight in here," she replied, getting squeezed by some exhibitors she recognized from the show. They tried to cram into the long line.

"I recognize you. You ride with the Carter Ranch, don't you?" He asked.

"Yes, how did you know?"

"My name is Lorenzo Ortega… uh, Larry. I bought a horse from Matt. He's being shipped up from Texas… I think, tonight."

"From Mr. Carter's ranch?" Julie asked.

"That's right."

"I got my horse from there. He's wonderful."

"Yes, I know. I've been watching you ride." He smiled and brushed against her as he reached over the table for cream to put in his coffee. "I just want a horse to trail ride… nothing fancy. I hope we can get to know each other. Maybe you could show me the ropes… show me around."

She realized he was hitting on her and suddenly wanted to get away.

"But," Larry continued, "I'm originally from Mexico. I've lived in the States most of my life. My brother has a business in Indiana. I work for him."

"What kind of business?" Julie asked.

"Import and export…"

Although Larry did most of the talking, Julie felt his attention was elsewhere. His eyes darted back and forth, circling the room before they came back and rested on her.

"It takes me out of the country frequently. Mostly down south to Central and South America," he said.

"How exciting for you." A pang of envy welled inside Julie. She wanted to travel but didn't have much opportunity.

"Some pretty exciting stuff is happening right here," Larry said, glancing around the room again. "Been riding with the Carter's long?"

Julie told him about getting Socks, and how Brenda had supervised their training program. She couldn't believe she'd come so far in such a brief time.

She wasn't sure Larry had been listening.

He asked, "Carters do some traveling themselves, don't they?" Once again, he glanced around and then focused back on her. She wondered who he was looking for.

"Horse shows mostly," Julie said.

"Out of state? I hear there are some pretty big shows in Ohio and Oklahoma. Planning on showing in any of them?"

"I can only dream," Julie answered. She meant it. She would have loved nothing more than to qualify and show at the World Show in Oklahoma.

"With Matt and Brenda, you probably will." Larry took a sip of his coffee.

Julie thought he would let up on the questions, but he didn't. "They have anything going to Oklahoma?"

"Maybe Brenda's gelding. The one she's riding today," Julie replied.

"Larry, glad you could come." Matt suddenly appeared again from nowhere.

"Got away from that brother of yours. Come to watch us show?" The two men shook hands like they were the best of friends.

Julie looked for an escape but couldn't find a polite opening.

"My Dad said he planned to ship your horse up last Friday. It should be here tonight or tomorrow. My wife can teach you a thing or two about riding. Hell, so can this woman. Eh, Julie?"

"Uh-huh," replied Larry. Matt took a step toward Larry, effectively blocking Julie from the conversation.

Julie wanted to get away but couldn't. She stayed, feeling awkward, as the two men talked—not excluding her altogether, but not including her either. She observed Larry closely. He was a handsome man with a slight but not overly pronounced accent. It was charming. But, despite his new interest in horses, something was not quite right about him. She couldn't put her finger on it. He had bumped into her—seemingly on purpose. There wasn't anything really wrong with the questions he asked, but Julie sensed that something just didn't fit. Maybe it was the wariness in his tone.

It was just that he reminded her of her neighbor, Mr. Murphy. When some kid had vandalized his property, Mr. Murphy would be really friendly to the neighborhood children—talk with them, joke with them, ask questions about their friends, until he'd ask the right question and then, as if by magic, he knew who'd tore up those flower beds. The man was amazing. He would have been dynamite in the CIA.

Julie wondered what Larry Ortega's real purpose could be in being at the horse show. Somehow, she didn't feel it was just about buying a horse.

Two men driving a red Dually and pulling a horse trailer, pulled into a small diner off Interstate 44 just outside of Springfield, Missouri. They were no longer able to outrun the storm that had tailed them from the Texas border, and now rain was pelting at their windshield so hard, they thought the glass might shatter. There were tornado warnings in the area.

The two men ran for it into the diner and shed parkas at the entrance.

"You guys made it just in time," a waitress said, smiling broadly and ushering them to a booth. There were just a few customers in the place, all travelers—refugees from the storm. "There are tornado warnings in the area."

The rain poured down, accompanied by lightning and thunderclaps, bursting at an interval of ten seconds apart.

"What'll it be?"

"Got any Scotch?"

"Sorry," she said. "Say, you're cute. What's your name?" The man was clean-shaven, blonde, with bright blue eyes and a ready grin. He looked as though he'd mastered the art of flirting.

"Bob. Bob Hanson. This here's my buddy Joe." Joe was the dark one of the two. He had wiry brown hair, a mustache, and hazel eyes, which penetrated Bob's impulsive behavior with a sour glance.

"Where you two from?" she asked, standing over the table, holding two menus.

"Texas, ma'am," Bob said.

"Well, Texas, ma'am. What'll ya have?"

They made their selections, and she turned, holding the menus, shouting directions at the cook. Then she shuffled over to other customers, leaving the two alone.

"How do you think the horse'll hold up in this storm?" Bob asked.

"Don't know. He's skittish… frightens easily at loud noises," Joe said.

"Matt knows about the switch?"

"Nope. The boss thought it was better he didn't. The kid's getting a bit out of hand, I hear. Teaching him a lesson in humility. Hah." He put a dollar in the table jukebox, and a country western number, 'Mama, Don't Let you Babies Grow up to be Cowboys,' came on.

"Hey, think anyone saw us last night?"

"Last night… why?"

"Yeah, when we… you know… cut the hose. I mean… suppose they fix it and send that other one up here anyway?" Bob whispered.

Joe bristled and half-stood. "Hey—are you nuts or something? Shut up."

Gusts of straight-line wind and ear-splitting thunder shook the place as torrents of rain poured down. Lightning brightened up a black sky in the middle of the day. Hail the size of golf balls pelted the metal roof of the diner, and the customers got unusually quiet. They moved away from the windows. Above the sounds of the violent weather, the two men could hear the horse screaming. Looking out, they saw the trailer rocking from side to side.

Bob turned toward the parking lot and the storm. "You think he'll break the damned trailer… turn it over or something?"

"I hope to hell not. We'll give him a tranquilizer when we get back."

"Yeah, if he don't kill us first."

The tray shook, and the waitress brought their hamburgers and milkshakes.

The weather was letter-perfect, as Julie showed in her classes. She made a stunning picture in a long, white-sleeved western blouse embroidered with tiny gold flowers, black chaps, and a black hat on top of her tall gray horse with a black and white saddle pad. Her saddle finished the picture with silver snips on its skirt. However, her concentration weakened, and she placed second and third, respectively.

Around four o'clock, gusts of wind started blowing sand from the arena, and some of it came flying into the now-emptying aisles of the horse barn. In their tack stall, Julie had to turn her back from getting flying debris into her eyes.

"Julie,"

Startled, Julie turned around to see Tom standing by the stall door.

"Uh… sorry, didn't mean to scare you." He looked serious. "There's something I need to tell you." He took her by the arm and brought her over to a far corner of the stall.

"What is it?"

"Greg's disappeared."

"He's what?" Julie gasped in disbelief.

"Shhh… I just spoke with Phil. They released him this morning. He was going to come back here, but he never arrived."

"My God, has this place gone crazy? Where can he be? Did he skip town, do you think? Skip bail? Was he afraid?" Julie's words came in gasps, trying to be quiet but hitting hard at the implications. Then, she envisioned Laurie. "Oh my God. Poor Laurie."

Tom took her hand. "I know. Phil told her to take the horses and go back to Kentucky. Julie, he's sending Laurie home with an escort. That's how serious this is."

"What's the count now? One drug bust, two murders, and two disappearances. This is as good as any novel I've ever read."

She almost laughed but realized that she would have cried instead.

"Look, we're pulling out of here. Paul's bringing the rig up now. You don't have to get too organized. We can do that when we get home. Let's get out of here."

"Are we in danger? From what? We're not involved with this."

"No, probably not. But still, I want to get back." Tom shook his head and looked concerned. "Brenda is talking to the show secretary and will be along. Just get ready to go."

"Okay."

Tom took her hand and held it. Then, doing something unexpected, he touched her cheek gently with the tip of his fingers. Some moments later, as if waking up from some dream, he released his hand and walked out of the stall, carrying her saddle.

Julie looked thoughtfully after him, suddenly out of breath—her heart racing.

As soon as Paul arrived, Brenda came from one direction, Matt from the other, and everyone grabbed a horse. Julie looked around at the vacating grounds, where so much had happened in such a short time.

Julie and Brenda decided to ride back with Tom, leaving Paul and Matt to haul the horses. The arrangement seemed to suit everyone except Paul. They pulled out just ahead of the Eagle Ranch van as Laurie flagged them down. Tom stopped, and Laurie got out of the camper.

"I want to thank you," she said. "You've made everything so much easier for me. Stay in touch, okay?"

"I will. I promise. I noticed you'll have some company on the way down?"

"Yeah, my bodyguards. I also have some great supporters from our barn. Friends will stay with me until Greg gets back. Thanks for offering to take us in. You're the best." She hugged Tom through the window and grinned at Julie, then turned, got back into the vehicle, and left with her entourage.

The sun was starting to set as they drove toward the Interstate. Julie sat in awed silence, still in love with the flat parcels of land and the rows and rows of yellow corn stalks maturing in the fields—*God's country.*

Brenda started humming an old folk song. Julie and Tom joined in with, "Here, *Blu oo oo, you're a good dog, too.*" Soon, all three were singing folk songs and trading tall tales. It was the first time Julie had seen Brenda laugh out loud with any spontaneity. She wondered if Tom had that effect on everyone. Out of the corner of her eye, she watched him drive. He chatted easily about the horse show, his dog, and the theater. She wondered why he wasn't married. As if on cue, Brenda came to her rescue.

"Tom, why aren't you married?" Julie turned back and looked at her. Brenda winked.

She's trying to fix us up, she thought.

Tom sighed. "I just haven't met the right woman, I guess. Acting creates an unsteady lifestyle. The women I meet aren't very anxious to be tied down, and their personal lives are unstable. Don't get me wrong. I've dated some nice girls. Unfortunately, a lady who could handle my acting career and my passion for horses and dogs seems to elude me."

He put his hand in the air as a gesture of frustration. "My dad tried to fix me up with a few girls. I wasn't interested in them."

"Because your dad suggested them?" Brenda asked.

"I don't know. Maybe." Tom said. "That was a very perceptive remark."

"Perhaps." Brenda replied, "But I know your history."

Tom glanced back at Brenda. "What about my baby brother? Does he have a personal life?"

Brenda hesitated and sighed as she turned toward the window. "No, not that I know of."

"How about you, Julie? Why aren't you…?"

"Cause she doesn't want to be right now." Brenda closed out the topic of conversation.

They pulled down the ranch's driveway around eight o'clock, helped by gusts of wind at their back. The sky was darkening with cumulonimbus clouds swelling with condensation. It looked like a nasty storm was brewing. Julie hoped she could get home before it started. A red Dually hitched to a silver four-horse trailer was parked in front of the barn. Splotches of mud caked the wheels and coated both vehicles as though they'd already been through severe weather. Two men got out of the front seat, one dark with a mustache, the other blonde and clean-shaven, wearing wet and mud-stained pants. They looked exhausted.

"Howdy," said the dark one, turning to Brenda, who'd just gotten out of the truck. "You the Carters?" Brenda nodded her head and looked at the van. "Got a delivery for you. Bob, bring out the horse, will you?"

"From my father-in-law's ranch?" Brenda peered through the back slats. "That horse has been sold to one of our new boarders. I'm glad to see he's arrived safely. New trailer?"

"Yeah. I guess. I'm just delivering. I'm Joe. You must be Mrs. Carter?"

"Please, Brenda." Brenda reached out to shake Joe's hand.

"Okay, Brenda. Where's Matt?"

"We've just gotten back from a horse show. He's still in the rig. Hang on. I'll turn the lights on for you." Brenda ran into the barn, the wind catching her hair and blowing it into her face as she reached for the light switch. Fluorescent beams flooded the area, and the local mosquito population immediately seemed to gravitate upward, many careening back down as they got zapped by the insect traps.

"Hey, Joe," Bob yelled. "Give me a hand."

Julie heard scrambling noises and hooves beating down on the van floor. She raised her eyebrows. It must have been a rough trip. Instinctively, she looked back toward the west and noticed fast-moving dark clouds starting to obscure a darkening sky. The moon rolled out from behind one cloud and then seemed to be pushed behind another. It tried one more time to illuminate the earth, then gave up and hid behind a larger and more authoritative shadow. It stayed there. For a while, its glow shimmered through, then dimmed, and finally gave up entirely. A blast of cold, damp air slapped Julie in the face.

Suddenly, her attention turned away from the sky to a coal-black body emerging from the out-of-state trailer. She turned to watch.

"Watch it!" Joe shouted, as the horse plunged down the ramp, nearly knocking Bob off the side. The rope pulled out of Bob's hands. Joe looked at Bob with disgust and shook his head. Then he turned back to Brenda. "Where do you want him?"

Silently, she turned away from Joe and picked up the lead rope, starting to lead the horse into the barn.

"Uh… you want us to take him for you?" Bob started to take the rope from Brenda.

The horse reared, and Bob jumped out of the way. Brenda grabbed his halter.

"That's okay. You two have done enough." She smiled and patted the animal's neck. As if by some silent signal, he snorted and settled beside her. As she rubbed him behind his ears, Julie wanted to laugh. The horse seemed to be telling Brenda all about his trip and these two clowns. As if in reply, she could hear Brenda crooning, "Easy son. It's okay. Rough trip? Thought so. Poor boy." She was amazed at how easily the horse followed her as though he'd known her all his life. That had always been true about Brenda. Somehow, she could take the wildest colts and have them eating out of her hand. Too bad she hadn't been able to do that with her husband.

Matt watched silently as Brenda disappeared into the barn.

"She's got a way with the horses, that's for sure…" Joe shrugged his shoulders and turned to Matt. "We outran a storm… got caught in Missouri, where we stopped for lunch. Damned straight liners nearly blew the windows in. Thought the horse would wreck the trailer." He looked down at his wet pants. "Stepped into some mud up to my knees."

Matt looked at them with an icy stare that Julie couldn't figure out. He didn't seem pleased to see them. The two men stood beside him, watching the horses unloaded from Carter's van. They were silent as though waiting for something.

As Julie unloaded Socks, she heard Brenda call over to Paul, "We need to put fresh sawdust inside the door before we leave. It's supposed to storm tonight, and we don't want a flood of water coming in under the door, okay? I'll get the back door. Also, we need to fix the grate on the black horse stall. It's coming loose from those splintered boards. The stall probably needs a new door."

Julie put on her jacket as she left the barn and looked up again at the sky. It was almost totally clouded over now. The last clomping of hooves beat onto the concrete, then fell silent as horses were put away and fed. She could still hear voices back in the barn.

The cool evening air felt good on her sunburned face. The lot looked deserted as Julie returned to the trailer to sort out the things that were going home with her. She moved quietly as if afraid she might break some enchantment. As she sorted, she heard voices coming from the other side of the trailer. Peering out through a small window, she saw Joe and Bob talking with Matt directly beneath. The arena lights shown directly onto the three men so she could catch their reactions as they talked.

"Joe, what the hell are *you* doing here?" Matt's face was livid with anger.

"Shh,"

"Nobody's here. They're all in the barn. Why are you here, and who the hell's this?" He turned to Bob.

"I'm a new hired hand working at the ranch. Came along to help."

"Yeah, but why? We were expecting a horse but not from you… and not this one. This *wasn't* the one that was supposed to be delivered here."

"We're just following orders, Matt. Just like you."

"I don't know nothing about any orders."

"No? Don't surprise me none. Maybe you weren't told."

"The old man tells me everything. I'm expecting a different horse. You guys get your sorry asses out of here before…"

"Before what? Listen, Matt. You don't call the shots, okay? You may be a big wheel up here, but you're still only one of us. Things have changed."

Julie could see the tension rise in Matt's body posture.

"What kind of things? And where is the damned animal we bought?"

Joe smirked. "Still down in Texas. He'll be there for a while until they get their van fixed. Broken gas line, I think."

"What…?"

"Your friend, Larry Ortega… One who bought the horse?"

"What about him?"

"You really don't know, do you? Stupid fuckin' hotshot."

Julie watched Joe toy with Matt. It reminded her of the old orange and black cat she once had before he pounced on a tiny field mouse who'd been unlucky enough to stumble into the house.

Joe grinned. It didn't seem like a pleasant grin. "He works undercover for the DEA."

"What?" Matt shook his head—wide-eyed, uncomprehending. "How do you know?"

"An associate… recognized him from a newspaper clipping during a drug bust in New Orleans. You sent a photograph of some of your so-called friends. Man, how could you be so stupid?"

Julie sensed Joe was enjoying himself. She wondered how long it would be before Matt would lose it.

"What associate… who?"

"Uh-uh, Matt. No names."

"What do you mean, no names? You work for me." Matt was angry and his voice was rising.

"Shut up, Matt. I don't work for you."

"If he is what you say, what's he doing here?" Matt asked.

"He's here spying on your ranch and on you, asshole."

"Me? Nobody's got anything on me."

"No? Then why did they send him here?"

"Maybe he just wanted to buy a horse."

"Yeah, right." His voice oozed with sarcasm.

"Well, that horse will kill him. I know him."

"Uh-huh… yep. That's the general idea. If not, kill him, hurt him. Bad enough to keep him from snooping any further into our business. The old man sent him up here as a kind of a gift… a warning. Maybe a permanent one." Joe was standing close to Matt and didn't seem intimidated by him. Julie sensed that Matt was backing down. The power lay in the hands of Joe.

"By the way, heard Eddie was killed this weekend. Know anything about that, Matt?"

"How the hell should I know? They arrested Richardson. He had a reason to kill Eddie." Matt was on the defensive.

"Hah! I think Richardson blames his brother's death on you."

"*Me?* Why? Because I sold him the horses?"

"Tony Richardson didn't sell drugs up here, Matt."

"How do you know? Maybe he had something going on with someone else. Look, we're better off without Eddie. He's a whiner and shot his mouth off. Whoever killed him did us a favor."

"Well, I'm not sure the boss looks at it that way…" Lightening lit up the sky, and thunder crackled in the background. Matt looked around and his eyes rested on the trailer window. Julie ducked just in time.

"Oh, and Matt…"

"What?"

"Boss wants to know how it's going at the old Eagle Ranch. The new apartment ready?"

"Yeah, the Smiths are already there. They've been making changes in the barn. Renovated the apartment."

"Okay, good. You take care of that wife of yours. It's gotten back to the old man that you're running around on her. He doesn't want to see her get hurt. She's important to this ranch and to our business. Her father…"

Matt almost exploded. "I damned well know all about her father."

Joe coolly turned his back on Matt and said, "Okay, Bob, we can leave now."

Bob nodded and said, "Nice to meet you, Matt." It wasn't exactly sincere.

As they pulled out, Joe called, "Matt, don't do anything stupid."

Matt stood rigid, almost shaking, as the trailer pulled out of the parking lot and down the driveway, then disappeared.

Julie was scared. She waited until she thought Matt was gone and picked up a few of her things. Then, taking a deep breath, she opened the door and ran headlong into Brenda.

"Oh my God, you scared me half to death," she said.

"Julie, you're white as a sheet. What's the matter?"

Julie was tempted to tell her the whole story, but Matt came right behind Brenda. Sheer terror gripped her. The look on his face said everything. He knew she had overheard.

"I must be overtired. I'll go home as soon as I get this stuff put away." She tried to control the tremor in her voice.

"Julie, go on. I can put your tack away for you."

"Thanks, I'd really appreciate that." Julie walked out toward her van and turned back. She saw Tom engrossed in conversation with Matt and watched Matt staring at her as he talked.

Completely unnerved, Julie drove home.

CHAPTER 8

Whan Julie finally pulled into her driveway and exited her van, she
involuntarily turned around to look over her shoulder. A car passed
her house, slowed down, then sped away. She hurried in and slammed the
door behind her, basking in the stillness of the house.

The noises started almost immediately, coming from the front bedroom. Startled, Julie began to hyperventilate, until she heard the reassur-
ing barks and whines of her vibrant and enthusiastic collie. Her neighbor
must have brought Annie home from her mini-vacation next door.

For the first time that evening, Julie felt protected. As she rumpled the
sable fur of her dog, she realized how much she missed her and how scared
she was.

"This is crazy," she said to Annie. "There's no one following me. My
God, I need a reality check." If her dog's ears had leaned further forward,
they would have fallen off her head.

Turning on the television to a late-night news broadcast, she stripped
off her clothes and got into a hot shower, putting it on as hot as she could
stand it. Besides getting off all the horse show dirt and grime, she started
to relax—body and soul.

She grabbed a blanket from the closet and dragged it into the living
room, where she curled up to watch the news. Julie dozed off and awoke
with Annie barking at the window. She jumped up, nearly knocking her
cell phone off the cocktail table, and went to the window to discover the
object of the dog's displeasure—the neighbor's cat.

"I'm really glad I've got you," she said, hugging Annie. "If anyone wanted to bother us, I'd at least know they were there. I guess that's some comfort." Still shaking, she walked into the kitchen, looking around for the lights as the evening shadows of the old oak tree danced onto her kitchen floor. The wind kicked up again, and the whistles emphasized her Gothic-terror mood.

Taking a glass from the oak cabinet above the sink, she jumped as Annie started to bark again. This time, the glass slid out of her hand onto the floor. It shattered, but again, it was a false alarm. Normally, Julie was used to her dog's barking. That's what collies do for a living, she thought. Part of the collie modus operandi. I teach school and write. You bark. She chuckled through her nervousness.

After cleaning up the glass on the floor, Julie got a plastic water glass and went into the bedroom. She put on a CD of some Mozart and set the player on *repeat*.

"This should calm me down," she said to Annie, who leaped onto her bed and settled for the night. The music played softly, and the moon crept between the mini blinds in her window. The loud ringing of the telephone shattered the stillness of the room. After regaining her composure, Julie picked up the receiver.

"Hello?"

A familiar voice said, "Julie?"

"Tom."

"I'm sorry to call you so late. I wanted to make sure you got home all right. You're there, so I guess you did." He paused. "I didn't get a chance to say goodbye to you," he said.

"I'm sorry I didn't wait. I was plain exhausted. You said goodbye. You're not going anywhere, are you?"

"Afraid so. I'm going back to the city tomorrow."

Julie felt an empty rush batter against her already knotted-up insides. She wondered why.

"Oh well, I'm sorry you have to leave. Although some awful things happened, it was a very nice weekend. When are you coming back this way?" She held her breath, waiting for the reply.

"Oh, a couple of days, I should imagine. I'm getting together with Phil and his wife for dinner. Julie…" he stopped. "Would you like to come with me?"

Julie didn't know what to say. She wanted to go with him but chose the safe way out. She declined. When she put the phone down, her whole body shook.

She remembered the last time she had been in love. Randy was good-looking, talented, and intelligent. They shared the same classes and interests and were both opera buffs. They often went to the opera, laughed, and even co-hosted parties. They got along as well as any couple she knew.

She remembered sitting in his apartment one night when he approached her with a glass of wine and suggested she move in. They were toasting each other and making love on his plush carpeted floor—an evening she would remember—always. As she looked back, he changed the subject or pushed back the date whenever she mentioned a time to move.

Shortly before graduation, Julie went to his apartment to surprise him. She brought Chinese food and a bottle of wine and waited. The phone rang. Julie remembered wondering whether she should answer it. Well, why not? We will be living together, so she picked up the receiver.

"Hello?"

"Hello. Who's calling?"

"It's Barbara. Is Randy there?"

"No, he's not back yet. Can I tell him what this is concerning?"

"Yes, you can," the woman replied, a coolness creeping into her voice. "Tell him it's his wife. It's about our anniversary next weekend."

"His wife?" Julie sat on the couch and held her breath.

"Don't tell me. Are you another girlfriend?"

"Another?" Julie was stunned. So, she hadn't been the first. "Yes, I guess I am. I'm sorry… I didn't know… that Randy was married. He never told me."

"He usually tells them up front so they have no expectations. How long have you been seeing him?"

"About a year. We were supposed to move in together."

"Oh dear."

"How long have you two been apart?"

"We aren't. We live in upstate New York, and while I finish school here, he finishes school in the city. He comes up every other weekend. We're planning on living in Europe after we both graduate. Out of curiosity, what does he tell you he's been doing during those weekends?"

"Visiting his family," Julie said lamely. "I guess he didn't lie about that. I thought he had an elderly mother."

"He does. She lives with us. I'm very sorry. Randy does some shabby things sometimes. I've known all along about his affairs. I didn't know that he was serious about anyone."

"Perhaps he's not. Maybe I was the only serious one in this relationship," Julie replied. "Please believe me, I'm not a home wrecker. Again, I'm very sorry." Julie hung up.

When Randy came home, Julie told him about the conversation—no temper tantrums, no tears. Calmly, Julie explained that it was over between them. Randy didn't say a word. His jaw dropped, eyes widening as if a jolt of electricity had hit him. Julie looked back at the scene and wondered why there was shock. Didn't he realize the phone would ring someday, and she would pick it up? Was he really that stupid? Or did he *want* his wife to find out?

She turned over, facing the yellow lava light that formed an eerie glow on the walls.

Annie grunted and rolled over.

Julie's thoughts were still on Randy. He was now singing in opera houses in Europe. Four years had done wonders for his career. On the other hand, she moved to Chicago and was now a schoolteacher working in the inner city. She ran away and thought that might be a more apt description. Maybe he did her a favor. She thought she'd never let anyone that close again. Not even the handsome Tom.

She tried to push the past out of the way and focus on what she would do. Julie decided to go to the barn early to stop whatever was going to happen—stay all day if necessary. She could clean up her horse—who didn't need cleaning. Or she could clean her equipment—which didn't need cleaning, or she could clean up her locker. Should she tell anyone? Who? Tom? Tom was Matt's brother.

Matt knows I overheard them, she thought.

Annie grunted and rolled over again.

She remembered that Tom and Matt had been involved in an intense conversation when she had left. Could Tom be involved with this, too? That's just too incredible. And what about Brenda? Could she be involved with her husband's activities? *Dear God, I hope not. That would be more than I could stand.* Julie did something she rarely did these days. She prayed.

She scratched Annie's rump, and the dog groaned in ecstasy. Would anyone believe that Matt could deliberately train a horse to kill someone?

What was going on? She had come in the middle of a conversation and didn't know what they said before. Maybe she'd imagined the whole thing, and nothing was wrong. Perhaps everything would look different in the morning. Sure, and maybe pigs fly. Julie fell asleep.

Then, the dreams came. First, she was riding Socks at a horse show around the arena, winning her class. Tom was there, smiling and helping her off her horse, when suddenly he changed. It was Matt grabbing her wrists and throwing her on the ground. When she looked up, Randy was on top of her. Then the scene changed, and she was in a cabin, with soft classical music playing and the rush of a waterfall in the background.

Julie could smell the pine outside and the crackling of a delicious warm fire in the fireplace. Suddenly, the music turned discordant, and the smoke from the fireplace turned back into the room. She was choking… Fighting for breath, she ran to the door. Finding it locked, she ran to the back door and found it also bolted. Julie ran to the windows, which were locked, too. She threw a chair at a window, and the chair bounced back onto the floor.

Just then, she heard a crash from the ceiling and saw Tom breaking in from the skylight. On top of him came Matt with a knife. The two rolled around the floor as the smoke choked out the last bit of breath left in her. Julie woke up with a start. Annie was lying close to her face.

She got up and ran out of the room and into the bathroom, throwing cold water onto her face. Breathing hard, she looked into the mirror, amazed and horrified to see how ashen she appeared. She sat on the edge of her bathtub and started to cry. Fear gripped her like never before, and she shook all over. She took her temperature and read it at 100.2. Not dangerous, but indeed a warning.

Julie went back to bed and slept until five o'clock when a crash of thunder woke her. She heard the rain falling outside her window and pulled the covers over her head.

At six, the alarm woke her up. She wanted to stay in bed until, maybe, forever… The rain still pattered away on the rooftop, and she heard the faint sound of thunder in the distance. Julie got up and let Annie out, made some coffee, and threw on her jeans, rubber boots, and a white tee shirt with two horses on the front. She pulled her hair up in a ponytail and attempted to put on makeup, but her head still ached. I look horrible, she thought. And I think I have a fever. Swell, she added in disgust, as she pulled out two Tylenol tablets and washed them down with water.

After bringing her dog in, wet and smelling fragrant from the rain, she bundled into an old army jacket her father had given her. Then, they piled into Julie's van. The rain was coming down harder now, and the distant thunder was making a comeback and getting closer. She saw streaks of lightning on the horizon and wondered if Larry would come out on such a dismal day. She thought he probably would as she remembered their indoor riding arena.

Fifteen minutes later, Julie pulled into the driveway and drove down to the barn. She parked her van as close to the door as possible to avoid getting wet and ushered Annie out of the van. She didn't budge.

"Come on, Annie, let's go."

Annie didn't want to get out of the van.

"Come on, you'll only be outside for a few seconds. We can get inside the barn without getting wet. *Come on!*" she said.

Reluctantly, the dog jumped out of the van, staying as close to her as possible.

Julie had trouble opening the big sliding barn doors as she went in. The sawdust was wet as it caught most of the water that passed under the door. Her boots made clear, fresh tracks as she and her dog went inside. It was dark and quiet except for the snorting and pawing of the horses. Weren't they fed? She walked down the aisle toward Socks' stall. The horses upped their anxiety. They neighed and whinnied. All seemed to be talking to her, telling her they hadn't been fed and how much longer it was going to be, anyway.

Julie went in to see Socks. He was covered with lather. Julie felt a new wave of panic come over her. Was he about to colic? She had seen horses having attacks before, and it always started with a cold lather breaking out over their body. She looked over at the horses on either side of his stall. They were full of sweat as well. What was wrong with these horses? Why hadn't they been fed or watered?

Julie left Socks's stall to get the water hose when a gut-wrenching howl drowned out the horses' sounds. Julie dropped the hose and ran to the opposite side of the barn.

"*Annie!*" she screamed. Annie was pawing the ground by one of the stalls and barking furiously at something. Julie pulled her dog away and looked at the stall occupied by the new horse. But something was wrong. The new horse was no longer in his stall. Julie wondered if Matt had come down earlier and moved him. She walked back down the aisle and investigated the other stalls. He was not there. Annie ran back and forth between Julie and the now-empty stall, and Julie wondered why she kept going back. Annie started to howl again, and Julie felt shivers traveling up and down her spine, wondering why she was avoiding looking into the empty stall.

"This is stupid," she said. "I'm going back over there."

Annie ran to the front of the stall and peered in, then looked at Julie. When Julie approached, she noticed hoof prints coming in and out of the stall and something red—something thick and sticky-looking—blood. She pushed her dog out of the stall doorway and stepped inside.

As she moved to take another step, she took an abrupt step backward. Lying face down on the floor in the shadows in front of the stall, she saw the lifeless body of Matthew Carter with his head bashed in.

CHAPTER 9

Julie took one look at Matt's lifeless body, whirled into the stall across the aisle, and lost her breakfast. The silence in the barn was deafening. Even the horses seemed to be holding their breath. The rain pinged off the metal roof, and thunder rumbled in the distance, now coming closer—again. Cold chills of fear returned, and she sat on a hay bale huddled close to Annie. The two shivered together.

Suddenly, a crack of thunder blasted so close that the whole barn jumped into motion. The horses neighed with fright, and Julie jumped up as though something had picked her up from behind. She ran to the office and picked up the phone, almost afraid that the onslaught of a lightning bolt would electrocute her.

"Hello?" Tom's groggy voice answered the phone after an interminable five rings.

"Oh, my God, I'm so glad it's you!"

"Julie, is that you? What's wrong?'

"Tom, get over to the barn now, please. Your brother…" Her voice trailed off, unable to finish.

"What about my brother?'

"Oh my *God,* he's… dead. Please, hurry." Still shaking and nearly missing the cradle. She hung up the phone and went back over to the stall. Within minutes, she heard two men running down the driveway. They were soaked as they plunged into the barn.

Tom and Paul investigated the stall where their brother lay dead. Without saying a word, they turned around and sat next to Julie on a hay bale.

"When did you find him?" Tom asked when he regained his composure.   "About ten minutes ago." Another crack of thunder startled her, propelling her into finishing her story.

"I got here around seven thirty and went to look in on Socks. The horses hadn't been fed or watered. They seemed restless, and Annie acted strangely. Then, she started howling, and I followed her over there. The stall door was open." She stopped for a minute to catch her breath. "At first, I thought that Matt or Brenda moved the horse somewhere, so I checked. I came back and found Matt lying there…" Once again, her voice faltered.

"Tom, Annie didn't want to get out of the van. When I got her inside the barn, she cowered by me. I thought it was the storm." Julie started to cry. "His head is bashed in. His *head* is bashed in."

"Easy, Julie." Tom rested his hand on her trembling shoulder. "I'd better call Phil."

Julie and Paul waited in silence, unable to move or speak. The silence inside was oppressive, magnifying the storm's power, and the rain was coming down in sheets. Paul got a horse blanket and put it over Julie's shoulders.

"Why don't you come into the office? We'll put on the heater," Tom said when he returned. "Phil will be here in a few minutes. He slammed the receiver down when I told him what happened. We've got to tell Brenda, preferably before Phil gets here."

Tom took Julie into the office, followed by Paul a few minutes later. As Tom dialed the phone, in a low and unsteady tone, Paul said, "Tom, that horse… he's gone. He's not anywhere." Tom raised his eyebrows and then spoke on the phone.

"Bren, you should get down to the barn immediately. Put on a heavy coat, it's cold down here and, Brenda, come through the office door, okay? I'll explain when you get here."

"When she gets here, we'll keep her in here. Keep her away from the stall until Phil gets here. You didn't touch anything, did you?" His voice was sharp and strained."

"No, unless throwing up in the stall across the aisle counts," she said.

"No, probably not."

Julie and Tom sat on the sofa, which taunted the atmosphere by displaying colorful Southwestern throw covers. Paul sat across from them, absently flipping through an old Quarter Horse Journey stacked on a driftwood and glass coffee table. Rows of ribbons lined the walls of the room, and trophies, some sterling silver, sat in glass-enclosed trophy cases.

Brenda came in wearing a heavy parker over an old sweatshirt and rubber boots covering the pants leg of her jeans. Her long, damp hair hung loosely over her shoulders, and Julie thought she looked about twelve years old without her makeup. She looked at them with a puzzled expression.

"What's going on here? What's wrong? Julie, why are you here so early?'

"Brenda, Matt's dead." Paul plunged in using the direct approach.

"*What?* What do you mean he's *dead?* If this is a joke, this is in very bad taste," she said.

"This is no joke," Tom said. "Julie found him this morning about twenty minutes ago."

"You did what? Matt's… dead?" Brenda shook her head as though not quite comprehending. "But, why… why were you here so early?"

"I just came in to check on Socks. I wanted to make sure he wasn't sore from the weekend." Julie looked at the puzzled faces surrounding her and suddenly didn't know who to trust. She decided to keep her information quiet.

"Why so early? "Brenda persisted. "I would have figured you'd be sleeping in this morning."

"The storm woke me up," Julie said. "There was a crash of thunder. Anyway, I'm programmed to get up early. It seemed like a good day to clean my tack, my locker, and whatever else. When I came in, the horses hadn't been fed, my dog started to howl, and that new horse was gone."

"The horse is gone, too?" Brenda asked. "Has this whole place gone crazy? You mean my husband is dead, and someone stole the horse?" Her voice sounded incredulous.

"It looks like it," Tom said.

Brenda turned to walk out of the office into the barn. Tom got up to stop her, but a figure blocked her path. It was the imposing structure of Phil Swanson.

"Good morning, all," he said. "That's a pretty nasty scene out there."

"Please let me by," Brenda said. "I want to see my husband.'

"I don't think that's wise at the moment."

Brenda clenched her teeth and muttered, "I promise I will *not* get hysterical. Let me see him, please."

Phil let her pass, followed by Paul.

"Don't let them touch anything," Phil said to a uniform nearby. The police officer followed Brenda as she passed from the office to the aisleway.

A few minutes later, Brenda returned, leaning on Paul's arm. She was deathly white.

Phil glanced at Brenda and Paul as they shuffled back into the office. "Now then, please sit down." It was not a request.

"Who found him?" he asked, looking directly at Julie.

Julie flushed. "I did. But I think you knew that."

Phil nodded. "Why were you here so early in the morning?"

Julie thought she would scream if another person asked her that question. She repeated why she was there and refrained from the sarcasm that she felt. Phil eyed her, as though reading her thoughts.

"When are the horses usually fed?" Phil asked, turning his attention to Brenda.

"We take turns feeding," she said. "This morning was Matt's turn."

"What time?"

"About five, I think. I don't know. I didn't hear him… uh… go out." Julie caught the hesitation in Brenda's voice and knew Phil had noticed, too.

"You didn't think anything of it when he didn't come back?"

"No. I fell asleep again. Tom woke me up when he called. I didn't even have time to comb my hair. Mr. Swanson, I didn't come down here to kill my husband," she said.

Brenda and Paul exchanged glances. Brenda looked away.

"Not implying anything like that. I want to get all the information that I can. I'm noticing some mud in this room. Did you bring it in?"

"Yes, Tom told me to come in through the office door. It's closer to the house."

"There was mud already in here when I called Tom," Julie said, looking at the doorway.

"Tom, did you and Paul come in through this door?"

"No, we came in through the barn door. It was already open.'

"Did you open the barn door?" he asked Julie.

"Yes, when I came in." Julie didn't like the way this was going. Brenda was deathly pale, and Brenda, well, Brenda held her emotions to her chest. She thought all hell would break loose if Phil decided to arrest Brenda.

"Had it been opened already?"

"I don't think so. It was shut tight. I had trouble opening it."

Phil grabbed a pad and pen. "Where do you think this mud came from?"

"Matt always came through the office when he fed in the morning," Brenda said. "It's closer to the house."

Phil turned back to Julie. "Notice anything when you came in?"

"Well, no. I wasn't looking for anything. There was sawdust under the door, absorbing the water, so it was muddy. There weren't any tracks there. Just mine, now Tom and Paul's. But what's so unusual about that? This is a barn, and it was raining."

"So, we have a horse who disappeared and couldn't have gotten through the barn door by himself because it was closed. We had no tracks there when Julie got here, then we had three sets of tracks, and now we have about six sets of tracks," he sighed. "Swell!" He sounded disgusted. "And we have two sets of tracks coming in from the office. Brenda and possibly Matt made those," he continued. "I have someone checking the back of the barn now."

Julie thought he looked much more formidable than the other night.

"Look, I'm sorry I have to do this, but it's my job, and we've had three possible related deaths in this community that happened—two within the past couple of days." He paused, not looking the least bit sorry. "Mrs. Carter, when did you last see your husband?"

"Last night, down here."

"Last night?" He looked at her curiously. "Mrs. Carter… Brenda, are you and Matt not sleep… er… estranged?'

Brenda blanched. "He wasn't home all night," she replied, looking down at the ground. Her face turned red with embarrassment.

"Go on," he said in a softer tone.

"We got back around eight. There was a van here from my father-in-law's ranch. They brought a horse for a new boarder. His name is Larry Ortega, and he's expected to come here this morning. Maybe he won't come with all this rain. At least, I hope he doesn't."

"Go on, Mrs. Carter. Did you know these men?"

"No, they weren't the ones that usually come up here. I didn't recognize the rig, either. It was a different one. I was too tired to notice anything. All I wanted to do was to unload our trailer and get the horses fed."

"Don't you have someone to do that for you?"

"Yes. We have a neighbor come in when we're gone. I'm talking about the horses we took to the show. We loaded up and left around seven o'clock. We stopped to speak to Laurie, Greg's girlfriend, on the way out. We pulled in around eight. Julie left a little after nine or so, didn't you?"

Julie nodded.

"When did you go back to the house?"

"Well, soon after that. Matt talked to the driver and his friend, then they left. That's really all there was to it."

"They worked for your father-in-law?"

"I assume they did," she looked at Paul, who nodded and shrugged his shoulders. "At least I didn't recognize those two."

"I'm surprised they didn't come in and stay overnight. Do they usually leave so abruptly?"

"I didn't think about it one way or the other. They didn't ask. I was too tired to care. If Matt wanted them to stay over, I'm sure they would have.'

"Is there any reason *why* anyone would want to steal that horse?" Phil continued.

"I can't think of any. Dad said he was a nice horse and well-trained for a beginner, but he had no papers. He wouldn't bring much on the market."

Julie looked at Brenda. Either she was a good actress or believed what she was saying. Brenda returned her look, raised her eyebrows, and looked away.

Then she looked at Phil, plunked down on a wooden bench in front of the heater, took notes, and observed. She suspected Phil's years on the force taught him to read people. He was looking at all four of them as though they were strangers—and liars. Even worse, he was looking at her that way, too.

He passed on Julie and continued, "Mrs. Carter, can you think of any reason why anyone would want to kill your husband?"

"I can think of many reasons why someone would want to kill Matt," Brenda said. "Phil, you know my husband wasn't a nice man. He used people, sold them unsound horses, and he cheated and lied. He was cheating on me with a girl from this barn. Matt didn't do right by people. Somebody got even. Why they stole the horse is anyone's guess. I just don't know." She stopped and sighed. "You may as well know this. Matt had business on the side. I don't know if it has anything to do with anything, but he spent a lot of time hauling horses for his Uncle George. I tried to learn more about it, but he shut me out. So, I left him alone."

Paul looked at Phil and said, "As far as I know, it was legit. I took over for him once or twice. There wasn't anything illegal about it. At least, I don't think so."

Phil shrugged and made a note. "Did you hear anyone drive in or out last night?" Phil looked like he was asking anyone who might have an answer.

"No, I didn't, but it was storming pretty hard," Brenda said.

Tom and Paul just shook their heads, puzzled.

"Damn it, if nobody drove in or out of here, how did the horse get out? The barn door was closed. Doors don't close by themselves. Wait… don't you have a back door that connects to a back pasture?"

Paul nodded.

They walked to the back of the barn, where they found the back door wide open. The still visible tracks were blotted into a muddy collage by the torrents of the night's rain. There was no way to determine whether someone had led a horse out that way during the night.

Tom and Paul led Phil and his two police officers out into the rain and through the back pasture to the gate. Julie and Brenda stood watching from the back door as the men stood, looking at the closed gate and shaking their heads.

Julie went back and stood by the empty stall, looking down into the lifeless body of Brenda's husband. The four-foot sliding door was wide open, the bottom half made of wood, and the top had a railing consisting of iron bars. One bar from the top of the stall door was missing, and the others seemed to hang loosely out of splintered wood. The stall was filled with sawdust and hay streaked with blood. Julie stooped to pick up the bar on the side of Matt's head.

"Don't touch that," a voice boomed from behind, and she turned around. "That's evidence," Phil said. "Whose fingerprints do you think might be on this?" He turned and looked at her.

"Probably all of us, from one time or another," she replied. We've all had access to this stall. "Wait, do you think this might be the murder weapon?"

"Maybe." He didn't say anything further but carefully picked it up with a rag by its two tips and placed it in a plastic bag.

"Brenda, was this door damaged before?"

"Yes. The bars have been loose for a while. A horse kicked it and splintered the wood where they were held. The door needed to be replaced. We just hadn't gotten around to it."

Two police officers were inside the stall, taking pictures and gathering fingerprints. The sawdust and manure, mingled with blood, made the process difficult. Looking inside the stall as they worked, Julie noticed a nail lying by the stall door. She went to pick it up and found another one.

"Wait, don't touch anything." An officer said.

"It's just a nail. I thought I'd pick it up."

"Uh, okay."

Julie thought this was not okay, but put the nails in her pocket and, turning to leave the stall, stumbled over an object lying underneath the sawdust.

"It's the halter he wore when he came in," Julie said. "I recognize it." She turned toward the officer and saw Phil standing at the stall door.

"Why would it be lying on the ground?" Phil asked. He took out a stick he found on the ground and picked it up, trying not to touch it with his hands.

Brenda stood behind Phil and peered over his shoulder.

"Could it have been removed and replaced with another halter?"

"Why, what's the point?" Phil looked back at her.

"I don't know," Brenda replied. "I know that I removed that halter last night and put it on the horseshoe hook right here," she said, pointing outside the stall door to a solid brass horseshoe hung upside down.

Julie thought the halter was significant, but she didn't know how. Whoever killed Matt could have flung a bridle and saddle on the horse and rode away, but it didn't seem feasible in all that rain. Nor did the horse seem temperamentally suited to that kind of thing.

"What the hell are we going to tell Mr. Ortega? He's going to be here soon, and he doesn't have a horse anymore," Paul said. He stood with his hands on his hips, a scowl covering his face.

"We're going to tell him that there's been a murder here and ask him where the hell was he early this morning," Phil said.

The rain started to let up as a voice came out of nowhere.

"Hello, everybody. What did you say about a murder, and where was I this morning?" It was Larry Ortega.

CHAPTER 10

Everyone turned to look at the man standing behind them. Phil turned to Brenda. "Let me speak with Mr. Ortega alone, okay? Brenda, we'll go into the office if that's all right with you. Give us a few minutes." He didn't wait for an answer but walked Larry down the aisle, and they disappeared into the office.

Brenda fought back tears. "Who does Phil think killed Matt? Me? It's always the wife who's accused after her husband's been murdered,"

Julie thought the tears might be more from anger than grief or fear.

"Do we know for sure he was murdered?" Julie said, sitting on a hay bale.

Brenda nudged her over and sat next to her. "Damn it, his head's bashed in. What else could it have been?"

"Maybe the horse knocked him into the bars of the stall, and he fell."

"With an iron bar? Then, he walks out of his stall, strolls down the aisle, out the door, into the rain, and disappears into the night. The criminal leaves the scene of the crime. Right…" Paul said, picking up a piece of hay, twisting it around his finger, and then throwing it down again in disgust. He sat on a hay bale across from the two women.

"He was hit pretty hard. His skull was…" Paul stopped as Brenda turned green.

"Sorry," he said.

Julie looked at Tom, sitting on the hay bale across from her, and caught his eye. He looked at her and then turned away.

He's mad at me, she thought. I think I hurt his feelings.

A few minutes later, Phil and Larry came out of the office. Larry grimly nodded his head and walked out of the barn.

Brenda scowled. "There goes one customer."

"What did you say?" Paul asked Phil.

"I just told him what happened."

Julie noticed Phil's eyes shifting upward. She wondered if that was his way of being evasive.

"What about the horse?" Paul asked.

"He's not worried. I guess he didn't pay for it yet." Brenda nodded her head in agreement. The paramedics walked by carrying the body, and Brenda turned away, nearly collapsing. Paul caught her and said, "Brenda, why don't you go up to the house and lie down? I'll take care of the horses." He nodded to Phil as if to say, "Leave her alone for now. She's not going anywhere."

Phil said gently, "Okay. I'll be back later when you're feeling better. Stay away from this area for now, although I think everything that can be done has been done. I'll be back here this afternoon. Don't go anywhere."

Brenda just nodded—again.

"Tom, I want you and Julie to come over to the station with me. I want to talk to you."

"You want to see me?" Julie asked. He either wants my help, or he thinks I killed him, she thought.

"Julie, I'll take Annie up to the house when I go. She'll be all right. Go on," Paul said.

Julie nodded.

Annie started to give her most ladylike dog snort.

Julie and Tom followed Phil in Tom's van, riding in silence. She didn't trust anyone anymore. The events of the last evening overwhelmed her, and she felt conspiracy all around. She thought Matt was capable of murder but hadn't imagined it about any of the rest of the family.

When they arrived at the police station, the last drops of rain dribbled from the sky, and the sun tried to peek out of the evaporating storm clouds.

Water was everywhere. Julie exited the truck and promptly stepped into water up to her ankles.

"Damn," was all she said. Still not speaking, Tom took her by the arm and helped her regain her balance. They went in.

"They're in Chief Swanson's office," the receptionist said without being asked.

"Sit," Phil said, pointing to the sofa and two chairs that circled the coffee table.

Larry Ortega sat at Phil's desk, drinking coffee and shuffling through some files. He didn't say anything but looked at Julie and threw a questioning glance at Phil, who ignored him.

After a few minutes of uncomfortable silence, Phil finally spoke. "You've met Larry."

All three forced smiles by way of acknowledgment.

"We've had three deaths—no, three *unnatural* deaths—in this area over the past year. All victims are members of our horse community and all…" He peered over to Tom, "Are suspected drug traffickers."

Tom raised an eyebrow, and his face flushed.

Phil continued, "I want to know as much as possible about Matt's activities."

Julie wondered why Larry Ortega was there. He looked up from his files, glanced at her, and smiled. She glanced at Tom.

Tom poured coffee for himself and Julie. "But I don't know anything about Matt's activities."

"No?" Phil took out a yellow pad and started scribbling notes. "Who were your brother's friends?"

"You know them as well as I do. He didn't have many, not close ones. He knew a lot of people, had business associates who he periodically screwed."

"Brenda said that he hauled horses for your uncle. What about your father? Did Matt ship horses for him, too?"

"Not really—just for our Uncle George."

Julie added, "When a horse came from Mr. Carter's ranch, his employees brought them. Brenda or Paul could tell you more, or… perhaps Larry could. He was a friend of Matt's, weren't you?" she said, glancing at Larry.

Larry looked back at her. Phil ignored her. Back to Tom, he said,

"Any enemies that you know about?"

"Probably lots," Tom said.

"Who?"

"Like I said, Phil. I don't know. He was a man who made enemies. The only specific one I can think of would be Greg Richardson."

Julie saw Tom casting his eyes down on the floor. He hadn't wanted to say that.

Tom went on. "I think Greg blamed Matt for his brother's death. The horses that Tony was shipping the day Eddie got stopped came from our ranch. I don't know any other reason."

"What about at school?"

"I didn't go to college with him. I don't know any of them."

Julie flushed in anger, remembering the conversation that Brenda had with Matt after Eddie's body was discovered.

Phil looked at Julie but continued to question Tom.

"Tell me what happened on the ride back from the show."

"I can't. Julie, Brenda, and I followed Matt and Paul in my van. We pulled in right behind them. When we got back, a van was waiting with Larry's horse. It had Texas plates. I helped unload our horses, so I was in the barn with Paul when Brenda brought that new horse into the barn. That's all I know. Julie was cleaning out her stuff in the van, leaving by the time I got out of the barn. It was pretty late."

Julie looked away from his eyes and across at Larry Ortega, who was still sitting behind Phil's desk. She wondered what he was looking for.

Phil sighed, puffed out his cheeks, blew, and stretched his arms over his head. "So, what happened after Julie left?"

"The van left. We just finished unloading and fed the horses. Then we all went to bed… end of story. You can call and talk to my father about those men. Like I said, I don't know who they were. They weren't friendly."

"Then what?" Phil ignored his last comment.

"I called Julie, and we talked for a few minutes, then I went to sleep. I was set to go back to Chicago this morning."

"Why did you call her?"

Julie saw Tom hesitate before he answered. "Wanted to know if she wanted to come to dinner with us. I thought she might enjoy meeting you and Marsha," he said, glancing over at her again and then turning back to Phil. "Anyway, I have some research into police procedures to do in Chicago, and my dog's there." He finished the rest of his coffee. "What the hell!" He continued, "Anyway, I woke up when the phone blasted away in my ear. It was Julie. You know the rest."

"What did you find out this weekend?"

"Not too much. Several barn thefts have occurred in the area during the past month. You probably know about those."

Phil nodded. "Think it could be related?" He looked over at Larry, who just shrugged his shoulders.

"Okay, what else? Who else has Matt pulled dirty tricks on?"

Tom noticed that Larry was no longer thumbing through the file. He was looking intently and listening to the conversation.

"Besides his wife? I don't know."

"What about the blond? What's her name, Lynette?"

"She takes lessons with Matt… or took lessons from him. I guess they're having a relationship. I understand that Lynette wants Matt to divorce Brenda."

Julie cut in, "Brenda told me about it. It started less than a year ago, just before Lynette moved in—when she was still over at Tony's barn."

"How long has Brenda known about this?"

"Always, probably. She couldn't help but know. We all knew. Matt flaunted it. It was as if he wanted her to know… to hurt her. It was quiet at first, but in the past few weeks, it's been escalating."

"How do you mean?"

"Lynette has been pressuring Matt to divorce Brenda. I heard them the other day. Matt put her off."

"Really? Who did Matt put off, Lynette or Brenda?"

"Both, but Brenda. She offered to give Matt a divorce sometime back. I think she wanted out of the marriage. He laughed at her," Julie continued. "He told her he would never give her a divorce. So, that was that. Lynette stayed at the barn, and Brenda has been miserable."

"Brenda told you all of this?" Phil asked.

Julie nodded.

Phil said, "Is it possible that Brenda killed him? Maybe she couldn't take it anymore, and in a frenzy, she hit him."

"Have you taken a good look at Brenda, Phil?" Julie asked. "There's no way that she could have had that much strength to bash in his skull like that. Besides, it's not in Brenda's nature to kill anything. Lynette had as big a motive for killing him as she did."

Phil looked up at the ceiling, nodded, and said, "Nice people can do some pretty nasty things under the right circumstances." He stopped and eyed her—probing. "Julie, what can you tell me about last night?"

"Me? Well, nothing." She stopped.

Julie looked at the three men staring at her, and the room seemed to close tightly around her. She didn't want to talk in front of Tom. Who was this Larry Ortega sitting on the other side of the room? Why was he here, and why would someone want to kill him? The chills came back. As if reading her thoughts, Phil asked the men, "Would you leave us for a few minutes? Tom, tell the front desk to hold my calls. I don't want to be disturbed. Don't go anywhere. I'm sure my receptionist will be delighted to keep you entertained. She might even have donuts." They left the room.

"Now then, Julie. Cut the crap." Julie looked up at him sharply. "You're playing a dangerous game here. You know something, and you don't want to talk about it. Why not?"

Nervously, Julie pulled her hair out of her ponytail and pulled it back in again. Despite her efforts, a tear escaped from one eye and dribbled down her cheek. She brushed it aside. Phil handed her a tissue from under a massive stack of papers on his desk.

"Yes, of course, you're right. I must talk to you." She folded her arms and hugged herself, trying to squeeze the chills away. "I'm very scared."

"Steady, girl," he said. "It's going to be all right. I'll make sure nothing happens to you."

Julie slowly sipped her coffee and told Phil about the conversation she had overheard in the trailer. She related the events of the previous evening when she hid in the small tack room in the horse trailer and overheard the men telling Matt how they were sending in a ringer—switching horses with the intent of killing Larry Ortega.

"They said that Larry was an undercover cop for the DEA. He was recognized from a New Orleans drug bust. Matt seemed surprised. He didn't know. They asked him about Eddie. They wanted to know whether Matt knew who killed him."

"Did he?" Phil asked.

"No. He said that he thought Greg might have. Matt also said something about uh… that he was trouble, and they were better off without him."

Phil whistled softly and shook his head. "You're right, Julie. Larry does work for the Drug Enforcement Agency. He's been assigned to investigate drug smuggling in this area. There seems to be a lot coming in and out of here in many creative ways, including shipping horses across the country. That's how Tony got caught. We got tipped off." He pointed to the coffee pot, but Julie shook her head. He poured some for himself and continued, "I got the call and brought in the DEA to investigate. That's why Tony's trailer was stopped at the border."

"Of course. I've heard rumors… about a relay. Pony Express style?"

Phil smiled. "We thought when Tony died that perhaps the drug running would stop. It didn't. So that meant that someone took Tony's place, or Tony wasn't doing it in the first place, or that he was in it with someone else, maybe Eddie Meeks."

"Oh!" Julie caught her breath.

"What is it?" Phil walked over and sat across from her.

"I heard one of the men in the van say that Tony wasn't working for them. Tony's getting caught running drugs appeared to have surprised them, so did his death—and so did Eddie's death. It was a bizarre conversation. I didn't hear the whole thing, just bits and pieces."

"Interesting. We started looking at Matthew as a possible suspect because Tony was hauling his horses. We thought that with Tony's death, the trafficking might stop. It hasn't. Larry Ortega was brought into it, posing as a boarder in Matt's barn. He could find out things without being suspected. Unfortunately, he's been recognized. I wasn't sure about Matt's involvement, but now I think he was involved up to his elbows." He shrugged his shoulders. "Who would have killed him, though… same person that killed Eddie and Tony? If so, Julie, a person is running around here who's killed three people already."

"I know. I hope it's not someone I know." She shuddered, and the chill came back in full force. Phil…?"

Phil looked at her as the question she dreaded asking started to spurt out. It came as a whisper.

"Why would that horse come from his dad's ranch? His dad…" Tom's dad, she thought.

"Maybe he didn't." Phil sat silent for a minute as she took in his last remark. "Maybe the horse didn't come from his dad's ranch after all. Where then?" He grew silent as if ingrained in thought. Then, he nodded.

"Okay. Julie, I'm going to bring back Tom and Larry. You need to tell them exactly what you told me. You can trust Tom… I've known him a long, long time." She nodded. "By the way, don't tell anyone about this. Nobody. You don't know who knows what or why."

"I thought there was something different about that man. He didn't seem at all what he pretended to be," Julie said, rubbing her forehead.

"Who?"

"Oh, sorry, Larry."

"You're really good, Julie. He's one of the best in the business. He's fooled a lot of people for a lot of years."

"Is there anything else you can tell me?"

"Actually, yes."

Phil stopped and turned to look at her.

She told him about the conversation between Matt and Brenda she had overheard.

He whistled. "Man, you're certainly in the right place at the right time, aren't you? Listen, with or without Tom Carter, I would love for you to meet Marsha. Come have dinner with us."

Julie smiled, then grinned and nodded her head. All was almost right with the world.

Phil called the two men back into the office.

CHAPTER 11

Puddles were everywhere as Tom's truck splashed its way back to the house. The air was crisp and smelled of hay fields and green pastures. Julie stopped for a moment to look over the landscape.

"Tom—look at that."

She pointed to the sky where a hawk was flying over the house, a snake planted firmly in his beak. The creature wriggled for a few seconds, then stopped as the hawk flew over a neighboring farm and disappeared. A flock of geese flew into view, their united honking contrasted with the stillness of the early afternoon. The sun suddenly burst through the clouds, providing comforting warmth. Tom stood beside her, pretending to look but focused instead on her zest for life. Tom had the sudden urge to kiss her right there, right now. He resisted.

They walked up the stairs through the screened-in back porch and into a large country room that exuded the warmth and charm of a kitchen from a bygone era. The wallpaper displayed colorful old copper teapots and brown spice jars, blending into wood paneling and brick tile floors. A wooden wheel light fixture with hurricane lamps towered over an oak table in the corner of the room. Freshly brewed coffee blended with faint smells from years of family breakfasts. At the far end of the table, Tom bent over a coffee maker and poured two cups of coffee.

Paul walked in and sat at the table. "So, you survived the Swanson third degree?"

Julie looked up and raised an eyebrow. "*What?*" she asked.

'What happened? When you got to see Phil," he replied.

"Nothing. He asked us a lot of questions, most of which we couldn't answer," Julie said. "I'm sure if you're really good, he'll get around to you, too."

Paul wrinkled his nose and asked, "So, we're all suspects?" He took a seat across from them.

"How could we be anything else? Our brother is murdered, and our horse disappears, apparently brought over here to kill a drug agent. Then another murder occurs at a horse show where we were, and you wonder why we're suspects?" Tom vented his frustration, nearly spilling the coffee. He didn't. Instead, he handed Julie a cup and decided to curtail his emotions. This wasn't Paul's fault. "Want some?" he asked Paul, a bit more gently, nodding at the coffee maker.

Paul shook his head and said, "Whoa—hold on a minute. Back up there, will you? To the part where you say, they brought 'our horse over here to kill a drug agent.' What drug agent?"

Tom told him.

"Larry? I thought Larry worked for his brother."

"Yeah, that's what we were supposed to think."

"Damn…" Digesting this last bit of information, he continued, "A drug agent here? Why?"

Tom looked at Julie and gave her a look that said, *Be quiet.* "Why don't you ask Phil?"

"Speaking of Phil, he called a few minutes ago to say that you and Julie would stay through the week. I'm glad. Brenda is in bad shape. She needs a friend right now. She's convinced that Phil is coming to arrest her."

"Oh no…no." Julie shook her head.

Paul continued, "Tom, I called Dad. He's coming up here tomorrow morning. He's devastated. I've never heard him break down before. As unpleasant as this is…"

Tom nodded."

"I know, we must talk about funeral arrangements. I'm glad you thought to call Wilson's…" he stopped. Paul hadn't mentioned that. It was just something he and Paul had done since they were kids. Telepathic.

He didn't know how, and he didn't know why, but they seemed to know what each other was about to say. It used to drive Matt crazy.

Paul grinned at his older brother. "We've got to talk about funeral arrangements, and I want to do it before he gets here. I did call Wilson's, and one of their people is coming here this afternoon. They're good at handling this stuff. I arranged to have Matt moved there." Tom nodded, and Paul continued. "Brenda is out of her head right now."

"Where is she?" Julie asked, turning her head toward the stairs.

"She's up in her room. But don't go up right now. She's out cold. I gave her something to help her sleep."

"Good, it sounds like you have everything under control. If you don't need us, Julie must get home and pick up some things. I have a couple of things to do this afternoon, too. Can you handle everything here?"

'Sure, no problem. I thought maybe Thursday might be a good day for the funeral. Is that too soon?"

Tom nodded. "That's fine."

"By the way, your dog is still down at the barn," Paul continued, "after everything that's happened, I thought it best to leave her there in case someone decides to return."

"Good idea. I think I'll check on her before we go. I don't know, but I want to look around. I wasn't thinking clearly this morning. I feel like I might be missing something."

"Who's playing detective now?" Tom asked.

Lynette Williams stood in the aisle brushing her horse and thinking about Matt. He would generally sit on a bale of hay teasing and flirting with her—making plans for a late evening rendezvous. She always hated sneaking around and smugly created a gossip line around the barn, tying herself to Matt and pushing Brenda into a position of nagging wife. It had been months since Matt promised to get a divorce, and it hadn't been until this weekend that she realized that might not happen.

On the surface, she appeared calm, but underneath, turbulence brewed, starting to bubble to the surface. She despised Brenda and disliked both Matt's brothers, especially Tom, but she really hated Julie. That stupid, stuck-up little bitch. Lynette brushed Irishman's neck just a bit harder, and he momentarily woke up and snorted.

Brenda. He didn't love her anymore. This had been an arranged marriage—because of the horses. So why hadn't he been willing to divorce Brenda and marry her?

Jealousy and envy ran through her veins as she thought of Matt having spent any time with his wife—with any of them. She didn't know why she had loved him for so long. At times, he'd been hateful—brutal. On the other hand, his charm and personality had captured her long ago. Then, she wondered if he had ever hit his wife. She was sure of it as visions of Matt's brutal outbursts entered her mind. Last night, for instance, all she said was, "When are you getting a divorce, Matt?" It had been enough to send him into a rage. She screamed, he screamed, and that led to the attack, which sent her flying back onto the bed. She wondered if the neighbors heard and if her makeup sufficiently covered her black eye.

She abruptly awoke from dark fantasies when she heard voices coming from the direction of the barn door. Shit—it's that redhead and Matt's brother. What the hell do they want?

She went on grooming, pretending she didn't see them. It didn't work. They immediately came over. Damn, she thought.

"Oh, hi. It's you. You two are becoming quite a little item, aren't you?"

Julie was not happy Lynette was in the barn. She was the last person that Julie wanted to meet. Tom prompted her, saying, "No, Julie, it's good she's here. She's on our list. Let's get it over with."

She bit her tongue as Lynette shot the crack at her and then felt terrible as she realized that Lynette might not know about Matt.

"Lynette, did you hear?" She gulped and took a deep breath before speaking. "About Matt," she said softly.

"Hear what?" The look of venom Lynette shot at Julie made her realize that this was a cobra in human form. Julie got ready for a poisonous verbal assault and spoke as softly and gently as she could.

"Matt was killed this morning in the barn. I'm sorry. He's dead."

All the hostility that had been there suddenly disappeared. Lynette turned white as paste and lost her balance. Tom grabbed her just as she was about to hit the concrete and helped her sit on one of the nearby hay bales, ready to become her horse's dinner.

"What do you mean he's dead? I just saw him…" She hesitated, then continued with "yesterday. How could he be dead? Wait a minute, you said he was killed?"

"Someone bashed him over the head," Tom said.

"No!" Lynette shrieked, scaring her horse. Tom pushed her out of the way just in time to avoid his hooves.

"You're *lying*." Her breath came in gasps. "You *must* be lying."

When she calmed down, she said, "So she finally went and did it, that bitch." The bitterness in her voice just edged out the proper amount of hysteria.

"Who?" Tom asked.

Lynette's voice turned shrill. "Who else but his wife? Have they arrested her yet?"

"No," Tom said. "They have not arrested her. She's under sedation and is in bed."

"Why do you think she did it?" Julie asked.

"Well, everyone knows they didn't get along. He was planning on leaving her."

"How do you know this?" Tom said.

"Because he told me. He was planning on divorcing her and marrying me." She got up as if for emphasis. "I could kill her for this. She was jealous of us, and she killed him. I know you two wouldn't believe that."

"Is there anyone you know that could have had it in for Matt? He did have a habit of collecting enemies," Tom said.

"Why the hell are you asking me for? He was *your* brother, Tom." Lynette pinched her lips together in defiance. "Look, I have nothing to say to either one of you. I don't have to answer any questions."

"Look, we're just trying to help," Tom said. "If I knew any of my brother's activities, I wouldn't have to ask you. But I don't. I've been away."

Tom's gentle tone seemed to soften Lynette.

"No… at least, I don't… don't really know. He could have, might have had enemies."

"Who are they, Lynette?"

"I don't know."

"You must have some idea? You hung around with him."

"He was busy with his horse business, buying and selling and transporting from place to place. Maybe someone could have been mad at him."

"Like *who?*" Tom asked, pressing her.

This time, Lynette didn't hesitate. "Maybe some of his buyers. I think Matt might have sold bad horses to some people."

"Did you have any problems when you bought your horse?"

"I didn't buy Irishman from Matt. I bought him from Tony Richardson. I'd heard not to trust Matt Carter regarding buying horses."

"Did Tony trust Matt?"

"No. Tony trusted the Carters. They always had a reputation for selling good horses. Tony knew his horses. He wouldn't have gotten suckered in, even by Matt."

"How long were you over at Eagle Ranch?" Julie asked.

Lynette flared up again at Julie. "What's it to you, Julie? Why should you care? Anyway, you were there when I was."

Tom soothed over the situation.

"We don't know, Lynette. We're just trying to fit some pieces together."

"Okay. About two years." She shrugged, glared at Julie, and focused back on Tom.

"He killed himself, didn't he? Did that strike you as odd?"

"How do you mean? Oh, well, Tony never struck me as the type to kill himself over anything. But some terrible things happened to him. His girlfriend dumped him, you know, then this thing—with the drugs."

"What about his girlfriend? Do you know who she was?"

"No. He kept her name secret even after they broke up. Anyway, last year, they were back together. Then, she got married, but I think she must have returned because I think she left him again because he got really depressed, and his brother had to take over the barn for a few days. I didn't see much of him after that." She paused. "He must have been dealing drugs because he got arrested. Soon after, Greg announced he was closing the barn and moving to Kentucky."

"Why did you come here?"

"I guess because it's the nicest barn in the area. Also, I knew Matt…" Her voice trailed off.

"Wasn't it true that you were already having an affair with Matt before you moved here?" Julie asked.

Julie waited for the sarcastic jab to come, but it didn't. Instead, Lynette said, "No, not quite. It was just starting. Matt came over to Tony's a lot back then. When I finished riding, he flirted with me and asked me for coffee or dinner. He needed someone to talk to. I guess things weren't too good between him and Brenda even then."

"Were you around the day Eddie took those horses to Kentucky?" Tom asked.

"Yeah, but not until that afternoon. I think Eddie left early in the morning. That was the day after Julie bought Socks, wasn't it Julie?"

Julie nodded. She remembered that day very well.

"So no, I wasn't. Hey, why all the sudden interest in Tony Richardson? That was over a year ago."

"Yes, I know. I guess I'm wondering if there isn't some connection. Lynette, was Matt with you last night?" When Lynette raised her eyebrows and scowled, Julie thought the question came unexpectedly.

"Why do you want to know that?" she asked. "I didn't kill him, if that's what you're wondering—or *implying*."

Julie noticed that she had grasped her hands, her knuckles had turned white, and her tone became shrill.

"No… no. I'm just wondering what could have happened between last night and this morning when Matt went to the barn."

"Well, isn't it obvious? He didn't come home last night, so Brenda got up early, went to the barn, and killed him."

"So, he was with you?"

"I didn't say that," she said sullenly.

"It would help if you told us," Tom said. "If you don't, Phil Swanson will come and interview you. He might not be so nice. He might see that you had a motive, too."

"Me?" Lynette flew into a rage. "I was in love with the man. Why would I have wanted to murder him?"

"Because you knew Matt wouldn't divorce Brenda and marry you."

"I knew *no such thing*!" Lynette's voice rose close to an octave above her standard vocal register. Annie started to bark from within the office.

"Calm down, Lynette." Tom's tone was forceful, and it worked. "It would help a lot if you just told us when he was with you last night."

Lynette sighed and settled down. "Oh well. Matt showed up at about one in the morning. He left at four to go back home and feed the horses."

"What did he talk about?" Tom asked.

"He talked to me about the show, about Brenda and how you showed up out of the clear blue. He talked about how well you showed, Julie, and how much he liked your horse."

"What else?" Tom said.

"Oh, he mentioned a friend having bought a horse delivered from his father's ranch."

"Did you talk about Eddie?"

"A little. We both knew him."

"What did you think of him?"

"He was an asshole. He would stab you in the back just as soon as look at you. He didn't like Matt much, and Matt didn't like him. He always talked about Matt as though he knew something about him that others didn't. I asked Eddie about Matt once, but he just laughed and walked away. He could be infuriating. He always wanted people to think he was important… that he knew something they didn't, even when he didn't. He was a jerk. I'm sorry he was killed, but I can't say I'm surprised or sorry that he's not around anymore."

"Do you think someone killed him because they thought he knew something which could get them in trouble?"

"Wouldn't surprise me. He might have pretended to know something that he didn't."

"Lynette, was Matt with you the night Eddie was killed?"

"Damn it, Julie, Matt was with me almost every night. I'm not making a secret about it anymore. Look, I know you two don't like me much. Brenda is your friend and your sister-in-law, Tom, but she has a dark side, too. She didn't like Matt. I did. I will miss the hell out of him even if nobody else does." Lynette removed her horse from the crossties and returned him to his stall. She left the barn to do her own share of grieving.

Julie and Tom watched her leave the barn, and Julie turned to Tom. "Maybe we should have asked her where she was at five this morning."

Tom turned toward her. "You think she could have killed him?"

"If she got mad enough, I believe she could," Julie said. "Wonder where she got that shiner?"

"Think they had a fight?"

Julie nodded.

"Maybe. Anyway, at least we know that Matt was with Lynette when Eddie was killed. So, it could be your theory is right. Maybe the same person killed both Eddie and Matt and maybe killed Tony as well. The only connection among the three is horses and drugs."

"If we can believe her," Julie said. She still thought Lynette had avoided directly answering that question.

"Well, well," Tom said, drawing out of his pocket the list of names Phil had given him. "The first person we see is Arthur Ashford, Tony's lawyer. Okay, Julie, let's go."

CHAPTER 12

"My heavens… it's Thomas Carter. It's great to see you. Come in." Lloyd Arthur Ashford, a man whose salt and pepper hair and boyish grin belied his advancing years, opened the door and showed surprise and genuine happiness to see Tom Carter.

"And who do we have here?" His interest immediately turned in the direction of Julie.

"Mr. Ashford, this is Julie Bishop, a very good friend of my family… and mine." Arthur took Julie's hand, and in the fashion of old Europe, he kissed her hand.

It was well known that, although he had always remained faithful to his wife, Arthur loved women, especially women with red hair, and Julie fit the bill perfectly. Arthur Ashford's advanced age had not slowed down.

He ushered Tom and Julie into the office of his two-story house in the upper-class neighborhood near the business district of Forest View. The office showed his personality. Pictures of his wife and him sailing on Lake Michigan, pictures of his children ice skating, and pictures of his family and their horses filled the walls. A prominent spot behind his desk hung a picture of the town mayor and Arthur jointly cutting a ribbon for the christening of a new office building. The most interesting picture on the wall for Tom was the picture of Tony Richardson at age 13, winning first place at the County Fair on his horse, Roscoe.

"What can I do for you, Tom? It's always a pleasure to see you, but it comes as a surprise. I thought you were living in Chicago now and didn't get back here much anymore."

"That's true. I came down here to visit Phil and to see Brenda and Matt show at the Forest View Quarter Horse Show. The real reason was that I needed some input about police work, and I thought Phil could help fill me in on police procedures."

"Oh, are you joining the police force?" he asked in amusement.

Tom told him about his work in the acting field. "It looks like I stumbled on a real-life murder. While I was in his office, we got a call from the fairgrounds. Someone finally found Eddie Meeks. His throat was cut."

The lawyer's smile left his face, and he frowned. "So that's it. I heard about it from one of my clients." He looked closely at Tom and said, "I suspect you have more to tell me."

"Yeah, I'm afraid so. They found him in Greg's trailer. It isn't very pleasant. Everyone's talked of nothing but during the duration of the show. There's more, I'm afraid. This morning, my brother Matthew was murdered. Someone hit him with an iron bar. It couldn't have been Greg. They took him into custody Friday night."

"My God!" The lawyer looked incredulous. "What in the name of heaven is happening?" He leaned forward over the desk. "Is there anything I can do to help your family?" he said, softer and gentler.

"I don't think so. The funeral will be on Thursday if you want to come. Dad will be flying here from Texas tomorrow. Phil thinks that a connection between the two killings and the death of Tony last year is a possibility. He wanted to know your feelings about it. Do you believe that Tony really committed suicide?"

"It's strange that you should mention that. No. It was not like that young man. He was desperate about his situation…" He looked at Tom thoughtfully. "But what do you mean? Do you want my feelings about it? Yes, I was his lawyer. I brought him back from his inquisition."

"Inquisition?"

"Yes, they grilled that poor kid for five hours, trying to get him to incriminate himself. When they finished with one line of questioning, they asked him the same questions in other ways. It was brutal. I stopped it a couple of times. Then, they incarcerated him overnight. I'll tell you, Tom, I've never been to one of these before, and I hope I never have to again."

"Do you think he did it?"

"They found cocaine in his trailer."

"Yes, but do you think he did it?" Tom persisted. "Could someone else have planted it?"

"It's possible. I never trusted that employee of his. The one that was killed this weekend."

"Why didn't Tony get rid of him? Why did he keep him around?"

"Tony never saw the bad side of people. He was naive, and that was his problem. Eddie did his job. He kept the stable up and made repairs around the place. He hauled horses and never got into trouble. At least, not that Tony noticed. Tony gave Eddie a place to stay, room and board. He didn't have to pay him as much in cash. It was a good arrangement for both. I'm sorry to say this to you, Tom, but the only person that Tony didn't completely trust was your brother."

"You're not going to hurt my feelings. I didn't trust him either. That's one of the reasons I left home, Mr. Ashford."

"Call me Arthur. It's become a kind of tradition. Not Art... not Artie ... just plain Arthur." He chuckled, then grinned.

"All right, Arthur. Why did Tony do business with Matt if he didn't trust him?"

"Force of habit, I believe. Your families worked together for many years. Tony didn't think about changing anything."

"Can you tell me what Tony said to you the day he died? It might be important to this whole mess."

"Well, you know about client-lawyer confidentiality. All right," he said. "If it will help clear any of this up, I'll remember what I can. He said he didn't do it and that someone was trying to frame him. I believed... *believe* him. I asked him to list anyone who might want to harm him or his business and any transactions he might have made during the past month or so. He said he would but died before he could. I came over that evening and found him…"

"Yes, I know. I'm sorry."

"I couldn't believe it when I saw him lying over his desk. I will never forget that, ever. Do you think someone killed him? It was his gun, found by his body on the desk. The computer was on with a note on the monitor."

"Had he started the list?"

"No, not that I found. I did find an empty frame on his desk, though. I don't know what was in it. The police questioned it but then decided it didn't mean anything. They established the time as late morning... just after I left."

"Could the person have been there when you brought him home?"

"There wasn't any car in the driveway. But there was a driveway leading behind the barn. So many people were coming and going; there would have been no way of talking about whose car was there. I believe people were riding there that afternoon while Tony was lying dead upstairs. Who would have known?"

"That's true. Do you know any of the people who boarded there?"

"Let's see. Yes, I believe a young woman named Lynette Williams kept her horse there. I have a file with the names of all the boarders and their horses. Tony asked me to keep it safe for legal reasons. I can give you those names if you want." He spun his chair around to the computer desk housed along the wall. It was a convenient arrangement for Arthur. It didn't clutter his desk, and he didn't have to get up. Pulling up the list of names on the screen, he clicked on *print*, and the trusty printer came alive. Arthur handed the list to Tom.

"Recognize anyone?"

"Yeah, almost everyone. Lynette Williams is now at our barn. The others... Julie, do you know any of these names?" They put their heads together and checked the names.

"Yes. I recognize Sarah James. She and her husband bought a small farm near Eagle Ranch. It's called *The James Place*. She shows her horses quite a bit. She showed last weekend. Her horse cut me off during one of my classes."

"I remember talking to her and another lady while I watched you and Brenda in the warm-up arena," Tom said. "I have her card."

Julie looked at him and couldn't help smiling. She remembered the way the receptionist at the police station looked at him. Tom was good-looking.

"There's Angela Smith." Julie pointed to the bottom of the list.

"That was the other lady I saw," Tom said.

"Wait a minute," Arthur said, looking at Julie. "Didn't you board there, too?"

"Actually, for about a week. I bought my horse from Brenda through Tony. I came out on the day he was... er, died. I stayed there until Greg closed the barn. Then Lynette and I moved to the Carter's."

"You're not from here, are you?"

Julie shook her head. "No. New York. Long Island."

"Ah." He said, "How did you end up here...?"

"The Richardsons are distant cousins. My aunt put me in touch with Tony before I left New York. That's where I'm from... where my family lives. Tony told me about Socks. He was supposed to have gone down to Kentucky with those other horses, but it turned out that they wanted mares instead of geldings. I came at the right time."

"So, you're Tony's cousin. I heard someone was coming out from the East Coast. You were getting away from..."

"Did Matt hang out at his ranch a lot?" Julie said, changing the direction of the conversation.

"I believe he came once or twice a week to see Tony. My guess is he had another reason, too. I remember Tony saying he thought Matt was trying to steal one of his borders—that Lynette Williams girl. I don't think Tony would have minded if she left. She caused trouble in the barn."

"What kind of trouble?" Julie asked.

"Just gossipy type stuff. But she also flaunted herself in front of the married men at the barn. Their wives didn't like it that much."

"Did Tony tell you who brought the sale horses over from the Carter Ranch?" Julie asked.

"I think it was Paul... could have been Matt, though." Arthur was now leaning as far over on his seat as he could without falling. He was interested.

"Could Matt have planted those drugs in the trailer?" Tom asked.

The lawyer looked surprised. "Could be... I know the trailer was being serviced the day before and wasn't at the ranch when they brought the horses over. Anyone could have planted those drugs. Tony wouldn't have suspected."

"No ideas on anyone else Eddie might have been working for?"

"None. I'm sorry I can't be of much help to you. The only thing I know of interest is that Tony mentioned Eddie spent time on the campus where Tony and Matt went to school. He hung around with Matt and a bunch of his friends. Matt was pretty wild..." He looked at Tom, trying to decide whether to go further. "I've heard Matt and his friends were into drugs. I guess you're not surprised. Otherwise, you wouldn't have asked whether Matt could have put cocaine into the trailer."

"Right," Tom said. "No, it doesn't surprise me. But why was he and Eddie murdered? And, of all people, why was Tony murdered?"

"I don't know, son... I don't know. I've always suspected Tony knew something. Maybe someone didn't feel safe and set him up. Maybe he knew who was running drugs and stumbled on it by accident. It's a well-known rumor that there's a drug ring operating within the horse community. People buy and sell horses and then transport them around the country. Along with the horses go the drugs, cocaine, heroin or otherwise."

"Phil seems to think so," Tom said.

"The big boys aren't from around here, so it seems. They have far-reaching connections. There's big money coming down around here. You see farmers who haven't had a pot to... well, you know, suddenly they're putting on a new barn roof and are all replacing the fences. There's been a flurry of buying and selling horses around here. It stopped after Tony died, but now it may pick up again."

"That's another thing," Tom said. "We had a new boarder at the barn. He bought a horse from my father, and it arrived last night. When we found Matt dead this morning, the horse was gone, stolen out of the barn."

"That's the first I've heard about horses being stolen around here. I usually hear about things like that." He stopped to take a breath and smiled sadly. "Who's doing your training these days? Was it Matt, or was it that wife of his? What's her name? Brenda?"

"Yeah, it's Brenda. I think Matt was going to train this new horse."

"Well, it was fortunate for the horse, at any rate."

"Yeah, that's true. Brenda is really the rider and trainer of the family. She and Paul both have a way with the animals. Matt terrorizes them." Tom stopped and changed the direction of his questions.

"Arthur, do you know anyone that Tony might have been seeing? A girlfriend?"

Arthur raised his eyebrows, looking like he wasn't sure what to say. "Yeah... yes. I think there was someone. He was involved with someone at school, but it broke up. I don't know why. The last time I saw him, no, just before that, he grinned at me and said that I might have a godchild yet. I asked him what he meant, and he just laughed. He said if everything worked out, he wanted to get married. That's all I know. I never met the lady. That always bothered me. Tony confided in me about a lot of matters. He never even introduced me to his girlfriend." Arthur lowered his head and shook it. "Tom, I'm not being too much help to you. If I think of anything more, I'll let you know."

Then, Julie put in her two cents. "Is there any other reason that Tony could have been killed? I mean, not related to drugs. Might someone have been jealous of him? Could it be related to his girlfriend or his horses? He had some good horses, I understand."

"Everyone liked Tony. I can't believe they could have killed him over horses. I know it's happened before, so I guess anything's possible." Arthur shook his head and shrugged, looking frustrated. "I want to lose my temper. I have no solutions for this—none. And you seem as angry at all this as I am."

"Yes, I am. But I don't know," Julie said. "I want to—need to check the possibilities."

"Why? Are you helping the police too?"

Julie nodded.

"By the way, Tom, how's that uncle of yours? George... George Carter. Still have that million-dollar horse operation in Texas? Doing okay, is he?"

"As far as I know. He has a knack for making money with his horses. He has a big place down there near Laredo."

Arthur nodded his head. "So, who will be hauling horses for him now that Matt's gone."

"Don't think we've gotten that far. I'm not sure that Uncle George even knows about Matt yet. We need to call him."

Tom got up and offered Arthur his hand.

"I guess we'd better get back. My family will be wondering where we are. Please let us know if you can think of anything that might help. You know our number."

Arthur grinned at them and then took Julie's hand. "You look like someone I used to date. Didn't work out. But my, she was pretty. I rebounded and married my wife. Best thing that ever happened to me. She's been gone for the past two years. I miss her. She and Ethel were good friends. She was a neat lady. Did you ever meet her, Julie?"

"She died before I came here."

"Pity. Ethel Carter would have liked you."

Tom looked at Julie and smiled. Arthur smiled at both as if sharing some unknown secret with himself.

"Damn," he said, just loud enough for them to hear. "Damn if he didn't look at her just the way I looked at my wife before I married her."

Tom looked back and grinned.

CHAPTER 13

"**W**here in the hell did that horse go?" Paul asked, as if to anyone who would listen. Paul sat with Julie, Tom, and Brenda at the kitchen table late that afternoon.

"What makes you think he went anywhere?" Brenda asked, picking at the tuna casserole that Julie made up in a hurry.

"He couldn't have disappeared into thin air. We went combing the countryside, stopping at farms and talking to anyone who would listen to us. No one saw that horse," Paul said.

"Maybe they took him from the barn when Matt was killed," Julie said.

"What makes you think it was *they*?" Paul shrugged. "Without anyone hearing a truck or trailer?" he asked, as much to himself as to the others.

"Could he have been walked down the driveway?" Tom asked.

"I didn't see any tracks when I entered the barn this morning. It didn't look like anyone had been in or out since last night," Julie said. "With all the rain, you wouldn't have seen tracks."

"How about the back pasture?" Brenda asked, sitting back in her chair. She swiveled her head to look out the kitchen window.

"Possibly… doubtful. They looked in the pasture shed at the other end, and the pasture backs into a field. Any trailer would have gotten stuck in the mud. There were no signs of him or anyone trying to break the lock on that back gate," Paul said.

Nobody responded. Except for the loud ticking of a cuckoo clock and the birds chirping away outside, the room was oppressively silent, and the atmosphere was glum.

"It's possible that someone who knew Matt entered, killed him, took the horse, and replaced the sawdust. In other words, he covered his tracks. The driveway was almost flooded. There wouldn't have been tracks leading down to the road."

"Brenda noticed that already. So, nobody heard anything last night?" Julie asked.

"Julie, it was pouring, and we were asleep. We wouldn't have heard anything. Damn, we need to get a dog or two around here," Paul said. "Tom, why don't you bring Jinx down here? Or Julie, leave Annie here. We could sure use them about now."

Julie said, "Hmm. Where Annie goes, I go."

"Not a bad idea. Anyway, around five o'clock, there was a loud crash of thunder. It shook the whole house. Woke me up. The lightning lit up the room like a searchlight. It was incredible."

"I heard it too," Julie said. "Annie huddled in bed with me. Some protectors she is. I had to protect her."

Paul laughed. "Yeah, right." He rose to look at the calendar on the wall. "What's tomorrow, anyway? I can't keep track of everything that's happening or what day it is anymore."

"It's Monday today. That makes tomorrow Tuesday. Yesterday was the horse show. Can you believe it? Last night, Matt was cussing everyone out. Now, he's dead. Go figure," Tom said, brooding over his coffee.

"Who's going to pick up Jonathan at the airport?" Brenda asked.

"We've decided that I'll do that," Tom said. "It'll give me a chance to talk to him in private. There's some stuff that I don't understand, and maybe he can clear it up for me. Paul, can you and Brenda get the house ready? I have a feeling there will be a lot of people here."

"The phone has been ringing off the hook. That's one reason Brenda and I decided to look for the horse. It was getting too much. We have a ton of people coming to the funeral, even those that didn't like Matt." He paused and added, "Maybe, especially those who didn't like him. I called Forest View Catering. They'll bring sandwiches, potato salad, and other stuff here."

Brenda shook her head and lowered it between her legs. When she looked up, her face had turned pale.

"Brenda, why don't you go back to bed?" Paul said, looking concerned.

She shook her head. "I don't want to get back into bed. I've been in bed all day. Julie, why don't you and I take a walk? Or, maybe, ride a horse. That always makes me feel better."

"You sure?" Paul asked. He stood and put his hands on Brenda's shoulders.

"Yes, I'm sure." She was emphatic.

Julie and Brenda left the two men to clean the dishes and walked to the barn. Brenda chatted about stuff that didn't matter much, and Julie figured it was to keep her mind off things.

"Julie, I didn't kill Matt," she said at last as they entered the barn.

"I don't think that anyone thinks you did. They think he was killed because of his involvement with drugs."

"Well, I believe that too. Julie, I think he might have had a hand in killing Eddie and maybe even Tony," she added.

"Why?" Julie stopped dead in her tracks. "Did you tell that to Phil?"

"Does that shock you that I think my husband could do such a thing? I think Matt was capable, all right, if he was threatened in any way. Believe me when I tell you that Matt could do the most awful things. I know him better than even his brothers do. He was a rotten person."

"Then, why was he killed?"

"Maybe because he killed the other two."

"Brenda, he couldn't have killed Eddie. He was with…" Julie stopped and looked at her.

"Damn it, Julie. Just say it. He was with Lynette Williams. If you can believe what Lynette says. She's the biggest liar of all."

"Maybe she did it. If they fought, maybe she followed him back here and killed him, hoping that the trail would lead to you."

"That still doesn't explain the disappearing horse act."

"True."

They separated and got their horses. The sun was setting as they rode across the road and into the fields across the street. The streetlights got dimmer and dimmer, and the moon lit the way as they followed the path through the hayfields. Julie relied on Socks to make his way and looked up at the sky where the stars came into full view. She thought she was in heaven for a few seconds, where everything was completely calm, beautiful, and utterly perfect.

The fields headed south and went on for miles. The trails zigzagged their way through the fields, then toward the edge of the fields surrounded by state forest preserves. This was one attraction that the Carter Ranch offered its borders. The evergreen—deciduous forests of the Northern Midwest states were among the loveliest in the world, and this one was no exception. The two riders rode into the woods and immediately noticed the smell of pine trees that lined the path on which they traveled. Further up the trail, towering oak trees rose like shadows. Their branches waved to them like arms reaching out to grab unsuspecting prey. The horses pranced nervously around, snorting at every sound and every shadow.

Julie was nervously enjoying herself, and Brenda sat on her horse and hummed a little tune that Julie did not recognize. For the first time in a while, Brenda seemed totally at ease. Now, she wished the horses would relax. Oh well, you can't have everything, she supposed. They rode on.

"Brenda, I hate to break this mood, but shouldn't we return soon? It's dark, and there aren't any lights in here."

"In a bit. The moon is full. Do you mind, Julie? I love to ride out here at night but haven't been able to for a long time. Maybe it's a dumb idea, but it's pretty safe. No one comes here much except riders and students on field trips."

"No place is really safe anymore," Julie reflected sadly. She didn't want to break the mood, but she wondered how safe they were in an isolated place where no one could hear them if they ran into trouble. "Maybe I'm too urbanized," she rationalized.

They rode on. The terrain went from flat to hilly. Julie supposed they were on the edge of some ice age moraine. It was a popular spot for riders and students exploring their geographic environment. The leaves rustled, and the wind kicked and whistled in Julie's ears. Socks looked in one direction and then another as he picked up a jog. Julie reined him back to a walk. Brenda's horse, Rummy, was also alert to the sounds of the forest. The two horses would walk, then jog, and bump into each other as they searched in the distance for undetected monsters. Suddenly, Socks became more animated.

His nostrils flared, and his eyes got big as saucers. He picked up his grey head and whinnied to something in the distance. Rummy started to prance around, and he, too, whinnied.

"Brenda, what do you suppose they sense?"

"Oh, probably nothing, maybe a deer or some other animal. There's lots out here." Brenda seemed confident, so Julie settled down and rode on.

The horses, however, did not settle down. The further they rode, the more animated they became. Socks pranced around like a racehorse parading to the post. Rummy broke into a lope and then galloped down the path before Brenda could bring him under control. Socks, being by nature a herd animal, followed Rummy.

"What's going on with these two?" Julie started to get nervous. She was out of her comfort zone when it came to trail riding at night. Most of her riding had been confined to the riding arena.

"Don't know," Brenda said. "Maybe we should start back."

They reined in their horses and tried to turn them around, but the animals had different ideas. They didn't want to go home. Rummy pranced around, and Socks bucked as Julie spurred him toward home.

"No," Julie said firmly. Then she heard Brenda say the same thing to her horse.

"Maybe we should go ahead and see what's up there," she told Julie.

"Do we have to?" Julie was now afraid and wanted to be anyplace other than where she was.

"No, but we should." Brenda rode on ahead.

Julie thought, *She's got a lot more guts than I imagined.* "Come on, Socks, let's go on."

Socks planted his feet and wouldn't move.

"Brenda!" she called. "Let's go back. This is crazy. Socks won't move."

Brenda didn't pay any attention and went on ahead. When her horse decided to catch Rummy, he had to run to keep up.

"Brenda, don't run. It's too dark to see where we're going,"

But Brenda kept going.

Finally, they reached the top of the hill. When Julie caught up, Brenda was staring down into a ravine. Julie looked down at where Brenda was pointing, and her horse suddenly reared as she did. Julie did all she could to stay in the saddle but wasn't prepared. She fell off to one side and started sliding down the hill. Over and over, she rolled, catching pine needles in her hair and jagged rocks scraping against her arms until she landed with a thud against a huge oak. As she rolled over on her back, she found herself staring into the fiercest pair of coal-black eyes she had ever seen. The monstrous head flared steam from its nostrils and reared its black body straight toward the sky. Julie first rolled over on her side to avoid the onslaught of the steel hooves. As she rolled, she realized this monster wasn't coming after her. The horse nuzzled the object of his panic as she finally got to her feet.

Slowly, she got up and felt for broken bones. Then, she realized that although she was hurt, if she had broken bones, she wouldn't have to feel for them. She reached up and petted the horse's neck, and doing her best to hold on to him, the two plunged up the hill back to the path where Brenda had gotten off her horse.

"Julie. My God, are you…" She stopped. Looking at what came up the hill and into view, she stood, unable to speak. "So," she finally said. Then, very gently, she reached up to the monster horse and said, "So, here you are, poor boy. You look like you've had a time of it, haven't you?" She put her hand on his neck and drew it back as the moonlight lit up the blood on her hand.

"Is this him?" Julie asked. Then she said, "Of course it is. What a stupid question."

"It makes sense. That he would come here, I mean." She was almost speaking to herself.

"You knew he would be here? Is that why you came out here tonight? You thought the horses would lead us to him?"

"I didn't know. I guessed. Where else could he have been? Paul and I checked the neighboring farms. They wouldn't take one of our horses. He broke away from whoever killed Matt and tried to steal him. He could have been a hundred miles away at some auction or worse. I didn't know he'd be here, but I hoped. And…" she added, "here he is."

"Yes," Julie said, looking at Brenda in a totally new light. "Here he is."

Brenda picked the halter off her saddle and put it on the horse.

You brought a halter along just in case, she thought.

They found their horses up the trail, and Julie went to get them, while Brenda hung onto the horse.

Surprisingly, as they mounted, he was quiet and sniffed the other horses gently as if to say, "Thank God, I'm coming home with you."

They rode back the way they came, and neither spoke a word as the wind rustled in their ears and the trees blew cold air over their heads. The oak tree's strange hands touched the tops of their heads as they rode by, and the pine trees looked solemn and questioning as they dared enter their domain. They rode into the fields.

The horse followed, stopped, and tugged at the halter, wanting to be free. Then, he relaxed and followed along behind. He stopped and drew back as they approached the ranch, nearly jerking Brenda out of her saddle. She held onto him and negotiated her horse around him so he couldn't pull her off. The horse ran backward, and Brenda held fast, her horse nearly jerking off his feet. He swerved. She and her horse came with him. They ran in circles. Suddenly, Brenda, holding on to his lead rope, took her feet out of her stirrup and leaped onto his back. He reared and bucked, but Brenda kept her seat, hanging onto his mane for dear life.

As suddenly as he started, the horse stopped, panting and pawing the ground. Brenda slid off his body. She remounted Rummy, and they walked up to where Julie was sitting on her horse. Julie hadn't taken her eyes off Brenda for one minute, fearing that if she even breathed, Brenda would be thrown and trampled. As she watched, Julie realized that there was no way that would happen. Brenda subdued a twelve-hundred-pound horse and rode like the devil himself.

She also realized that she could have very easily bashed the living day-lights out of Matthew Carter, and it would have been over before he could turn around.

CHAPTER 14

As the two women rode silently up the driveway, Tom and Paul waited in the barn office. Julie and Brenda had been gone well over two hours, and twilight had already turned dark. Julie's collie lay at their side, eyes closed, ears poised in an alert stance for when her mistress returned.

The men talked quietly about the farm and the business, and Tom discussed his acting career. The phone interrupted Tom's account of his play. Annie lifted her head in anticipation and then went back to sleep.

"Yes, hello. Oh… no, it's Tom… hi, Dad." Tom felt a slam in the pit of his stomach when his father didn't recognize his voice. He had asked to speak to Paul. "Hang on a minute, Paul's right here."

"Hi, Dad. No, nothing's new. Yeah, I arranged for the funeral for Thursday at noon. There will be lots of people here, people who know our family. We must expect that. You're coming when? Oh, tomorrow morning? Good. We'll arrange to pick you up. Midway? Okay.

"Uh, Dad. With all the mess that's happened, I forgot to tell you. That horse you sent up here? Well, it disappeared when Matt was killed. Huh? Wait a minute… yes, I said 'Your horse.' You know, the one you sent up here for our new boarder."

Paul's face turned pale before he said, "What do you mean you didn't send up the horse? He arrived with your two men last night… what?"

"What?" Tom asked. He was half out of his seat, trying not to pull the phone out of Paul's hand.

"Ssh, wait…" Paul returned to his conversation.

"It was cut, by whom? Oh, the horse is still at your ranch. Okay, I'll be at the airport at ten o'clock. Dad, I love you. Bye." Envy swelled in Tom's gut, formed a cold lump in his throat, and stayed there. He had never said he loved his dad since he was a little kid. He needed to say it now, but he wasn't given the chance.

"What? What did he say?" Tom fought past his feelings.

"Tom, he didn't send the horse up here. The gas line in his van was cut, which looked like sabotage. They just got it fixed. He was going to call and tell us, but then we called about Matt, and he forgot.

"Sabotage? What kind of crap is that?" Tom stood, phone in hand, bewildered. "Who would do such a thing?"

Paul shook his head.

"Someone who wanted to send their horse instead," Tom answered his own question, reflecting on the morning's conversation. "Someone who wanted Larry to have that particular horse."

"Tom, just who the hell is this Larry Ortega?"

Tom just shrugged his shoulders.

"You don't know, or you won't tell me?" Paul looked Tom squarely in the eyes, and Tom knew he couldn't lie to his younger brother successfully. He wanted to tell him but remembered Phil's edict of silence. Fortunately, their conversation abruptly ended when they heard horses coming up the driveway. The two dogs were already headed into the barn, barking and carrying on—each trying to be the first to reach the door.

"Thank God they're back. We should give them hell for scaring the living crap out of us," Tom said.

"Tom, this conversation isn't over yet." The two men locked eyes, and Tom turned and walked into the barn.

They didn't give the women hell when they saw them, they were too stunned. Julie and Brenda slid off their horses, Brenda, still holding the black horse.

"Where...?" Tom asked.

"How?" Paul stammered. It was the only word that would come out of either mouth.

"He was in the forest preserve," Julie said.

"Julie fell on top of him," Brenda grinned.

"She did… what?" Tom sputtered.

"The horses got crazy as we were riding along the trail. We had trouble holding them. Socks reared up when we came to the top of a hill, and I fell off. I rolled down a ravine and landed just in front of his feet. I rolled back just in time not to get creamed by his hooves."

"Julie found him," Brenda said. She grinned.

"Was this the halter that was on him?" Paul asked. "I thought that belonged to Rummy."

"It does. I brought it with me," Brenda said.

"Why?" Paul asked.

Brenda ignored his question. "He's hurt. I don't know how badly. He was also frightened of coming back here. I need to clean up his scratches."

"We can't shut his stall door anymore," Paul said, checking the horse's stall. "Somehow, the hinges came loose. There's an empty stall on the other side of Socks."

Tom entered the office and pulled out the medical kit he handed Brenda. He stood next to Julie, watching Brenda croon in a deep voice as she cleaned up the scratches—some deep. The still wary horse kept looking around as though waiting for something—possibly bad—to happen. But he never moved his body—just his head. Tom marveled at the effect his sister-in-law had on horses.

"What a mess," said Brenda, reaching down and examining his foot. His rear left leg had a gash running down his leg to the rear hoof, which had a giant crack where the shoe had been torn off. "That is the only reason I could subdue this horse tonight, Julie. The *only* reason." Tom looked questioning over at Julie. She glanced at him and shook her head.

They closed the barn for the night and walked back to the house. Annie led the procession, Brenda and Paul whispered, while Tom walked beside Julie, not knowing exactly what to say. He was confused and tongue-tied, trying to find the right questions to ask. When Brenda and Paul entered the house, he pulled Julie aside and asked, "How did Brenda know the horse would be in the forest preserve?"

Surprised, Julie answered, "I don't think she did."

"Then, why did she bring that halter along?"

"Don't know. I wondered about that, myself."

"Julie, did he have anything on at all? I mean, another halter?"

"No... nothing." Julie related the events that happened in the hay field. When she finished, Tom stood close to her and put his hand on her shoulder. He wanted very much to kiss her and yell at her. He had been scared when they hadn't come back. She started to pull away, and he pulled her back.

"Julie..." He started.

"Julie?" came a voice from inside. She turned and, brushing past him, ran up the stairs and into the house with Annie. Tom followed close behind, then stopped and stayed out on the porch.

He wanted to know what the hell was wrong. Is it with her or me? Maybe there's someone else, and she's not telling.

He looked over the arena with the light from a full moon staring down and wondered about her. He thought he saw a spark in her eyes when she talked to him. Sometimes, he caught her looking at him when he wasn't looking. Usually, that was a good indication when a woman was attracted. Nevertheless, she'd pulled away when Brenda called her—a convenient excuse to escape. He tasted disappointment mingled with something else. Was it relief? Maybe he felt scared about feelings that were coming on all too fast. He sighed and went into the house.

Tom and Julie arrived at Midway's arrival area in a flood of morning traffic. Cars were pulling in and out all around them. Taxis beeped their horns and pulled in front of cars that had to stop short to avoid a collision. Tom found a spot and pulled in near the entrance.

"God, what luck. Julie, move over to the driver's seat, okay? If you have to, pull out and drive around. What a pill. I hate airports." He exited and slammed the door as a taxi flew past him, nearly knocking him over. Julie moved into the driver's seat and waited.

Tom went into the terminal and found the luggage area. He saw a group of passengers heading down the long tunnel, heading right for him. Tom recognized his father in the middle of the pack.

"Tom. I thought Paul was coming to pick me up."

Disappointment swelled up somewhere in the inner recess of Tom's psyche, and he reverted to his childhood shell. No matter what he did, it wouldn't be right—he couldn't make it right. Was his father upset that it was him and not Paul who'd come to pick him up? If he hadn't come, his father would have been hurt—now, was he hurt that Paul hadn't come? He hoped his feelings wouldn't show, but he knew they had. "Paul is at home nursing Brenda and making arrangements for the funeral."

His dad nodded.

"Son, it's been too long," Jonathan Carter said at last, looking at his son. "You've grown up. I can see it in your eyes." Then, Jonathan did the unexpected. He gave his son a hug that nearly knocked the wind out of him and brushed tears away from his eyes.

"Sorry, it's the dust. Seem to be allergic to the stuff," he said.

It was too late. Tom had already picked up on it. Unknown to his father, it was the biggest moral boost Tom could have gotten. He suddenly realized how alike they were. They supported a front so the other couldn't see into his vulnerabilities.

"Dad, let's get your luggage. You point, and I'll pick them up." Tom and his father pushed through the crowds and waited until the massive conveyor belt started churning out the luggage from the airport trucks. Tom squeezed through two burly men to snatch up the suitcases. His father grabbed the smaller of the two, and they walked out of the terminal and up to Tom's truck.

"Dad, this is Julie Bishop. She has a horse at the ranch and is staying with us for a while, helping out." Opening the passenger side door, he flung the suitcases into the back and squeezed Julie into the middle as he got into the driver's side.

A dark green Suburban with no windows in the back pulled out into the traffic just behind Tom's van. No one got in the car, just as no one had gotten out. The driver seemed intent on his business. He followed as Tom drove out of the airport maze and onto the expressway leading south, keeping up at a close distance in the same lane.

Jonathan Carter turned to Julie and said, "Nice to meet you, Julie. I'm sorry we had to meet under such sad circumstances. I appreciate your helping us out. This means a lot to me and my family."

Jonathan had hoped his sons would find women who loved him the same way Ethel had. Well, it was too late for Matthew. Had Brenda loved him? He thought she was the perfect wife for him. She could handle and train horses in ways that Matt could not. She could deal with people in ways that Matt could not. Could she control his temper? He thought perhaps she could not. She could tame horses, but not his son. That had been the tragedy of Matt's life.

"Dad, Julie owns Socks. He came up from your ranch last year.

"My goodness, is that the grey horse?"

"Yes, he's grey," she answered.

"I remember him. He should be about four or five now, isn't he? I raised him at the ranch. I think Tony Richardson had a buyer for him. That was you?"

Julie shook her head. "Actually, no. The other person wanted mares instead. Brenda recommended him to me. I was the lucky one, though. I'm glad I took her advice."

"Ah, so you're Tony's cousin, then. Tragic about him. My sincerest condolences." Jonathan wondered if that was the same group of horses that stopped at the border last year. If so, the horse had lucked out, too. The mares had been confiscated and sold at auction—part of the standing drug policies.

"Well, it's nice to see he's got a good home and you're doing something with him." He changed the subject, which would have sent them all crashing to their emotional floors.

"She practically cleaned up in the amateur division with him last weekend." Tom found the perfect topic.

"Good for you!" Jonathan said, warming up to this girl.

She was getting better and better in his eyes. He loved matchmaking, and he thought she might be good for Tom. Unfortunately, with Tom, he had to be careful. If he claimed something was white, Tom would immediately call it black. The two could not agree on anything. Jonathan thought there might be some jealousy over Matt. Matt was the eldest. Jonathan had always indulged Matt in ways he never did with the two other boys. He still didn't know exactly why he did that. It hadn't helped Matt—probably made him worse. He thought that maybe he'd overcompensated for some other things. He focused on Julie, who was talking about her horse and the classes at the show.

"Tell me more about this murder at the horse show," Jonathan requested. "I want to know everything, don't leave anything out."

"I can't tell you everything. I don't know much, and Phil Swanson's handling the case. He's asked for our help. So, we're helping," Tom said, maneuvering his truck to the right lane and trying to lose a green Suburban on his tail.

"Stupid van." The van's windows were tinted.

"Patience, son," his father said. Jonathan wondered why he felt the need to say something he knew his son resented. He couldn't help it.

Tom went on to tell his father everything that had happened during the past four days, up to Brenda and Julie finding the horse the previous night. Jonathan sat in silence and listened.

"So…" he said slowly, not being able to help focus on the original conversation. "They think Tony was murdered last year. They think Eddie's death was somehow connected and that Matt's being killed had something to do with all of this, as well. They further think that Matt was dealing drugs and perhaps was involved with Tony and Eddie in the trafficking of cocaine. Is that about it?"

"Yes, I guess that's about it," Tom said.

"Well…" his father said. "I can tell you right off that your cousin would never be involved with something like that. His being arrested for drugs is appalling. I thought so at his funeral, and I'll repeat it. He was not involved… as for Matt…" His conversation faltered as the Suburban cut in front of Tom's truck, making Tom step on the brakes. The van in back honked and moved to the center lane.

After a mutual sigh of relief, Jonathan said, "Nice maneuver, Tom," hoping to make up for his previous remark. Then he continued, "So, the horse is back. I'll want to see this magical disappearing animal. Maybe later, after I've settled, we can go to the barn together."

There was no time for a response. The Suburban crossed back into the center lane and slowed down to parallel Tom's vehicle. Then, slowly, it inched its way back into the right lane, and there was no time to brake. Jonathan saw his life flash before him as the Suburban bumped into the van, scraping—metal on metal. It moved back over to the center line, and as Jonathan breathed a sigh of relief, the van lurched back again, harder. Jonathan put his hands on the dashboard for support. He saw his son's expert maneuvering momentarily—first slowing out of impact range, then suddenly accelerating as the other van slowed with him. He wondered why, throughout all their lifetime together, he'd never seen how competent his son was. Nor had he been able to tell Tom how much he loved him—and how proud he was of him. As he felt another, more substantial jolt forcing them further to the right, he thought it was too late.

Tom navigated off the expressway onto the grassy embankment just seconds before reaching a hundred-foot drop into an underpass filled with construction traffic. The Suburban sped away, leaving Jonathan, Tom, and Julie speechless and staring at each other.

"Nice driving, Tom," his father said. This time, he meant it.

CHAPTER 15

After they dropped Jonathan Carter at the ranch, Tom and Julie quietly drove to Bruce Warner's, the next name on the list.

Once again, Julie felt a cloud hovering over her life, threatening herself and the people she cared about. This time, having Tom Carter on her side made all the difference. The threat became more of an adventure-mystery novel in which she and Tom had leading parts.

"So, who do you think would want to kill us?" Tom jolted her back into reality.

"Do you think that was an actual attempt to kill us... or merely frighten us?" Julie asked. "I think if they had been out to do severe damage, they could have waited a few more seconds. We'd have gone over the edge, becoming a highway statistic."

"Maybe that sun is bright. Hand me my sunglasses in the glove compartment, will you?" Julie dug into the glove compartment and pulled out sunglasses from under some photographs. She handed him the glasses and looked at the pictures.

"Who's she?" Julie looked at the face of an exquisite girl of about eighteen years old with long black-brown hair and bright blue eyes.

"Oh, that's where they went to. I was looking for those. She's an old friend. I haven't seen her in several years."

"Didn't work out?"

Tom looked at her, then gave a sad little chuckle. "No, I'm afraid not." Julie put the pictures back into the glove compartment.

"Sorry," she said. They drove through the small Indiana town of Lowell, continuing east toward Crown Point.

"It's a long time ago. She was older than me and married my Godfather. I got over it."

"She's pretty enough."

"Yes. Yes, she is. Inside as well as out."

"How did you get over it?" Julie asked.

"Some things you never get over completely." Then, more quietly, he added, "Some things you should never get over."

"Oh… well put, Tom."

"Why do you ask?"

"I was seriously involved with someone a couple of years ago. I also had to end it. It was devastating," she stopped and stared out the side window for a few minutes as they drove by farm after farm.

"You said that you ended the relationship," Tom said, prompting her to say more.

"He was married."

"Oh, good Lord. I'm sorry, Julie."

"I didn't know until I picked up the phone at his apartment, and his wife answered. He'd led two lives. He spent the week in the city going to school and every other weekend upstate with his real family. He told me about an elderly mother. He omitted the part about his wife."

"How long did you…"

"About a year. We were supposed to move in together. What a jerk. I never saw it coming." She changed the subject. "I liked your dad, Tom. I mean, I like him very much. You're a lot alike."

"You didn't have to grow up with him."

"I'm sure. Our parents always seem great to everyone else." She paused. "Tom, I want to ask you a question, but I'm unsure how you'll take it."

"Ask away. You won't ask me anything I haven't thought of myself."

"Do you think that your dad is… could be involved somehow in the drug trade? Maybe he did ship that horse up here?"

"I stand corrected. That thought never crossed my mind. Do you mean that my father has been instigating all of this? That he has been heading up a drug ring and was responsible for the deaths of three people? How?"

"No, maybe not the murders. Maybe he was involved with just the drugs and found out about the DEA's investigation. Somehow, I think the murders are related, but it seems that the victims were either suspected or known to have been drug dealers. Tony, Eddie, and Matt."

"My dad involved?" Tom repeated, half to himself. "I can't see it, somehow. Julie, you'd have to know him. He's so damned straight, your typical pillar in the community. I don't think he'd ever risk ruining his reputation. He's in total denial about Matt. I don't think he knew about his activities, let alone being part of them."

"Tom, those men knew Matt."

"I'd never seen them before, and that wasn't my father's truck."

"Of course not. Why would he send a van up here with known employees?"

"I don't know. If that was the case, why were we almost killed a few hours ago? And why kill Matt? My father doted on him, and he looked at Richardson's almost like extended family."

"Maybe we weren't supposed to be killed, just eliminated as suspects," Julie answered, almost like a question. "Or could there be a rival drug operation? Someone who wants to cut into the territory up here. That could explain the attempt on our lives today."

"Hadn't thought of that possibility."

"And, Tom, I think you're wrong about your father being in denial. . . about Matt, that is."

Tom turned toward her so sharply that he nearly wrenched his neck. "What do you mean?"

"Do you remember our conversation before we were forced off the expressway? We were talking about Tom and Tony connected with drugs. Your dad said that Tony would not have been connected. He was adamant. Remember?"

Tom nodded his head. "Yeah, so?"

"Well, he didn't say the same about Matt."

He glanced at her before forcing his eyes back to the road.

"Nothing makes any sense to me now. Nothing," he replied.

He drove along a tree-lined street with an eclectic mixture of old homes and modern-style ranches. Looking at the mailbox numbers, he found the right one at the end of the street and pulled up the driveway.

A woman in her late fifties answered the door. She looked first at Julie and then at Tom as though sizing them up. "Can I help you?"

"We hope so," Julie said, smiling at her and extending her hand. "We need to speak to Bruce Warner."

"I'm Mary Warner. My husband isn't home right now, but I expect him any minute. I hope you're not allergic to dogs. We have seven."

They shook their heads.

She ushered them through the door into the house as three collies bounded out of their playroom to greet the newcomers.

"Dogs, bed." They scampered back in the direction from which they came.

"Sorry," she said. Julie wasn't sure whether she meant that for them or the dogs.

She led Julie and Tom into her dining room, where they sat at a round oak table with matching chairs perched on rollers. Julie noticed you could roll anywhere in the house and never leave the chair. Pretty neat, she thought.

"Coffee?" she asked. "It's already made. I always keep a fresh pot going. My husband is a coffee freak."

Julie sat and observed Mary entering the kitchen to pour coffee. The interior of this sprawling ranch house in the early fifties style had plenty of room for two people and seven dogs. Julie noticed that the oak cabinet on one wall had a collection of cut-glass pieces and trophies that had been won at various dog shows.

When four mugs and a glass coffee pot were set on the table, they sat discussing horses and dogs. Mary chatted about her thirty-something years of showing collies, and Tom joined in, discussing his years showing horses as a kid. Laughter followed ring disasters, and tears came as they talked about the great horses and dogs they'd been privileged to know. The time passed quickly until all hell broke loose in the back bedroom. The dogs started barking enthusiastically as a thinly built man of medium stature walked in with friendly but inquisitive eyes toward the guests in his home.

"Bruce, this is Julie Bishop and Tom Carter. They want to talk to you, dear," she said.

"Me?" he asked with raised eyebrows.

"Mr. Warner, I'm Tom Carter, Matthew Carter's brother. This is my friend, Julie."

Bruce's eyes narrowed, and his face tensed.

"Matt was killed yesterday morning… murdered. We're helping the police investigate his death. We're researching his past, just talking to some people involved with Matt's life. I understand you were Matt's school advisor, and I was hoping you could tell me something about Matt while he was in college. Something to help us catch the person who did this."

Bruce sat down at the table. "I'm very sorry to hear about your brother. How did he die?"

"Someone bashed him on the head."

"Good Lord. I'm sorry." Bruce relaxed a bit and took a sip of coffee. "You're right, of course, I was his advisor. I'll help in any way I can. I hope you can take what I might have to tell you."

"I know my brother, and he wasn't an angel. His wife hated him, and I wasn't very fond of him either. He hurt a lot of people, especially those closest to him."

"Yes. Yes, I can see that." He looked thoughtfully at Tom. "Very well, what do you want to know?"

"First of all, what kind of people did he hang out with at school? Who were his friends?"

"He wasn't a real popular kid, except for the girls. They seemed to like him. He liked one, but she gave him a run for his money. I guess he finally married her. I'm sorry they weren't happy together. That's a shame. He really went after her. I remember telling him once that we couldn't always get what we wanted all the time. He just laughed and said that he always got what he wanted. I just shut up at that point."

"Did you ever meet Brenda?" Tom asked.

"No. I heard that she's a decent girl and a superb horsewoman."

"She is," Tom said. "Go on, Mr. Warner."

"His other friends were a bad lot. Some of them didn't go to that school but hung around campus, causing all kinds of trouble. The administration tried to stop them, but they always seemed to know whenever the authorities came. Then they would disappear.

"The campus police suspected that drugs were used on campus. Nobody could prove it, but everyone knew it existed. The cops planned raids on the dorms, but in every case, the drugs were gone by the time the police got there. Matt was suspected as being involved, but nothing was ever proved."

"Did you know a kid named Eddie Meeks?"

"What? Matt's friend Eddie? They were best friends. Eddie flunked out of school during his second year, and then suddenly, it seemed, he got rich. He drove fancy cars and had girls hanging all over him. He and Matt were thick as thieves, went everywhere together."

Julie and Tom looked at each other. "Lynette said that Matt hated Eddie, and the feeling was mutual. What changed?"

"I'm trying to find something nice to say about Matt. I can't. He pulled a real nasty trick on me."

"What did he do?"

"I used to try to help my students with their term papers. They'd come to my office and borrow research materials. I didn't mind. They did their own papers and used my projects to supplement their observations and research. Matt came to me for help one day. He was studying different methods of training horses. He asked me all kinds of questions, and the subject came up about training horses… as a weapon to kill people. I had just finished a research paper on the subject, so I told him about it. This paper wasn't for publication. I wouldn't have wanted the paper to get into the wrong hands. I made the mistake of showing it to him. We talked for hours about the subject. He seemed genuinely interested in the psychological profile of horses. He wanted to take it with him, and I said no. When I came in the next day, the lock had been broken, and the research paper was missing. I spent a long time on that paper. It was gone, vanished. I do have it on disk, but still… I can't prove it, but I know Matt took it. Strange, though, I checked with all his teachers about his term papers. He never used that topic."

Julie and Tom exchanged glances.

"Were you Tony Richardson's advisor, too?" Julie asked.

"Tony? Of course. It was tragic about his death."

"What did you think about Tony?"

"Tony was a nice kid. Quiet but smart. I mean, not intellectually, but he had good sense and good instincts for horses. He worked hard and was well-liked by everyone. It was sad to see him knocked down in the prime of his life."

"That's an interesting way of putting it," Julie said.

"Yes. He had a rough go of things for a while, which made this even harder."

"What happened?"

"He fell in love. Apparently, there was a secret engagement. I don't believe many people knew. She went to the school, but I never saw them together… except once. I saw them in the cafeteria. He ate with many different people, but there was something different about how he looked at her.

I think she broke it off. Her parents, I gather, disapproved of him. Don't ask me why. I can't see why any parent wouldn't be tickled to death to have their daughter marry Tony Richardson, but that's only my opinion. I tried to get Matt to hang around with Tony more. I knew that their families had always been tight. Matt only laughed at me and said that Tony was a bore. Once again, I left him alone."

Bruce sat as though locked in his thoughts as Julie tried to filter through everything she'd just heard.

"Well, have I helped you at all? I don't know anything else that I can tell you."

"You've helped a lot already. I wish we could find Tony's girlfriend. She seems to be a major player, and we can't find her. There were no pictures of her at Tony's house. The police checked on that last year. Even his lawyer didn't know."

"Arthur didn't know. How strange. He was close to Tony. I was going to suggest that you talk to him."

"Thanks, we did that already."

They sat drinking their coffee and looked around the room at the various pictures of dogs on the walls.

"So, you folks show horses?" Bruce asked.

"Yes," Julie said. "I had some pictures taken last week, just before the show last weekend. We showed at the Forest View Fairgrounds Quarter Horse Show. We did quite well for our first major show, and Brenda took high point open rider."

"You have the pictures with you?" Mary asked.

Julie took them out of her purse, and the four passed around pictures, "oohing" and "aahing" at various horses and riders. Suddenly, Bruce took one of the pictures and said, "This one, here. Who is this? Who's the rider?"

"That's Brenda," Julie said, passing the photo to Bruce.

"That's Matt's wife?" he asked with a funny tone, making everyone look up at him and stare.

"Yes, that's Brenda. Why? What's wrong?" Tom asked.

"There's no mistaking it. That is Tony Richardson's girlfriend."

"But you only saw them together that once," Julie said.

"I won't ever forget how those two looked at each other."

They stared at him, and Tom recovered first.

"Are you saying that my sister-in-law was Tony's girlfriend?"

"Absolutely."

"She left Tony to marry… Matt?"

"I guess she must have. What kind of connections did your family have with her family?"

"I'm not too sure. I think her father knows my Uncle George. Brenda's family was into horses. They rode on the hunter-jumper circuit back East. I believe her father is in the chemical business and has his own firm. They're very wealthy. I came home for Matt's wedding, but I can't say that I know Brenda very well.

"I've gotten to know her more in the past two days than I did over the past three years. She married him about three years ago. I didn't know that she even knew Tony. She never mentioned it to me. Even when she saw Greg at the horse show, she didn't mention anything. I don't think that Greg knew his brother dated her."

"Greg was here?" Bruce asked.

"Do you know him?" Tom was stuffing the photos back into an envelope.

"Not well. I met him at Tony's funeral. I felt very sorry for him. He looked like a little lost dog without his brother. His loss was so acute. It was painful to watch."

"I'll bet that Matt knew," Julie said.

They all looked over at her with surprise.

"If Matt was as ruthless as you seem to think, what stopped him from killing Tony last year? Maybe Matt set him up."

"Why? He was already married to Brenda. He would get more out of gloating with Tony alive."

"Would he? Supposing Brenda planned to leave him and run off with Tony?"

"Matt would never have given her a divorce."

"Maybe that's why Matt's been playing around with Lynette."

Bruce and Mary's eyebrows involuntarily rose toward the ceiling as if on cue.

"No, maybe he started with Lynette to get even with Brenda. Someone said that Tony's girlfriend came back for a while. Tony was happy. He told Mr. Ashford that he might be getting married. Maybe Matt found out about them, set up Tony, and killed him. The police wouldn't suspect it was anything other than suicide. Also, if Matt were suspected of being part of a drug ring, maybe implicating Tony would get the police off Matt's back. Kill two birds with one stone, so to speak."

"But then, what about Eddie's death?" Tom asked. "And, why in the world was Matt killed?"

"Maybe Tony's death is the reason for Matt's death," Mary said. They all looked at her. "Maybe, when Brenda found out that Tony had not committed suicide, she figured out that Matt killed him, and so she bashed his head in. Maybe the wife did it." With that, Mary went into the kitchen to get everyone some cake and to refill the coffee pot.

CHAPTER 16

"So," Julie said as they headed back to the ranch.

"So?"

"So, Brenda was Tony Richardson's girlfriend. Doesn't that beat everything? *She's* the missing piece in this puzzle. We've been going crazy about a mystery woman, and it's Brenda."

"Do you realize what this means?" Tom turned his head toward her as they headed home. The dwindling light from the sun blinked under the horizon as blue, pink, and orange merged in and out of fluffy clouds, way too beautiful for their moods.

"I'm afraid I do. It means this would be an additional and powerful motive for Brenda to kill Matt. And she doesn't have an alibi except for being asleep when it happened."

"I woke up when I heard that crash of thunder, and the electricity went off when the generator in town got hit. However, I honestly didn't hear anything other than that."

"What's that you're wearing?" he asked.

"You mean these slacks?"

Tom drew a slow grin and gazed at her eggshell slacks and forest green tank top tucked in and held together with a gold belt. Pretty, yes. However, his nose was doing most of the work, not his eyes.

"I mean the perfume—gardenias."

"It's called *Gardenia.* You're very observant."

"I've been told that I have a rather sensitive nose. It's nice."

His truck rode too close to a ditch, and Tom swerved back onto the road.

"Ouch!" Julie hung onto the dashboard. "Thank you," Julie said. "Watch the road."

"You're welcome—okay." He grinned and focused back on the road. "Now, how could Brenda have pulled this off? She's way too fragile, Julie. Matt would have seen her coming, and she would have been the one lying in that stall."

"Not that fragile, Tom. I saw her stop a 1200-pound horse last night, and he was fighting her the whole time."

"You believe that Matt trained that horse to kill someone?"

"Well, yes. Don't you? Bruce confirmed it this afternoon. Matt took his ideas and put them to practical use."

"Brenda rode the horse and wasn't killed... and she rode bareback."

"If Matt trained the horse at your ranch, Brenda must have known him too. Brenda's a great rider, and she was prepared—she knew his problem. Anyway, we're avoiding the issue. She was pretty strong last night."

"Do you think Brenda killed Matt?"

"Actually? No." Julie was firm.

A white Cadillac was the only car in the lot as Brenda walked through the open entrance into the barn. At first, she didn't see Lynette as she strolled down the aisle and over to the black horse's stall. Half staring and half dreaming, she watched him. She didn't move until a voice—brutal and ugly—woke her.

"You killed him, didn't you?"

Startled, Brenda turned and faced Lynette, who was almost upon her. Lynette, eyes narrowed and wild with fury, went for Brenda like a mare about to defend her young.

Oh shit. Brenda took a deep breath, crossed her arms in front of her, and didn't move a muscle. She exhibited an expression she used to stop Matt cold, for protection. Usually, it worked. It was a glare in the eyes that had turned fury into fear and hate into apprehension. Lynette stopped.

Lynette stopped and sputtered, "You ki...ll...ed him because he was... go...ing—"

Through clenched teeth, Brenda said calmly, "Going to what?"

Lynette didn't answer but stared at Brenda.

"I didn't kill him, Lynette, and you know it. And, no, he wasn't going to leave me. I only wish he would have. You don't understand. We were both his possessions. He wouldn't give up on either one of us without a fight. You're wrong if you think I killed him. I didn't, though. I think I know who did." With that, she looked hard into Lynette's defensive eyes.

"You...you don't think that I...?" Lynette gasped and backed up a few steps. She turned on her heels and ran out of the barn. Brenda's gaze never left her.

Brenda walked into the office and looked into the mirror. She shocked even herself. Her face was drawn and pale, and her hair was uncombed. She pulled a bag from the desk and picked a brush and some berets. Brushing her long, straight hair back, she braided the sides and pulled them back. Next, she took out some rouge and lipstick and gently, almost lovingly, put them on her face. Then, she took a step back and looked at the results.

"Well, I look almost presentable… almost, not quite." It started as a soft chuckle that turned into a laugh that started coming from her inner being until she realized that it wasn't laughter but sobs—almost screams. She let it go, giving it all she had until there wasn't anything left to give. The woman realized that was the last tear she would ever shed over her husband—her *deceased* husband. Her grieving process was over. Anything more would be a lie.

She walked back out and quietly approached the black horse. Walking into his stall, she checked on his scratches. Most were entirely gone. She ran her hand down his right leg, looking at his hoof. He flinched and moved as she touched him.

"You poor thing. You've had a time of it, haven't you? "

"Hello, Mrs. Carter, how are you feeling today?"

Brenda jumped up and whirled around, facing Phil Swanson, who stood in front of the stall door. The black horse whirled and kicked out, nearly landing his hooves on Brenda's back.

"My God, you scared me." She walked to the back of the stall. "Whoa, honey." The horse snorted, checked the stranger standing by his stall, then started munching on some hay. Brenda turned back to Phil. "Don't do that."

"Sorry," Phil said.

"Everyone's up at the house except for Julie and Tom. They're not back yet. Did you check up there?"

"No. I was looking for you."

"Oh?"

"So, this is the lost horse?"

"Yes, that's him."

"You know him?"

"Me? No, I… Maybe. I've trained so many horses. He looks familiar." She didn't know what else to say, so she remained silent.

"Can we talk somewhere?"

She took him into the office, and they sat in silence. Finally, Phil said, "I'm not your enemy, Brenda. I'm not."

"You think I killed my husband."

"Did you?"

"No."

"I think you might have had a good reason."

"Just about everyone who knew him had a reason."

"Who's everyone?"

"Lynette Williams, for one."

"I know. You told me. He was having an affair with her."

"I did? Oh well, perhaps I did. You're right. Matt wouldn't have married her. Perhaps he told her in his arrogant manner. He could hurt you sometimes."

"Do you think that Matt could have hurt Lynette enough for her to kill him?"

"Maybe, Phil. But probably not. She's not a killer." Brenda started to relax.

"Who do you think killed your husband?"

"I think you need to find the owners of that pickup from Sunday night. The ones who drove this horse here."

"Do you know who they are?"

"No. At first, I thought they were from my father-in-law's ranch. I was wrong. He usually sends two of his hands up here with his horses. But I found out Jonathan hadn't sent the horse up at all. Someone had messed with his trailer, and it was out of commission."

"Do you recognize the horse they brought in?" He looked closely at Brenda's reaction.

"All right, I know you'll find out about this sooner or later. Yes, I recognize him. He was here last year. He was Matt's project. Matt trained him and then sent him on his way. He brought him in here and told me to stay away from him. I never saw him ride or train the horse. One day, he hauled him away and wouldn't tell me anymore. I felt sorry for him because I knew how mean Matt could be with his horses. I still feel sorry for him because he's so messed up."

"How do you know he's messed up?"

"Because I got on his back last night. I don't know specifically what happened, but I know that he wasn't trained normally."

"Brenda, do you think it's possible to train a horse to kill someone?"

"Kill someone? A horse… on purpose? Was that what Matt was up to?"

"Don't know for sure," Phil replied. "Possibly. Is it possible, do you think?"

"Yes, absolutely. It's easy when you know what you're doing. You don't need to train the horse to be mean. Teach him to respond to normal signals in abnormal ways. The horse processes what you teach him."

"Someone would have to be pretty sick to try that."

"Yes, he would."

"Do you think that Matt was that sick?"

"Phil, do you think that Matt trained this horse to kill someone? My God." Brenda shook her head and looked away, blinking away tears that she thought were gone forever.

"Brenda, did you kill your husband?" Again, Phil looked for Brenda's reaction. This time, she defied him. She got out of her chair and, with a huff, turned on him.

"Mr. Swanson, if you think I killed Matt, then, damn it… prove it!" She walked out of the office leaving Phil to contemplate the walls all by himself.

He sat still, watching those walls briefly, reflecting on all he'd seen and heard during the past few days. Damn. He didn't have experience dealing with people when it came to murder. His little world was topsy-turvy, and he didn't like it—one bit. These people were his lifelong friends, and he had to come in and practically accused them of murder. Still, when death occurred, there had to be a motive. The nearest and dearest relatives usually had the strongest motives. Why do people kill? Greed, hate, jealousy, money? In this case, many people had reason to hate Matt. Brenda would inherit at least a portion of Matt's estate, and she had reason to be jealous of his involvement with another woman. The other woman had reason enough to hate Matt as well, and none of them had an alibi. Then, there were the two men who brought the horse. Did Matt somehow double-cross them in some way? What was the key?

He walked over to the black horse's stall and looked at him. Could this horse have been the motive for his death? That was an angle that he hadn't explored. But how? The horse approached the stall door and stuck his nose through, asking to be petted. Phil stuck his fingers inside and stroked the horse's nose.

"Brother," he said softly. "You're some killer. What do you do, lick your victims to death?" Phil walked out of the barn and headed back to his office.

Jonathan broke the dinner conversation by questioning the upcoming funeral arrangements scheduled for Thursday. "Your Uncle George is coming tomorrow night. He'll be flying up from Texas."

"How's Uncle George? Are you two talking again?" The family sat at the kitchen table eating Kentucky Fried Chicken, which Tom had bought on the way home. The edge in his tone shocked everyone at the table. Julie dropped her fork and stared at him.

"Tom, cut it out. He's your uncle." Jonathan's eyes narrowed for a moment, then softened.

"Sorry." Once again, Tom reverted to past feelings of inadequacy, like he was not meeting his father's approval. He felt even worse when his father continued as though the exchange had not happened.

"Anyway, I guess he's just fine. I called him to break the news. That's all. He's terribly upset. He should arrive sometime late tomorrow night. He said something about renting a car at the airport, so we don't have to pick him up." Jonathan dug his fork into the coleslaw like he was spearing it to death.

"It seems Matt was supposed to transport some horses for him. He'll need someone to take over."

"You mean he drove down to Texas just to pick up horses?" Julie asked with surprise.

"Not necessarily," Paul said. "Uncle George usually had a full van going both ways, around the country. Sometimes, someone would drive up here, and Matt would take over and finish the run. Sometimes, local buyers or sellers would have horses that needed transporting, and Matt would do it for them. It provided extra income for us. Occasionally, I did it for him, but Matt did, mostly."

"You transported horses for your Uncle George?" Julie asked.

"Like I said, sometimes."

Tom's thoughts ran wild, wondering why Matt wanted to spend so much time on the road. Then, he thought of a new possibility, making his blood run cold. Paul. Could he enter the picture somewhere? How about Brenda? His imagination ran wild. No.

"You made many of the runs, didn't you?" Brenda asked. It was more of a statement than a question.

"Not many. Just sometimes, when Matt wasn't available, it was income."

"Dad," Tom said, "Do you suppose someone he worked with killed him? That rig down here Sunday night. It didn't come from your ranch. We don't know who the driver was. Matt seemed to know him. Maybe they doubled back, killed Matt, and tried to take the horse back."

"How did he get into the forest preserve?"

"Don't know," Tom said. "Maybe he got away from them."

"Getting that trailer down here again without anyone hearing it would be difficult. It's not impossible... just improbable. Maybe they parked it up on the road. Still, Paul and I talked to all the neighbors. Nobody heard anything. The people next door woke up to the thunder and looked out. There wasn't any movement at all out here." Brenda spoke up for the first time during the conversation.

"Maybe they tried, and he ran. It rained so hard, maybe they slipped."

"Maybe one of them broke his ankle, or better yet, his neck. One can only hope," Julie said.

"Eat your dinner," Jonathan said.

"Anyone want coffee?" Brenda rose and went over to the coffee pot.

"Paul, Phil Swanson was down at the barn."

"When?"

Brenda was washing the dishes, and Paul helped dry and put them away.

"Just before dinner. Lynette was there and accused me of killing Matt."

"That bitch…" He slammed the towel down on the counter and looked at her.

"That's not all," she added. "Phil Swanson came in and started interrogating me. He thinks I killed him, too. Everyone thinks I did it."

"Bren… Maybe I should tell them. Maybe we both should tell them."

"No… At least—" Her conversation ended abruptly. Julie came in from the porch.

CHAPTER 17

Wednesday night, Julie did not sleep well. The nightmares of the day worked their way into her dreams during the night, and reality became fantasy, and fantasy became reality.

It started innocently enough. She and Tom visited the next name on their list, Eagle Ranch. No longer the Richardson's farm, it now belonged to a couple from Missouri named Marion and Daniel Smith.

"Have a seat," Marion Smith said as she showed them her favorite gathering place. It was a large farmhouse kitchen with plenty of room for a long pine table and antique chairs that stood over brick vinyl tile. As Marion said, they repaired the vinyl three times because of broken pipes. "It was," she said, "a decorator's nightmare."

Julie looked at the treasures displayed in the kitchen. A turn-of-the-century sidebar reminded her of the one she had at home, and an old dresser painted green had an old-time radio displayed on top. Various painted plates of Arabian horses and original oils of show horses were hanging on the wall.

"Where in the world did you find this tablecloth?"

Marion, a thin and rather tall woman with light brown hair sprinkled with grey, was still in excellent shape for her early forties. Julie guessed that she rode her horses a great deal and probably trained them herself. She looked like a performance rider.

"Oh, we're antique shoppers. We found it at a flea market. It's from the 1940's." Marion fingered her tablecloth as though it were made of a most delicate material.

"Beautiful."

"We're glad to meet you," Daniel said. "But we're not sure how we can help." Daniel was a man who was also in decent shape. He was muscular but on the thin side. Julie decided he could be a construction worker. Then, looking around at all his electronic equipment, Julie thought he might be an electrician. He glanced from Tom to Julie, then back again. His face looked hard, tense with wary eyes, but a smile never left his face.

Tom caught Julie's eye. Then, he smiled and turned back to Daniel. "We're not either. We're investigating the death of my brother, Matthew. He was killed Monday morning. Somehow, his activities lead us back to Tony Richardson and Eddie Meeks. We thought maybe you could show us Eddie's apartment in the back of the barn."

"I'm sorry to hear about your brother's death. I'd gladly show you the apartment, but it's different now. We renovated it for our foreman, who's still with the horses in Missouri. I'll take you back there if you want to see."

They walked out of the house and down to the barn. As they entered the entrance, a long row of stalls with beautiful cherry wood doors and iron bars over the stall windows stood at either end of the large aisle. There were large stalls, some ready to accommodate brood mares waiting to foal. Julie was impressed. "Wow!"

"Ah, you've been here before?" Marion gave Julie a questioning glance.

"Last year. My horse was here when I bought him."

"From Richardson?" Daniel asked.

"Actually, from Mr. Richardson and Brenda. This certainly has changed since the last time I was here."

"I'm sure it has. We've replaced all the stall doors ourselves and enlarged the stalls. Cost a fortune," Daniel said.

"I'll bet," Tom said, looking over to the large riding arena with mirrored walls. Do you train your horses for dressage?"

"Yes, we do. That's what mirrors are for. My wife's ridden on the dressage circuit for years. That's why we like the Arabian horses. They're smart, small, and flexible, unlike the larger warmbloods that are popular now. You're into the quarter horses, aren't you?"

Julie nodded.

Daniel took them up a staircase at the back of the barn, which led to a beautifully decorated two-room apartment on the second floor.

"You, see? Everything new. We paneled over the old walls in a knotty pine. Some of the walls had to be removed completely. The floors are all new. We almost gutted the place, didn't we, Marion?" His wife smiled and nodded, and Julie looked around in awe. She didn't know anyone who could build something like this from scratch. She went over and felt the paneling. Knocking on the wall, she heard an echo from behind a wall.

"Can you remove the paneling?" she asked.

"Yeah, I suppose. Why?"

"Oh, for pipe repairs or something like that."

"Oh well, no pipes run along that wall. The only pipes up here are those that run from the bathroom. We've paneled that part with doors." Julie entered the bathroom and looked at a panel door that slid open. Behind it, there was a crawl space filled with copper pipes. It was obviously new.

"Thanks for showing us around," Tom said. "Now, Julie, I think we'd better be getting home."

"You folks married?" Marion asked as they walked back down the staircase.

"No," said Julie and Tom almost simultaneously.

Julie felt for the shoulder strap of her purse. "Oh, sorry. I left my purse up there. I'll be right back." Julie turned and tore upstairs before anyone could turn around. She went back into the living room and knocked on the walls again. Again, she heard the hollow sounds. She checked in the bathroom and slid the panel door open again. Crouching down, she crawled into the space and pulled the light chain, illuminating the crawl space.

She thought someone had been doing something in here when she noticed signs of something being pushed in and taken out again. Whatever had been hidden inside was now gone. She turned the light off again and slid the door shut.

"Find it?"

Julie swung around into the face of Daniel Smith.

"Oh. You scared me. Yeah, here it is. Thanks. I'll be going." She hurried out of the bathroom with him right behind her. She started down the stairs and got halfway down when her foot slipped out from under her, and she plummeted down the rest of the stairs, just veering off to the right into a stall—fortunately, filled with hay.

"Julie, are you all right?" Tom raced in and knelt beside her.

"Yes, nothing broken, I don't think. Ouch…" She touched her back where she landed as Tom helped her to her feet. Marion and Daniel were right behind Tom.

"Are you all right?" they asked.

"Yes, thank you. I must have tripped over my feet. I didn't know that I was that clumsy."

Julie thought about their visit as she lay in bed that night. She and Tom hadn't discussed it on the way home. He wanted her to see a doctor, but Julie insisted she was all right. She fell asleep and dreamed about the beautiful barn with the cherry wood stall doors. She saw the staircase and feet. Rows and rows of feet. Then the scene changed, and she was in the apartment, standing in the middle of the living room, as men hauled in hundreds of boxes. She was invisible as they walked through her in a zombie-like fashion, putting the boxes into the crawl space.

She woke up from the heavy dream-like state and lay as though in a trance between the world of day and night. She suddenly knew she hadn't tripped over her feet. She tripped over Daniel Smith's feet. No, he tripped her on purpose. And there was more. As they walked from the barn back to Tom's van, she noticed—barely visible—a green van parked in an alcove behind the house.

Looking around at the other bed in the guest room, Brenda was curled up, looking like a ten-year-old girl. Phil can't honestly believe that she killed anyone, she thought, getting up and fumbling for her navy terry cloth robe that lay strewn about on a rocking chair next to her bed. She tiptoed out of the bedroom, and Annie woke up just as she stepped over her. "Ssh." She walked downstairs and onto the back porch as she scrambled to keep up with her, yawning and stretching.

Julie stared at the moon shining down in the outdoor arena. She removed her terry cloth robe and threw it over a rocking sofa in the center of well-maintained wicker porch furniture grouped for easy conversation on long summer evenings. She lowered the top of her nightgown to her waist and stretched, letting the breeze reach her upper body as she stood, mesmerized, watching the sky.

Annie sat next to her, and they watched silently, looking at a specter of dark and light-mingled shadows. She felt the cool breeze from the distant lake, which felt good on her bruises. Suddenly, she felt another presence on the porch, and turning, she looked into Tom's eyes.

"Oh." She suddenly remembered that she was half naked and pulled the top of her nightgown back up where it belonged.

"Sorry… if I scared you. I heard a noise and came down to see what it was."

She noticed his voice was shaking, and his eyes were trying to focus on her face. Chills started moving up and down her spine, and it intermingled with hot flashes. She felt as though she might faint—but controlled herself.

Julie replied, "I couldn't sleep. I kept seeing paneled rooms and rows of feet," trying to keep her voice steady.

"It's been quite a week for you. I'm sorry for bringing you into our family crisis."

"You didn't. I was already in the middle of it."

"It's something, isn't it?" he said, moving over to her side and glancing at the moon.

"Enchanting," she said. "The moon has a hypnotizing quality about it. It's so far away and yet so near. It makes people do strange things."

"Like fall in love," Tom said, almost in a whisper.

She turned around to face him, and he pressed against her. The moonlight made his face look almost translucent against the dark background. She finally admitted to herself how much she wanted him, no longer wanting to resist. She responded to his closeness in a way she had not experienced for years. It frightened and fascinated her, and she wished his hands would touch and caress her.

Shaking off desire, she said, "Tom, I've been a friend to this family since I came here. They've taken me into their lives and helped me in ways I can never repay. It's my turn to give back to them."

"Ssh… you don't have to talk, just because… are you cold?"

Julie noticed that she was shaking.

"No. That's not why I'm shaking. Tom…"

He moved closer and brushed her hair out of her eyes as a strong breeze blew onto the porch. The top of her nightgown fluttered off and, on her skin, she heard Tom gasp.

"What? What's wrong?"

"You have to ask me that?"

Julie stared into his blue eyes, which simmered with passion and felt an unveiling of prehistoric desire that engulfed both animals and mankind. She wanted her nightgown to fall off her body like the shedding of unwanted skin. The nerve endings in her body tingled, and the tension felt unbearable.

As if in a trance, Tom pulled her toward him. His hands lightly brushed her breast as he gathered her in his arms and kissed her. Hard.

"Hey… who's out there?"

The shock of the unwanted voice tore them apart. Annie barked and jumped onto the rocker and Julie's robe. Julie pushed Annie off her robe. Annie yelped and scrambled to catch herself before falling onto the floor.

Julie quickly put her robe back on, tightly tying the sash. Annie pranced around the newcomer, with visions of doggy bones dancing in her happy head, and Julie turned to face the voice.

"Whoops. Did I interrupt something?" Paul looked from Julie to Tom and broke into a grin.

"No, I couldn't sleep. I must have woken Tom because he came down. Now, I woke you up, too." Julie tried to sound casual but failed.

"I've been pretty shaken up myself… slept badly. I heard every noise inside and out. What time is it?" He looked at his watch and answered his own question. "Three-thirty. It'll be time to feed the horses soon. What the…?" He looked out to see a car's headlights moving slowly down the driveway. "Who could that… probably Uncle George."

Annie started to bark, alerting everyone on the porch that there was an intruder. She jumped on a chair to get a better look.

The car pulled into the parking area by the house, and they heard the door slam. Paul turned on the porch light and an imposing figure walked up the porch steps. Julie gasped. He had the face of Jonathan Carter, but as he moved closer into the light, Julie thought he had Matthew's eyes. She shrank behind Tom despite herself.

"Good evening. Everyone up? I didn't expect a welcoming committee at this time of night. Paul, Tom…" The man stopped to look at Julie. "Oh, Hello. Who are you?"

"Uncle George, meet Julie Bishop. She's a friend of the family."

"Hello." Julie nodded her head at him.

They heard a commotion coming from upstairs, and the lights in the hall lit the stairs as Jonathan came down with Brenda at his heels. Everyone gathered in the kitchen while Paul put on a pot of coffee. Uncle George settled his stocky frame onto a kitchen chair and settled back, eyeing his brother's family.

"You're in late. You flew up and rented a car?" His brother looked around to see if anyone else had entered the house.

"Yes. All my men are tied up now. I came as soon as I heard the news. If I find the person who did this to Matthew, he won't have to wait to stand trial. What was all this about a horse?"

Paul explained.

"Who found him?" George asked.

"I did," Julie said.

"You did," Uncle George looked at Julie and appraised her as he would a prime piece of Grade-A meat, "So, you have a horse here?"

"Yes, I do." She explained about Socks and her involvement with the Carters. As she did, she noticed Annie. She had sniffed Uncle George when he arrived but stayed as far away from him as possible. That was not like her sociable self, who was interested in everyone.

With some curiosity, George looked at Julie and, occasionally, over at Tom, who was looking at her. Yes, the boy was interested in her. Was she interested in him? Oh well. He had always taken an interest in all the boys, but his favorite had always been Matt. He hoped that Matt would take over his business someday. Matt was brilliant and ruthless. He had something his brothers didn't: the ability to manipulate and get away with it. It was a quality he had fine-tuned in his own life. With Matt gone, all his future ambitions seemed to have gone with him. Could Tom be the one to take over for Matt? Paul wasn't hard enough. Way too soft. He'd have to investigate this other one—the one making it alone.

"What time is the funeral?" Uncle George's voice cracked under the strain of events

"One o'clock," Jonathan said. The family sat, drank the rest of the coffee, and watched the sun come up through the kitchen window.

CHAPTER 18

Thursday morning, Julie helped the family do chores. She was keenly aware of Tom's presence, how the blue in his eyes matched the blue in his shirt, how the sun shining in just the right position enhanced the gold in his hair, and how the dimples on either side of his face didn't quite match. They bumped into each other and devised small talk on several occasions, but they never spoke about the previous night.

Brenda entered the barn as Julie filled up one of the water buckets. "Julie?"

"Hmm?" Julie answered, her mind far away.

"What's with Tom this morning? What's with *you* this morning?" Julie missed the bucket and soaked her pants' leg.

The morning rolled by. Julie stayed away from Tom but couldn't get him completely out of her mind. He would walk by, carrying a bale of hay, and there would be the scent of his aftershave—a *lingering* scent. Her body tensed, sweat covered her forehead, and a strange vibration hit below her waist.

I wish he hadn't worn that this morning.

Another thing Julie couldn't keep off her mind was the dive she took down the steps at the Smith Ranch. Her body was still sore from the fall, and it hurt to move her neck. She hadn't spoken of it to anyone and wondered if Tom had. Probably not. He thought it was an accident.

She hurried on with busy work. She helped the caterers put away the food for after the funeral. She helped clean the house and watched Uncle George when she thought he wasn't looking. He interested her.

He resembled Jonathan Carter and Matt. That wasn't so strange. What she found interesting was that he didn't look like Paul or Tom, and they greatly resembled their father. So, what was the difference? She mused over these thoughts as she dusted the gold punch bowl Brenda won at a horse show. She continued dusting and daydreaming and nearly collided with Tom on the staircase. He steadied her, and she involuntarily jumped as he touched her. Tom looked at her as she ran up the stairs.

"Julie?" She turned around briefly, and he smiled and winked at her as he nearly collided with Brenda.

"Tom, look out."

"Sorry."

"What the hell?" Brenda stood with her hands on her hips, looking after him. "What's *with* you two?"

There was a presence of something in the air. Julie felt it. Everyone seemed on edge, and it wasn't just the funeral—that would be enough to make anyone jittery. What was it? Suddenly, Julie recognized it—the presence of fear—fear and something else. Julie stopped dead in her tracks and suddenly felt afraid. There was evil in this house. She went about her business and, turning around a corner, ran headlong into Uncle George.

"Whoops, careful," he said.

"Oh, sorry. I'm so clumsy. None of us are ourselves today." Julie shrugged him away.

"You've been a great help," he said. "Come on, let's have some coffee. I'm buying," he led her into the kitchen.

"Here," he said, maybe too cheerfully, handing her a cup of coffee. "So, Julie. What do you think of all this? Did you know Matt for long?"

"When I came out here during the summer to visit Tony and Gregg. We'd come over here and play games in the barn." She looked down at her fingernails. "And, since last year when I bought Socks."

"I've heard about him. I want to go to the barn to see your wonder horse when the funeral ends. I hear you're a good rider."

"Thank you."

"You and Tom are trying to solve Matt's murder?"

"Oh, you know about that?"

"Of course. I know everything that concerns my family." Uncle George leaned over the table in a conspiratorial manner and asked, "Find anything interesting?"

"We're just talking to some of Matt's friends, that's all. But no, we haven't found anything yet."

Uncle George had an ageless face, even though he was in his early sixties. His stocky frame shook when he laughed, and he had devastating steel grey hair and icy grey-blue eyes. Julie thought some of that weight was pure muscle, and she wouldn't want to get involved in a wrestling match with him. She thought he could be mean if provoked. As Uncle George pumped her for information, Julie started to feel uncomfortable. She wasn't sure how to handle his questions, and she caught him maneuvering his subjects between the murders and his ranch.

"You know. We race our horses."

"Our?" Julie asked.

"Well, my ranch. I refer to it as ours, I guess, because I feel it belongs to the Carters as well as to me. Matt would have inherited it. Now, it will go equally to Brenda, Paul, and Tom. It's a multimillion-dollar industry, horse racing. The stud fees of some of my stallions are worth more than fifty grand. Astonishing?" He grinned at Julie's surprised expression.

"Why?" he continued. "Because when those babies are ready to sell, they'll bring six figures on the auction block, maybe even over a million."

"I didn't know that quarter horses brought so much."

"I don't just have quarter horses. I have thoroughbreds as well. They're the primary money makers. Although, the quarter horses do well, too. Ever see a quarter horse race?"

Julie shook her head. She was fascinated by this man's rants about racehorses and breeding programs and listened in awe. Nevertheless, she was relieved when Tom and Jonathan came into the kitchen.

"Hi there, Uncle George," Tom gazed at Julie and sat beside her.

"How's your neck?" he asked Julie.

"Still sore," she said.

"Sore? From what?" Uncle George rose and headed to the refrigerator. "Anyone want a beer?"

Julie perused her friends. They were nodding. "I think we all do. Thanks, Uncle…"

"Oh no, George, please. You're not seven anymore."

Julie grinned.

"So?" He continued.

"Oh, I fell…" Julie said. Then, before Tom could say anything and before anyone could ask, she said, "I was in the barn, and I tripped over the hose. I wrenched my back when I landed. It's sore but okay."

Tom cocked his head to the left side, and his eyebrows rose. What interested her more was that Uncle George had the same peculiar look.

The funeral procession was somber, with many local horse people attending the service. Julie gazed around the stone Episcopal church in the heart of town, two blocks from Phil's police station. It was a lovely little church with stained-glass windows that reflected the sunlight as it streamed in through the many colors of Christ and his sheep.

Julie sat with the immediate family in the first row between Brenda and Paul. Next to Paul was Tom, and Jonathan and Uncle George sat on Tom's other side. She looked at the colors reflecting on Tom's face and turned away to observe the faces of the congregation.

She realized most were not there because of their love for Matthew but out of respect for the Carters. Some came out of curiosity. They were a closely knit group, and when something traumatic happened to one in the community, it affected everyone. She saw Lynette sitting with some other boarders from the barn. She wore a shawl-collar jacket in dark green with matching pleated front trousers and a crocheted lace blouse that buttoned down the front. The outfit accentuated her hair, and Julie thought she looked stunning. No wonder Matt had been crazy about her.

She noticed Phil Swanson's brooding face sitting in the back of the church and thought he might be wondering if anyone in the congregation had enough reason to kill Matt. That might include quite a lot of people. She glanced at a woman sitting beside him, holding his arm. She had exquisite features and very pale skin with mahogany brown, almost black hair. She glanced at Tom as he turned around and smiled back at them. That probably was Phil's wife, Marsha.

Jonathan gave the eulogy and spoke about the positive gifts that had blessed Matthew's life. Julie knew few from the congregation bought into some of those gifts. She noticed her feelings seemed to be reflected on the faces of others present. Suddenly, she felt uncomfortable and, looking up, she saw Uncle George looking at her. Tom turned and looked at him, and Uncle George turned away. She met Tom's eyes and smiled. Last night everything had changed between them, and she wondered how their relationship would play out. During the eulogy, she fantasized about what would have happened if Paul hadn't come out onto the porch. It was probably just as well that they were interrupted.

Julie rode to the cemetery with Brenda and Paul, while Tom rode with his father and Uncle George. Listening as Brenda talked easily with Paul, she noticed that not once was she guarded about their conversation. They would have been a good match, she thought. A glance at Paul's expression as he talked with Brenda finally made Julie jump to attention. She wondered how long Paul had been in love with her. Her mind continued to race. Would that be another motive for Brenda to want her husband out of the way? Julie's imagination ran away with her until well after the burial service ended, and they were back in the house.

A flood of people poured in from the funeral, offering condolences. Julie's attention floated between all those faces. Their expressions read that Brenda was better off without him. She suddenly felt depressed and wondered where Tom was hiding. She didn't see him in the crowd anywhere, and she hadn't seen him since the service in the cemetery.

Walking into the kitchen, she picked up a tray of au'doeuvres and passed them around as Phil and Uncle George walked toward the study, engrossed in conversation. Julie followed the tray, but they reached the door before she could catch them. Phil pushed the door so that it closed almost—but not quite—all the way. She moved just close enough to the crack to overhear bits of conversation.

"Yes, I have some ideas. We believe he was dealing drugs, Mr. Carter. That should give plenty of people a motive for…"

"I want answers. I want you to find the person…"

"Being so close to the border, your ranch is in a prime area for bringing drugs in from Mexico."

"My what?"

"You'd be a good suspect yourself, so, for that matter, would your brother. What a perfect setup, Mr. Carter. You have your drivers run around the country selling horses and running drugs at the same time."

"Go on." Hostility crept into Uncle George's tone.

"What a cover. Pilots fly over the border without anyone detecting them right into your ranch. Great. Then your employees remove the stuff from the plane and load them into the horse trailers along with the horses."

What kind of game is Phil playing? She imagined how Uncle George must look, his face tense and swollen. She wondered if it had turned red.

"Where do you keep the stuff once it's up here until it's ready to distribute? Here, in this house? Should we search from top to bottom?"

Julie was starting to move away from the door when Uncle George exploded. "Search away… *if…* you have a search warrant. But you won't find anything. You don't have any evidence against us, and you can't prove any of that garbage. I'm surprised at you for even bringing it up, especially today… a day of mourning. We've lost a beloved family member. If you think that either my brother or I are the heads of some drug ring, then prove it. You want to search this house? Fine. Again, if you have a search warrant." His voice lowered to an almost seductive tone. "You're grasping at straws, Sheriff. I'm not the enemy. I'm on your side. As for me, I run a legitimate business."

As she turned to leave, Julie was bumped by someone coming out of the bathroom, and her tray nearly landed on the floor. She landed against the study door. The two men looked at her with astonishment as she fell inside and tried to regain her balance.

"Oh, I hope I didn't disturb you. Just wanted to see if you wanted something to eat," Julie said with a wide-eyed, innocent smile. She felt their eyes on her as she left the room.

So, Phil suspected Uncle George was some drug kingpin and had the nerve to tell him to his face. If it were true, saying so would have been a dumb move. Maybe he had a reason. Maybe Phil was pushing so that Uncle George would make a mistake. Maybe she'd been watching too many movies. Suddenly, Julie nearly dropped the tray.

I know, she thought. I know where they take that cocaine. I need to talk to Tom. She looked around but still couldn't see him. Where was he? She entered the kitchen and put the empty tray on the counter.

"Brenda, have you seen Tom?"

"No. Not for quite a while." Brenda stood by the phone, playing with the collar of her navy-blue cotton dress. Her long hair was pulled back in a French twist, and with her thin frame, she looked like a model from Vogue. The phone rang.

"Hello? Oh yes, thank you. No. He's here somewhere. Can I have him call you? What's your name? Ellie? Okay, Ellie. Will you call him back? All right. Thanks."

As Brenda spoke, Julie noticed Lynette sitting at the other end of the table. She wondered what they had been talking about.

"Julie, if you find Tom, tell him someone named Ellie called. She'll call him back."

"Ellie?"

"She's from Chicago. I think she's from his theater group, but I'm unsure. Julie, I meant to tell you. I love your suit."

Julie relaxed for a moment. She had on a black suit with a mandarin collar jacket and a white draped cowl neck tank top suitable for the changeable Illinois weather. Her hair was pulled back and tied with a black velvet band, and she wore gold hooped earrings. Around her neck, she wore a simple, small gold cross. She sat briefly with Brenda and Lynette and talked briefly about the service and the people visiting the house.

"Julie, I want to go to the barn to check on the horses. Or maybe I need to be alone. Would you take phone calls while I'm gone?"

"Oh, Julie," Lynette said. "I just remembered. Tom mentioned something about going up to his room. There was something he needed to find concerning his uncle and Matt. You'll probably find him up there." Brenda went outside, and Lynette left the kitchen as Uncle George came in looking for a drink.

"Oh, hello, Julie. Smashing outfit. Need something to drink?"

Julie shook him off and maneuvered her way up the stairs.

She knocked on the door. No answer. She knocked again.

"Tom?" She knocked a third time. When she heard a crash coming from the closet area this time, she walked into the room.

"Tom?"

"Oh, hello," he said, shaking old photographs off his head and carrying an album full of pictures and dust. He pulled off some cobwebs and sat on the bed. Julie laughed and came over and sat beside him. He had changed from his dark navy suit into jeans and a polo shirt.

"See this?" he asked. "This was Matt and me when we were he was four years old, and I was three." It was a picture of two kids riding ponies with a young Jonathan standing proudly beside them. On the other side of the boys was a pretty woman with blond hair and a sweet smile. "That..." he said, with a sigh, "was my mom."

"Oh."

The phone rang, and Julie reached over to the nightstand.

"I'm on phone patrol. Oh, there was a phone call for you from Chicago. Someone named Ellie."

"Ellie?" Tom raised his eyebrows. "Who?"

"Hello?" Julie said.

Julie sat numbly on the bed, listening to the woman on the other end of the phone. She turned chalk white and looked at Tom with disbelief. Tom shook his head and shrugged his shoulders.

"What is it, Julie? What's wrong?" His eyebrows curled up with a questioning expression."

"It's your fiancée, Tom. You know, the girl you're engaged to. She wants to know when you're coming home."

Tom looked at her with his mouth wide open.

"Damn you… Tom!" Julie flung the phone onto the bed and ran out of the room, fighting back tears of anger and hurt.

Julie ran down the stairs and angled her way back through the crowd, trying not to cry. Uncle George caught her by the kitchen and said, "Listen, I'm sorry, but it's important. Your neighbor called and said that there was some kind of emergency at your house. You need to go home right away. Julie is something wrong?" he said seeing the tears streaming down her face.

"No, thanks, I'll go… home." It was all the excuse that Julie needed to get out of that house. She picked up her car keys from the top of the refrigerator and went out the back porch.

CHAPTER 19

om ran downstairs, trying to catch Julie. "Paul, where did Julie go?" he shouted over the crowd's noise.

"Tom," Paul yelled back from across the room. "Emergency in the barn." Paul tore out of the house with Tom on his heels nearly knocking over Lynette, coming up the back porch stairs.

"What's wrong?" she called as they raced past her, hardly noticing she was there.

"What the hell?" Phil saw the commotion and followed them, rushing past a group of people on the way to their parked cars.

Paul opened the arena door, and they went into the office. It was dark and quiet except for the horses' gentle breathing, which contrasted with their heavy panting.

"What? What's the matter?" Tom, catching his breath. "What the hell's the matter?"

"There was a call from the barn, saying to get down here immediately. I thought it was Brenda," Paul furrowed his brow and looked perplexed.

"It was from a woman?"

"Sounded like it to me."

"Hey, what's up?" came a voice behind the office desk.

"Damn, Brenda. Shit, you scared me. What's wrong? Did you call up to the house?" Paul went over to the desk where she sat, thumbing through a Quarter Horse Journal.

"No, why?"

"You've been here all this time?"

"Yes."

"Anything happen? Anything wrong?"

"No. Everything's quiet. I was thinking about feeding the horses. It's past their dinner time. What are you doing here? Why were you running?"

"Brenda, we got a phone call saying there was an emergency and to get down here immediately. It was a woman's voice that sounded like yours," Paul said. Then, he added, "You were going to feed the horses dressed like that?"

"Hey…where is everybody?" Larry Ortega asked, his head popping through the open office door.

"Larry! I thought you were out of town."

"I had to come. Listen, I have Julie's purse here. This is her purse, isn't it?"

Brenda nodded. "I think so, why?"

"Well, she tore out of the house, got in her van, and drove off like a bat out of hell."

"What? Why?" Phil asked.

"Don't know. I thought you might. Driving like that, she'll probably need her driver's license."

"Where could she have gone?"

"Oh, that I know. She went home—an urgent message or something. Her next-door neighbor called. Your uncle told her."

"Well," Brenda said. "I have her neighbor's number for emergencies right here. Let's call her so she can tell Julie that we have her purse." Brenda dialed the number.

"Hello, Mrs. Rosselli. This is Brenda Carter from Carter Ranch. Could you tell Julie that she left her purse here and that we have it locked up? Is everything okay?" Brenda listened, and gradually, a puzzled expression came over her face.

"Everything's fine? Didn't you call here a few minutes ago telling her to come home? You didn't?" She cupped her hand over the phone.

"Phil, Mrs. Rosselli never called. There is no emergency at Julie's house." She returned to the phone. "Thank you, Mrs. Rosselli. Yes, that's strange. You will? Thanks," Brenda hung up. "She says she'll call Julie and tell her it was a misunderstanding."

"Holy shit…" Tom said. They looked at each other, stunned.

"Tom…" Brenda said, a cloud covering her pale face, "Is Julie in trouble?"

"God, I hope not." Tom sprang into action and started running to the door.

"Wait," Phil said, stopping him. "You're not going alone. We're coming with you."

Tom, Phil, and Paul leaped into Phil's truck. "Hold tight. You're in for the ride of your life." He hit the gas pedal hard, and they shot down the road. Phil picked up the phone and dialed. "Can't you make this thing go any faster?"

"Who're you calling?" Paul said.

"Julie. To get her out of her house."

The phone wasn't responding. "Damn this thing," He floored the gas pedal.

"Hand me that cellular deal in the back, Paul." Paul reached for the portable case beside his seat and pulled out the phone. The phone rang.

"Give me that." Phil snatched it with his one free hand.

"Yeah… what is it? Oh! Yeah, Brenda. Really?" Phil glanced over at Tom. "Okay, I don't know. I'll ask him. Yeah, talk to you later. Listen. Call her neighbor and tell her to run next door, okay? I have a bad feeling about this. Thanks." He drove on, then picked up the phone again. "Julie, this is Phil. Get out of your house… now. Go over to your neighbor's or get back in your van and come back here. But get out!"

Tom and Paul looked at Phil curiously as he continued to drive. For a few minutes, he didn't speak.

"Why was Julie crying when she left?"

Tom shook his head and stared out the window. Paul and Phil looked at him.

"You know something about that, Tom?"

"Yes. Um, no." He hesitated and then sighed. He didn't want to talk about what he didn't understand. "Julie came up to talk to me about something. The phone rang, and she picked it up. The next thing I knew, she told me it was 'my girlfriend, the one I'm engaged to,' and it was dead when I picked up the phone. I ran after her, but Paul yelled that there was a problem at the barn."

"Another emergency…" Phil said.

"I know that my friend Ellie called. She's a friend from Chicago. She's also happily married to my director. They're both friends of mine. She'd never pull that on me. She'd call to see if everything was all right, but that's all." Tom stared out the window for a few minutes without speaking.

Phil whistled as he activated his police siren. He ran a red light and plunged down the ramp onto I-57. They hit 80 mph on the interstate. Cars pulled over, and drivers craned their necks, trying to figure out what was happening.

"Timing is incredible. Julie came looking for you, and someone told her you were in your room. A phone call is made. Julie is on phone duty, right? She picks up the phone. Angry as hell, Julie runs downstairs. Then, there's an emergency phone call, and Julie is told to go home. Exit Julie stage right. Then, you get a phony phone call from the barn distracting you. Exit stage left. We knew her phone call was phony because she had forgotten her purse, and Larry was in the right place at the right time. You, my friend, were gotten out of the way."

Julie floored her van from the parking lot onto the road. Her tears caused intermittent blindness, and she stopped her van before entering the ramp to I-57.

God. What a fool I was. What an unmitigated little fool. How could I have been so stupid? I never saw this coming. Never. What a liar! En . . . gaged. How could he? She sat back and took a deep breath before the flow of tears started to overwhelm her again. She had fallen for him—hard, harder than she had known. The anxiety that plagued her on and off for the past few days came back, and she struggled to keep her wits.

First, someone tries to run me—us off the road, then someone pushes me down the stairs," she thought. And I'm worried about a damned man? She knew she was concerned about not just any man but *that* man. She took another deep breath. She looked at herself in the car mirror and couldn't believe she was staring at herself. Her eyes were puffy and red from crying, and her face looked haggard. His girlfriend probably doesn't look like that, then burst into tears again. She remembered how they met and then everything they went through together. Then, she thought of the conversation when he told her he wasn't seeing anyone.

Liar. She thought of Randy and said it even louder, banging on the steering wheel at the same time. "Liar!" She screamed at the top of her lungs. Only the wind and a few crows heard her.

She thought of her fall and realized she hadn't told anyone it wasn't an accident. She meant to tell Tom, but she forgot. A love affair between her and Tom had begun last night.

Oh boy, is he good, she thought? He had me going. How could I be so blind? God, it hurts so bad. She started to cry again and realized she was hyperventilating.

This is stupid. I have to stop. There's an emergency at home, and I've pulled over to the side of the road because I'm crying too hard to stop. This is stupid." She forced herself to quit and started down the ramp onto I-57. Her thoughts turned to Brenda, and she wondered how she was holding up.

Did Uncle George tell Brenda that I left? Her thoughts flowed freely onto the murders and drug dealing. Which one was it? Was it Uncle George or Jonathan Carter who was involved in the planning of a massive distribution of cocaine to residents of the Chicago land area? Or was Phil on the wrong track altogether? Were the Smiths the head of some sinister operation? She fervently hoped it wasn't one of the Carters as she drove home.

Julie got out of the van and looked for her purse. Damn. *I left it there along with Annie… and my heart.* She choked back a sob, then pulled herself together. She took out her ignition key that had the spare. She thought that maybe she'd instead not ever go back there again. Perhaps she'd move Socks out to another barn and start over again. She had done that before. Maybe she would do it again.

No. She wouldn't entertain those thoughts. She didn't need to start crying all over again. She pulled down her street and looked over at her neighbor's house. Should she go over there first? Julie thought about it, then decided to call Mrs. Roselli from home.

She opened her door, and for a minute, she felt she was missing something. Annie was still at the ranch—but that wasn't it. Contrasting the commotion at the ranch, here it was abnormally, almost deathly quiet, and she felt threatened. Why? She turned on the living room lights, which turned on her radio, and the sudden noise made her jump. Walking into the kitchen, she took a glass from the cabinet and filled it with ice water from the refrigerator. She drank it down with a shaking hand.

What's wrong? What's wrong is that nothing's wrong.

She walked through the hall past the bathroom and thought about washing her face. The closed door seemed to take too much effort to open, so she walked into her bedroom and turned on the light. As an afterthought, Julie switched on the lava light, which cast a dim yellow light against the wall, giving her strange comfort. She went to the nightstand by her bed and turned on her answering machine.

Beep. "Julie, this is your mother. How did the horse show go?" Oh Lord, she had forgotten to call her mother. Beep. "Julie, hi, this is your neighbor. It wasn't me. Sorry you had to come all the way home. I never called." That was strange. She'd have to go over there and straighten this out. Beep. "This is Phil. Get out of your house—*now*. Go over to your neighbor's or get back in your van and come back here. *But get out!*" What? Julie's heart began to race, and she thought about what she was hearing.

She got off the bed and stood for a moment. If there was an intruder in the house, where was he? The only room that was closed was the bathroom. The bathroom. What's wrong with that? Then, she remembered. Before she left, the bathroom door was open.

The sinking feeling of imagined danger turning into reality made her physically ill. How would she get past the bathroom and out of the house? Maybe she could run and hope that the suddenness of her movements would catch him off guard. Him? How did she know it was a *him?* She tiptoed out of her bedroom and ran. Too late. Out of the corner of her eye, Julie noticed the bathroom door fling open. The intruder was too quick for her to outmaneuver. He grabbed her from behind and pulled a clothesline around her neck. Struggling, Julie turned to face her attacker and briefly succeeded, but he was too strong for her. She twisted and turned and tried to pull away. He pulled the cord tighter, and she gasped for breath. The harder she tried to escape, the tighter the noose became, and the man laughed. He was enjoying his work. Julie's consciousness started fading in and out, finally leaving her altogether. As she fell, the last thing she heard was the clatter of the brass bowl when she fell over the coffee table and onto the floor.

CHAPTER 20

Tom dove out of Phil's car before it even stopped in the driveway. Running and stumbling over the stoop, he pulled open the front door, nearly knocked down by the other three men following behind.

A scrambling noise followed an object crashing on the floor, followed by "crap" as the back door creaked open and slammed shut. Phil tore through the kitchen, followed by Paul. Larry turned and ran out the front.

At first, Tom couldn't see her. He noticed the couch was slightly out of place, and the throw cover pulled off the coffee table.

His feet nearly slid out from underneath him as he ran over to the other side of the room and stopped dead in his tracks. Lying face down on the floor was Julie, the cord still wrapped around her neck.

"No!"

Tom fell to his knees beside her body and gently removed the cord from around her neck. He turned her over and cradled her in his arms, feeling for her pulse.

She gasped for air and opened her eyes.

"Tom?" For a brief second, she pulled away. Then, realizing who he was and wouldn't harm her, she relaxed.

"Julie. Thank God you're alive."

"I can't breathe… wait," she shifted positions to catch her breath.

"Let's see your neck," he said. He looked at her and saw the rope burns outlining her neck like a tight necklace. In another instant, she could have been dead.

Julie put both arms around his neck and hung on for dear life. Then she cried, and Tom hung on to her, the warmth of her body consoling him. The crying turned into sobs and gasps and slowed down as she tried to breathe normally.

"Ooh… I'm not sure I can do this."

Tom felt her panicking when her breaths came in short wheezes and pants.

"Lie down," he said, maneuvering her over to the couch.

"Tom, I have to throw up." Julie pulled away from him and hurried toward the bathroom, stopping and falling to her knees. Tom held her up and carried her the rest of the way. Gently putting her down at the foot of the toilet bowl, he lifted the lid, and she wretched into the bowl with him guiding her upper body.

"*Oh God! Please help me!*" She whimpered and slunk back to the floor. He sat next to her, and she threw up again.

"Here, turn around." He took a washcloth and soaked it in cool water, placing it over her face and neck. Julie started to breathe normally again.

"Is Julie all right?" Paul walked into the bathroom.

"Someone tried to strangle her," Tom said. "She's all right, but she's sick as hell. Is there any Ginger Ale in your refrigerator?" Julie nodded her head.

"Paul, would you?" Paul nodded and went back over to the kitchen.

Julie started to cry, and this time, she couldn't stop. Tom held on to her until she had to throw up again. Paul returned with the Ginger Ale. It helped.

"Paul, would you… er… I need to be alone with her."

Paul nodded and left.

"Shhh…"

Her blouse was soaked through. Tom pulled the soft white tank top over her head. He reached for the washcloth and wiped her neck and her upper chest.

Julie continued to hold onto him as though if she let go, she would slip into the bottomless, darkest hole in Hell.

"Could you turn the light down… please?" Tom lowered the dimmer on her bathroom switch. They sat together on the bathroom floor.

"What's wrong with me? I'm not dead. Why am I… so… sick?"

"Honey, you've had a strong shock to your system. Someone tried to strangle the living daylights out of you, and you ask what's wrong with you?"

"Why? Why would anyone want to kill me?" she whispered.

"I don't know, honey, I just don't know."

He took the washcloth, washed it again, and helped her clean up. Then, he reached for her back and unhooked her bra. She let it fall to the floor. "Do you want to, or shall I?" he asked, offering her the washcloth. She just shook her head, too weak to move. Carefully cleaning her up, he reached for the bathrobe on the hook of the bathroom door and put it on her. Then, gently lifting her, he carried her into her bedroom and shut the door. Setting her down on the bed, he helped her out of the rest of her clothes and wrapped her in her robe. Then, he sat next to her. She closed her eyes as his hands stroked her face, tears still trickling down her face. She struggled to sit up.

"No, lay down."

"Tom." She lay on the bed, her head on three pillows, looking up at him. "About last night."

"Julie, honey…"

"I guess I thought… well, I'm not sure what I thought…" She was too weak to continue.

"Julie, please, listen to me. I don't know what that phone call was about. You've got to believe me." His eyes showed what his heart wanted to tell. "I'm not engaged to anyone."

"Thank God," Julie whispered. "I thought… that woman said…" A new flood of tears welled in her eyes, and she turned to her pillow, burying her face.

"Julie." Tom handed her a tissue on top of the radio on her nightstand.

"Please turn off those lights. They're hurting my eyes."

"O… kay." He patted her cheek and walked over to turn off the switch. The lava lamp made strange shapes as the main light went out, reflecting against the walls. Globs of pale yellow danced against Julie's face.

Tom sat back on her bed and continued with his story, gently holding Julie captive with his hands on her shoulders and his eyes looking down at her. The sash of her robe started to loosen, and the material began to pull apart on top. Tom compelled himself not to focus on that direction and concentrated on her face. He couldn't bear that this—his beautiful, wonderful, and loving woman, could think of him as despicable.

"My friend Ellie called. She's married to my director… my boss. Whoever you spoke to was not Ellie."

"We were set up, Tom," Julie gazed up at him. She tried to get up again, but Tom propped her against her pillows, gently caressing her hair and cheek.

"Just when I came downstairs to stop you, there was a phone call saying there was an emergency in the barn. Paul took the call. We went down there, and no one was there, Julie, except Brenda. There was no emergency. We knew you were in trouble because Larry saw you forgot your purse, and Brenda called your neighbor." He stopped and then changed the subject. "Did you see him? Did you know the person who attacked you?"

"Yes. I saw his face when I tried to turn on him. Tom, it was Daniel Smith."

Tom whistled. "No! Daniel Smith?" Tom sat back, incredulous.

"He was hiding in my bathroom and came up behind me. I got my messages, and the last one was from Phil, telling me to leave the house. I tried. He sprang out and grabbed me, pulling the cord around my neck. Oh, *God*." She shuddered. "Tom, if you hadn't come…"

"Julie, we *did* come, and you're all right." He pulled her up and put his arms around her, pressing her body against his. "Julie, don't you know how much I…"

There was a knock at the door. Julie quickly tightened her robe. Tom noticed his palms were sweating.

"Come in."

Phil entered with Paul and Larry at his heels.

"Did you get him?" Julie asked.

"No, he got away."

"Oh, no." Julie slunk back with disappointment and dread showing in her eyes. "They're going to come after me again."

"They?"

"Someone's trying to kill me. And I think I know why."

"Why?" They looked at her. Phil sat in the rocking chair in the corner while Paul and Larry stood by the door, waiting for her to continue. Finally, Julie spoke.

"Tom and I went to Daniel and Millie Smith's ranch… one of the names on the list. We were escorted to Eddie's old apartment, where they had completely renovated the structure. They put up new paneling and a new pipeline into the bathroom. I wanted to look closer without them, so I left my purse behind. When I returned, I opened the sliding panel door in the bathroom and saw a cavity wide enough to hold a whole storage of stuff. I also saw the residue of some white powder that had been dragged along the floor.

"That's when Daniel caught me looking inside. When we started downstairs, I tripped and fell into a stall. Tom knows about that. What you don't know, Tom, it *wasn't* an accident. Daniel tripped me… You wanted to know where they're storing the cocaine when it comes up here? They're bringing it there. Maybe they've been doing it all along, even when Tony lived there, without his knowledge. Or perhaps they decided to buy the place and put up a false wall. That's why he's trying to kill me."

"It was Smith? Did you see his face?"

"Yes, briefly. It was definitely him. I thought that when the bad guys tried to kill someone, they put a paper bag or something over their head so that nobody would recognize them. He knows I know him." She buried her head in her hands. "He's going to try it again."

She lay down again and closed her eyes.

Phil said, "Tom, I've called a friend, a nearby physician. He will come over here right away and check out her neck. If she's okay, we need to get her into protective custody." Larry nodded his head in agreement.

"Can we do anything in the meantime?" Paul asked.

Tom took over the conversation and said, "Yeah. Could you leave us alone for a minute? I need to clear something up." They left the room and shut the door.

"I'm all right now. At least, I think I'm all right. I'll…" She took a breath. "I'll put some clothes on and come out." She reached for Tom's hand and tried to get up. Then, she sat down again, pulling him back on the bed with her.

"I'm worried. Do you think they'll try again? Come back here in the middle of the night?"

"Honey, I won't leave you alone."

"Tom," she stroked the sleeve of his shirt. "Thank you,"

"For what?" He placed his hand on her hair and stroked it gently, flipping coils of cinnamon strands around his fingers.

"For saving my life, loving me, and not being engaged."

She broke the tension, and he laughed, partly because of relief, partly because she was funny, and partly because—because she realized he loved her.

"Julie, I know we haven't known each other for a long time… but you've got to know how I feel about you."

"How?" Her eyes twinkled, and she smiled for the first time. She was playing this out. She was giving him his chance—a chance he wouldn't blow.

"Look, damn it. I've only been in love once in my life. Er… that I know of. But…" Now, it was Tom's turn to hyperventilate. He took a deep breath and took the plunge.

"I just want you to know that…"

"Tom?" Paul knocked on the bedroom door.

"Oh no… go away," Julie said with a moan. Tom smiled. She unwittingly answered the question that was plaguing him.

"The doctor is here."

"In a minute," he called back.

"You were saying?" she asked.

"Okay, here goes. I think I'm falling…"

The knock on the bedroom door came again. "Tom, what are you doing in there?" It was Phil.

"Wait a minute," he called back.

Julie took matters into her own hands.

"Tom," she sat up again. "Hold me, please."

Tom gently and protectively put his arms around her and kissed her on her forehead.

"No!"

"What?" Tom sat back, not understanding what she wanted.

She grabbed him by his collar and pulled him down on the bed with her.

"I want you to hold me like a man holds a woman when he's desperately in love with her."

There was another knock on the door.

"Damn," Tom said—loudly.

"Tom, can I believe you? You're not engaged, married, involved with anyone?" They lay close together–face to face–eye to eye, the sash to her robe completely undone, her breasts resting against Tom's chest.

The reflection of the lava light bounced over her and formed a kind of halo accenting the copper tones in her hair. He sat back and opened her robe, moving the material away from her body. He was mesmerized by her beauty and desperately wanted to make love to her. She lay back, naked and vulnerable, looking at him, desire flaming through her eyes—her soul. He knew now what he wanted to know. Julie loved him.

"Julie. There's no other woman in this world for me other than you. When I came in here and saw you lying on the floor, I saw my future lying there with you," he said with his voice cracking and hoarse. "I'm so in love with you. I don't think I can stand it anymore."

There came another knock on the door.

"Is everything all right in there?"

"Can you make him go away?"

"No, probably not… but Julie…"

"What?"

"I think both of us know we love each other, so no matter what happens in the next few days, we can carry that with us. You think?"

"Yes. Tom." Julie said, faltering, speaking words he knew she hadn't spoken for a long time, "I do love you."

"Good," Tom said.

CHAPTER 21

A swarm of men—and Julie—sat around a small, square oak table. Situated in the dining area, it backed the window on one side and the Victorian-era sidebar on the other. The only remnant of the 20th century was the portable phone that rang, shattering a confused silence over the group. Larry Ortega gently pulled it out of her hand as she answered it.

"Ssh," he said. Julie gazed at Phil, who looked as puzzled as she was.

"Are you going to be home? Okay, I'll be over in a few minutes." He put down the phone.

"That was your neighbor. She wants to know what happened." Everyone looked at him with perplexed gazes. "Our little game of playing detective seems to have backfired, and the two of you got in deeper than you even know." In one sentence, Larry had everyone's undivided attention.

"And… Julie nearly got killed. It seems the Smiths are up to their ears in whatever is happening here, imminently respectable, running a legitimate business, and… crooked as hell."

"Who are they, really?" Julie asked.

Larry pulled out a pocket computer and keyed in *Daniel and Millie Smith*. "Their real name is Smith. Daniel and Millie. No record, but under surveillance for the past several years… on and off. One of the reasons they moved here from Missouri. They were suspected of providing a storage and clearance house for drugs. The trouble was that no one could get anything concrete from them. We couldn't find out where they were running their operation. They really are genuine horse people, and they do raise Arabian horses."

"Who do they work for?"

"That's what we would like to know. We have suspicions that it ties into what is going on up here. I think they knew they were being watched. That's why they moved up here. Uh… sorry, Tom, but my guess is they're working for George Carter."

"My uncle." It was no longer stated as a question. Phil silenced him, and Larry continued.

"In any case, my dear Julie, they're on to you, and we need to set a trap. They have been planning this attack, probably since you came to see them."

"They set up that whole emergency scheme?" Tom asked.

"Oh yeah. And… they weren't alone in it. It took more than them to set it up. Julie, who told you there was an emergency at home?"

"I believe it was Uncle George," she replied. "But I think he was responding to a telephone call."

"You know that for sure?"

"No."

"Paul, who told you there was an emergency at the barn?"

"I thought it was Brenda, but it was a woman."

"The mysterious Ms. X," Larry said. "The plot thickens. It could have been George…or it could have been Millie Smith."

"Or, it could have been Daniel and Millie planning the whole thing," Tom said quietly.

"For Heaven's sake, why Uncle George?"

"Or, it could have been Daniel and Millie, Tom, just like you said." Larry's expression suggested that it was not just Daniel and Millie Smith.

"Anyway, two can play this game. We say things we want them to hear and let nature take its course. They believe you're dead. I want them to go on believing that. Tom, if your Uncle George is involved in this, and I'm about ninety-nine percent sure he is, you can lead us right inside. He suggested that you take over for Matt, didn't he?"

Tom nodded.

"Good. Uncle George will probably ask you again when Julie is out of the way. If he's legitimate, nothing will happen, and you will take a tour of the country and earn extra cash. And you'll finally get us off his back.

"If he's not, we'll find out how he runs his operation. The van will probably be loaded with cocaine, and the horses will be loaded as cover. If you get to… er, if you finish the run and come home, your last stop will probably be the Smith Ranch, where we suspect a great deal of crack will be unloaded—to be distributed to the dealers in Chicago.

"We'll be checking up on you along the way. Someone will cover you when you get down to his place in Texas. If he makes it down to Texas."

"Who?"

"Exactly what do you mean… if… he gets home?" Julie asked, interrupting the conversation. "And it still doesn't solve the 'who killed Matt' problem."

"No, but it will. The rats will come out squealing when that million-dollar empire is blown sky-high. Phil knows, but I'm not sure you do. This will be one of the biggest sting operations in years. Tom," he said, speaking softly and very seriously. "This is not a two-person operation. Millie and Daniel are only sergeants, maybe lieutenants, in a highly structured, militarily run empire.

"We hear about the street kids getting killed or arrested. The law can't touch those kids cause they're too young. They do the dirty work for these bastards. Those kids work for other kids—a little older. Then there are the adults who run around in their Mercedes. Do you think they're the ones running the show? Uh-uh. They're the ones getting the stuff from the Daniels and Millies. The ones running these shows are the cartels run by highly respected businessmen. But there's more."

"More?"

"Yep. My spies in Texas tell me they're setting up another lab." Larry moved his chair closer to the table. "Ever hear of Fentanyl?"

"Yeah," Phil said. "It's supposed to be far deadlier than either heroin or cocaine. The kids are getting it in their schools."

Larry said, "Right. They are. Well, your Uncle George is getting his hands on it. My sources say he will discard the cocaine and focus entirely on Fentanyl."

"Oh boy," Tom said. "How evil can you get?"

"Very," Larry said. "Very. We want this lab, and his whole empire stopped. But we need it infiltrated."

The room became quiet. The ticking of the clock seemed to grow louder.

When the cuckoo chirped, the room exploded, with everyone spouting out their ideas.

Larry controlled the room. "Tom, don't think I'm sending you down there unprotected."

"My Uncle George? It seems incredible. First the cocaine and now Fentanyl?"

"I hope I'm wrong, but I'm staking my reputation on it. Look, we've been tracking this for several years. We knew that there was a lot of activity going on around here. We know the known drug dealers and all points always lead back to Matt. We could never catch him. When we caught Tony, it was Matt's horses he was hauling. We thought maybe Tony was involved, but no one was convinced. I bought a horse to get a closer look inside your ranch," he said to Tom and Paul. "Sorry, but it had to be done."

"You still don't have proof of this," Paul said.

"When the Smiths are caught, I believe they will have a great deal to say. They aren't the type to go to prison without taking a lot of people with them. They may not know who is behind it all. Frequently, there are communication holes in the layers of the ranks."

"Meaning?" Julie asked.

"Daniel and Millie might not know exactly who they're working for. They may know who they report to… probably George, but not what he is to the organization. So, we need Tom."

"By putting him in danger?" Julie asked.

"Yes."

"What would you like me to do?" Nick Delaney, an assigned ambulance driver, sat quietly in the group, barely noticing. Nick normally wasn't only a paramedic. He worked undercover with the DEA, taking on odd assignments that came along as needed. He and Larry went back many years.

Larry turned his attention back to Nick. "Julie's attacker left her on the floor, unconscious. I don't believe he knew she was still alive when we burst through the door, and he rushed off through the back. I think that it would be a good idea for them to think she was dead. That's why I got you down here." Larry looked at Julie, who began to protest, and he waved his hand. "No, Julie. Really. I know you want to help, but it would be more helpful if you were dead now."

He smiled.

She scowled.

"Them?" Paul asked.

"Oh, yeah. Daniel Smith is in the area with access to your Uncle George. I'm sure he already knows what you discovered in their barn, Julie. He probably gave the orders for you to be hit. It was set up well. You were deliberately gotten out of the way and separated from Tom, then lured back to your house and attacked."

"But why… why Julie?" Paul asked.

"To keep her from telling anyone what she saw in that apartment. They probably assumed that she'd already told Tom. He'll be next on the hit list, you watch."

"Me?"

"Oh yeah. I honestly believe, Tom, that the reason your uncle wants you to haul his horses is to find out what you know and then either recruit or, somehow, kill you. It would probably be an accident on the way back."

"So, the itinerary will be a sham?"

"Hm, probably. I'm only speculating about this. It's how I survive. I also want the two of you to survive. Of course, he may try to recruit you…"

"Hell of a way to make a living," Julie said.

Julie glanced at Tom, sitting next to her, and, without thinking, leaned her body closer to him and brushed her arm against his. The electricity of their chemistry sent sensations up and down the back of her spine, and they landed in some of the more personal and intimate parts of her body.

Dear God, I can't lose him now. Out loud, she asked, "What about me? Where do I go to play dead?"

Phil cleared his throat. "I would love you to stay with us for a few days. The kids are visiting their grandparents in Michigan, and Marsha is there by herself. You should be safe. I don't think anyone would look for you there, especially if the word is out that you were killed. Would that be suitable?"

Larry nodded his head. "Julie, when you get there, you're not to leave the house for any reason, understand?" Julie suddenly felt like a child being chastised by a parent. She also felt left out. She said so.

"Nevertheless, that's the general idea. You're safer that way."

Julie pursed her lips together and nodded. "Yes. I understand. I don't like it, but I think you're right."

"So, when do we carry out the body?" Nick asked.

"We'll take Julie out in the stretcher, for real. You'll take her into the ambulance, to the morgue, where she will be heavily disguised as hospital personnel, and then driven back to Phil's house. You, my dear lady, will remain there until this is over."

Julie nodded meekly, a trait that did not fit her personality.

"What about my mom and Brenda? Do they have to think that I'm dead?"

"I'll call your mother before we leave. I know she'll be worried, but at least she'll know that you're safe, and we'll tell her what to say in case anyone calls her for information. Verifying that she's really dead." Julie looked at Larry with questioning eyes.

"Oh yes, that's possible—someone will probably call her. A very innocent and solicitous call. 'So sorry to hear about your loss, etc.'" Larry looked disgusted and shrugged his shoulders. The others just waited for him to continue.

"As for Brenda, she's too close to be safe. Uncle George may charm her into telling him that Julie's alive. No, we can't take a chance on her."

"I can give you my personal guarantee that Brenda will not be charmed into doing anything that she does not want to do," Paul said. "I can guarantee her character. I think that it would be cruel and rotten, especially now, with her husband dead and everyone hurling accusations at her, if she thought that her best friend was dead or that we didn't trust her enough to let her in on this. Don't you dare do that to her." Paul was so forceful that all heads turned to look at him. "Damn it. I'll take responsibility for her, okay? You can trust Brenda. She won't tell Uncle George. Besides, she doesn't like Uncle George. He's too much like Matt."

"Okay," Larry said, overcome with the unexpected intensity. "I give up. But you tell her when you go home, in private. We call her from this phone and tell her that Julie is dead." He suddenly looked up with a look of curiosity on his face. "Why, specifically from Julie's phone?"

"Because," he replied, "I believe it's tapped."

"What?" All eyes shot toward Larry. He got up, got Julie's phone, and unscrewed the base. Sitting there was a tiny silver metal cap, about 0.5 centimeters. It had a hole in the center.

"What's that?" Julie asked, perplexed. "It looks like a microchip."

"That's the transmitter. They can listen to them on phone calls. They probably set that up after you visited them that day. I didn't know, I suspected. I'll bet the phones at your house are tapped, too, Paul."

Total silence—stunned silence filled the air. "So, will you do what I've asked you to do?" Larry asked. He tapped his pen on the table.

"If you have to."

"I have to."

"So, I'm going to be hauled out of here with a sheet over my face? In an ambulance? Can Tom come too?" A mental picture of her under the sheet with Tom flashed through her mind. She shook it off and focused on reality.

"No. He gets to ride in the big police car behind the ambulance."

Tom got up and came behind her. Putting his arms around her shoulders, he gave her an affectionate kiss on the cheek. Julie knew he was telling everyone they were a couple, and she liked the feeling.

"Now's the hard part," Larry said as he handed the phone to Tom. "Call."

"Me?"

"You're the actor, older brother," Paul said.

"Okay, okay," he dialed.

"Brenda? No, I'm afraid it's all bad. Julie was attacked in her house. We got there too late. I'm sorry. Julie's dead." He waited for the reply at the other end of the phone. There was a long silence.

"We'll be back in a while. You'd better tell Uncle George and Dad about it, okay?"

Tom hung up the phone and looked shaken. "That could have been for real."

"Okay, now. You follow the ambulance. I'm going to call Julie's mother from my car, and Paul, you can call Brenda back."

Julie was strapped down to a stretcher with a sheet placed over her, and they carried her out to the ambulance. Neighbors gathered on lawns to watch, and Mrs. Rossellini came over. Larry had a quiet and private conversation with her, and she returned to her house. The ambulance pulled away, and Phil and Tom followed behind. About ten minutes later, Larry and Paul pulled away in Larry's car. Down the block, another car slowly pulled out, following the ambulance at a distance. The driver picked up the phone. "Where are you? What happened? Shit, you bungling fool. You sure she's alive? Damn it! Okay, they're putting on a show. I'm going to follow them and find out where they're taking her."

The ride to the hospital was bumpy at best. Nick humored Julie by telling ambulance jokes and setting off the siren. She managed to unstrap herself from the Gurney and sat up, looking through the front of the ambulance.

"Hey, you can't sit up with those straps on," he said. "How did you manage to get out of them anyhow?"

"They weren't tight. I used my fingers to manipulate the buckle. It's no fun being strapped down." She thought about Tom holding her down when he forced her to listen to his explanation about the phone call. She rather liked his overpowering manner when he was intense.

She wanted him and wouldn't have a moment's peace until… her thoughts about what she wanted Tom to do to her as he held her down, was interrupted by Nick.

"We're almost there," he said. She focused on her job of playing dead.

They pulled up to the ambulance's emergency entrance, and several staff members in white coats opened the back door. A man in a business suit jumped into the ambulance in a white coat as other staff members passed by, getting ready for the next shift.

He was the fifty-year-old administrator of St. Sebastian Hospital. Although he had worked in his position for nearly ten years, his knowledge of the hospital expanded for close to twenty-five years. His appearance, however, belied his age, and he looked closer to thirty than fifty. His wife claimed he had the kind of baby face that appeared ageless. He helped Larry from time to time in his witness protection program and trusted his staff implicitly.

"Hi," he said. "I'm Adam Westmore. How in the world did you get the straps undone?"

Julie told him.

"Hm, clever girl. We're going to strap you down again. Then, we'll take you to the morgue, where you'll change clothes and be taken out of here."

"You think all this is necessary?"

"I don't know what's going on, but if Larry says it's necessary, then it's necessary. Lie down." She lay back down on the Gurney, and one of the white coats strapped her back down. They covered her back up with the sheet, and Julie was carried into the hospital and down the corridor to the morgue, followed by Phil and Larry, with Tom and Paul close behind.

The man and woman known as Millie and Daniel Smith connected several blocks from Julie's house. They listened to every word that went on in her house from the other electronic devices placed before the attack. And before they'd debugged the place after the meeting.

CHAPTER 22

The kitchen table was the favorite gathering place for the Swanson family. Everyone who came into the house was greeted with a hot cup of coffee or hot chocolate in the winter and a choice of lemonade, cool-aid, or iced tea in the summer. The kitchen and dining room combined to make the room an ideal place for entertaining and dining—a place to prepare, eat, clean up, and talk. When the house was custom-built for the Swanson family, Marsha chose the layout of the rooms, and Phil was glad she had. It was a comfortable home with enough play area for the boys and enough privacy for themselves. Each room fed into the next, with the dining room/ kitchen leading out to the back porch on one end and into the living room on the other. The boys and the family's three Rottweilers could wipe their muddy feet on the porch before entering.

Julie chose the iced tea as she thumbed through some of the photo albums from Swanson's childhood. Julie was fascinated by how their family history intertwined with the Carters'. There were photos of both families together in many of the pictures. Sitting in a black lacquered chair with a wicker seat, Julie thumbed through page after page on the matching dining room table with a polished oak top. She looked around the room and realized how comfortable she was, especially with sniffs of spaghetti and garlic bread. This was the place to hide if she had to go into hiding.

"Julie, more iced tea?" Julie nodded as Marsha let in her dogs. They scrambled into the kitchen, slipping on the polished floor and scampering toward the living room until they stopped dead by the dining room table. They spotted Julie.

"Hi, *dogs*." The dogs, in turn, were delighted and nearly knocked her off the chair in their enthusiasm. Julie provided affection right back, patting and saying something nice to each one in turn.

"Okay, Julie. I can tell that you like dogs, so introductions are necessary. This is Karl, Khan, and Rottie. Boys, meet Julie." The dogs gave Julie their paw, each trying to get there first. She laughed and realized she was completely relaxed for the first time in three days.

Marsha shooed the dogs away and handed her a replacement glass of iced tea. She joined her at the table. "Phil tells me you and Tom have been working together to solve Matt's murder. Have you known Tom for long?"

"No, actually, we met at last weekend's horse show. It seems so long ago. I've only known him a week." Julie checked herself and realized that she had known him for such a brief time. She told Marsha about their meeting and how they got involved in helping Phil with the investigation. She also talked about her involvement at the barn and how Brenda brought Socks up from her father-in-law's ranch. She found Marsha easy to talk to and talked nonstop for about half an hour as they devoured spaghetti, salad, garlic bread, and a glass of Chianti to wash it down.

"My God—I've told you my whole history. You must be getting bored."

"No, not at all. Julie, I'm afraid I'm a fraud. I'm used to talking to people. It's what I do. I lure people into a false sense of security, and they talk themselves to death. Sorry. I have an ulterior motive. Phil tells me that you and Tom are becoming close. I've never been one to stay out of anyone's business yet."

Julie found herself laughing.

"I have a reason to want to know about you and Tom. You see, Tom and I went together in high school. He had a crush on me."

"He did?"

"Yes. I liked Tom a lot, but more as a friend. I was head over heels in love with Phil, and I couldn't get him to notice me no matter what I did. We double-dated. Me with Tom, and Phil with other girls, older girls, from around town. Sometimes, I thought Phil was acting as a chaperon.

I didn't mind. I liked him being there. I just wished it were him with me instead of Tom. I don't think Phil ever knew Tom's feelings for me, but he didn't know my feelings for him, either." She stopped and looked at Julie with concern in her eyes. "Does that sound horrible to you, Julie?"

"Goodness. *No.* It had to have been hard on Tom, though. Did he tell you?"

"Yes. One night, after one of the high school dances, he took me home and told me he loved me. He wanted me to wear his ring. One look at my face told him the truth, and he put it away. Then, he took me by the shoulders and made me tell him the truth. I couldn't lie to Tom. There's something about him, Julie. You can't lie to him."

Julie knew that was the truth. She couldn't lie to him either.

"Anyway, I started to cry. I sobbed right there in the front seat of his little red Ford. He was utterly taken, unaware. I hurt him badly that night. I told him how I felt about Phil. Tom was so good about it, Julie. He held his arms around me, but it was no longer like a boyfriend. From that moment, he became my brother, and he's been that way ever since.

"He went to Phil and told him. I could never have pulled it off the way he did. It turned out that Phil had never asked me out because of his friendship with Tom. He would never move in on his best buddy's girl-friend. The following week, Phil asked me out, and I went. We fell in love and have been together ever since. Julie, Tom has never been serious with anyone since then, at least not that I know of.

"Since he's been away, Phil talks to Paul, and Paul shares what Tom tells him. I know that he's had girlfriends. But they weren't serious, just dates or friends. That's why I must know about your feelings for him. He's a very special person to both me and Phil. I'd hate to see him get hurt."

Julie looked at Marsha and could tell what attracted Tom to her. She was pretty, but even more than on the surface, she had a deep inner sensual beauty. Her dark eyes and almost black hair were a marked contrast to her white, pale skin, and the difference was stunning. She was highly intelligent and possessed a unique sense of humor. She could see why she loved Phil and Phil and Tom loved her.

"Oh, wow," Julie remembered the incident from the afternoon's phone call. "Marsha, wait and let me get control of myself. First, you don't have to worry about me hurting Tom. I like—love him. I…" She stopped, overcome with the emotions she felt for him. "This afternoon, a phone call came for him. The woman said that she was his fiancee. It nearly drove me crazy.

"I was so upset that I ran into the trap, eventually bringing me here." She started to cry and didn't know whether it was from fear or the memory of thinking that Tom was engaged to another woman.

"They got you good. You poor thing," Marsha said, trying to comfort her.

They sat in silence for a moment until Julie recovered. "But I'm glad about you and Tom. Phil told me that he has it bad for you." Julie looked up, startled. "Oh, Tom didn't tell him, but Phil can read Tom like a book. You can put it away right now if you doubt Tom's love for you. I think he'd die for you, Julie.

"I didn't know you, but now that I do, I'm glad it's you. You never have to worry about him cheating on you or being disloyal. He isn't like that. He's a terrific guy who's been needing a good woman for a long time. I don't think he realizes that, but Phil and I do."

Julie dried her eyes with a tissue that Marsha pushed in her direction, saying, "It seemed so out of character that he would be engaged to someone and not tell me upfront. I didn't see it coming. After my relationship with Randy, I've been cautious about getting involved with anyone."

"Yes, I should think so. The bastard," Marsha said, with such vehemence that Julie reeled back in shock. She wouldn't want Marsha to be mad at her.

"Marsha, you know so much about the Carters. Can I ask you a question?"

"Of course,"

"What caused the falling out between Jonathan Carter and his brother? And, what caused the estrangement between Tom and his father?"

Marsha raised her eyebrows.

"When you ask a question, you come out with both barrels blasting, don't you? Okay, here goes. I don't know the whole story. Some things are sheer conjecture and speculation. I'll tell you what I know. Even Phil doesn't know the whole story. Lord, I don't know what he would do if he did. I've kept it secret because of what I do on the side."

"You're a teacher, aren't you?"

"Yes, but more than that, Julie, I run a shelter or halfway house for battered women."

"Where?"

"Right here. That's why Phil thought of bringing you here when you were in trouble."

"Before Phil and I got married and bought this property, my mother and father were deeply involved with church work, and they ran a shelter for battered women. My mother told me the story. It happened when I was just a little girl. About three months after Jonathan Carter brought Ethel, his wife, to Illinois, she ran away and came to our church. My mother was talking to our pastor when she came in, beaten black and blue. She told them she had been raped. My mother asked her who had done this to her, and she just shook her head. They all assumed it was her husband.

"She said she was afraid to go home in case the man should return. She was so young and innocent. She had the most gorgeous blue eyes imaginable, all swollen and puffy from her beating. Mom said that it was horrible."

"Why did your mom tell you the story?"

"It was after I'd started to go out with Tom. She knew his brother, Matthew. She was afraid Tom took after the male side of the family. I think that she was afraid for my safety. She didn't want me to date Tom, you see."

"Oh."

"Anyway, when she met Tom and got to know him, she changed her mind about him."

"So, what happened to Ethel?"

"She stayed at their house for about a week until Jonathan came and picked her up. It must have been brutal for him because everyone suspected that he was a wife beater."

"They suspected Jonathan Carter. That's so hard to believe."

"Yes, it is hard to believe when you get to know Paul and Tom. When you get to know Matt, it's not so hard."

"Did she ever get any explanation?"

"Sort of. Mom said that Ethel told her Jonathan was not the one who had beaten her up. She was terribly in love with him and dreaded that he could see her like that. When Jonathan came and picked her up, he was so crushed by her appearance that he was livid with rage. He thanked everyone for caring for Ethel and then took her home. Jonathan and Ethel have been one of our staunchest supporters throughout the years. Ethel never went back again as a client. But I saw her at church and school functions, and she and Jonathan seemed very much in love throughout the years."

"Oh, then you don't know why Jonathan and his brother didn't talk to each other?"

"No, just conjecture. I know George was up here at the time and left shortly after Jonathan brought Ethel back home. Their family life settled down, and Matt was born nine months later. Tom came a year after Matt, and then Paul came."

"Could Uncle George have been her attacker?"

"Whoa… what? What made you think of that, Julie?"

"Maybe George's personality. It wouldn't surprise me that he would attack a woman."

"It could have been him. He was up here at the time. I thought that perhaps George was fooling around with Ethel, and Jonathan flew into a rage and beat her up. It could have been the other way around. I think that George and Ethel went out together before Jonathan married her. Who knows? Anyway, Matt inherited some of that brutishness. Paul and Tom didn't. Those three boys are enigmas. They're so different."

"What about Tom and his father? That was my original question. What happened with them?"

"Yes, right, sorry. Your question was about Tom and his father. It goes back to when Ethel died. She was killed in a riding accident, you know. Tom was broken up more than I've ever seen him. He's always been at odds with his dad, probably because Matt was Jonathan's favorite. Tom wanted Jonathan to look into her death and have it investigated. He thought that some strange circumstances surrounded her death. His father refused, saying it was an accident, pure and simple, and to leave it alone. Tom walked away."

"Why did she have to die?"

"That's a strange question, Julie."

CHAPTER 23

Afigure stood in the shadows outside the Swanson house, listening to the conversation filtering out through the open window. He took a deep breath of the warm summer night air—with the smell of lilacs and roses in bloom, and his adrenalin made him form a half giggle—half gurgle—sound somewhere from the deeper part of his throat. He was an assassin, and he enjoyed his work. Of all the duties performed for his employer, killing was his favorite. His assignment was simple. "Kill her, I don't care how. Make it look like a madman—not a professional hit." He had been interrupted the first time. He wouldn't fail the second.

This redhead was the prettiest of all his hits. As he stood underneath the window, he thought that maybe he would have a little fun before he slowly throttled the life out of her. Slowly, he thought. Slowly. This would be fun. He looked through the window and caught the shape of the curves underneath the button-down shirtwaist blouse tucked neatly into her jeans. He'd have some fun unbuttoning those buttons slowly as he pressed her down, slowly choking the life out of her. He'd read somewhere that sex was most fun when—but there were two of them. How could he get the one out of the way so he could have fun with the other? He'd wait. She'd have to go out for something. Or maybe she'd go to bed, and he could attack the redhead in her bedroom. Or, even more fun, he could get two for the price of one. He visualized what he'd do and just how he'd do it. Then, he heard the words he'd hoped to hear.

"Julie, I'm going to the store. I'll get some stuff for breakfast tomorrow. Any favorites? Dislikes? Speak now forever hold your peace."

He heard Julie laugh softly and say, "My mother used to say that to me. No, whatever you want is fine with me."

"Good, I'm taking the boys with me. They love to ride in the truck. We'll probably be back in about an hour. Don't leave the house. But you know that already. Boys, come."

He heard the faint sound of the porch door closing and the footsteps of Marsha and her three dogs walking to the truck. Then, the truck door slammed, and the engine started.

The man laughed and decided which way he would enter the house. He fantasized as he plotted. He'd done this before and loved to see the shock and anger turn to fear. He'd heard all kinds of pleadings. The men were always fun to see die, but the women—that was another matter. He didn't think an hour would be nearly enough time. Oh well. He silently went to the back porch and tiptoed up the stairs. Cautiously, he peered into the kitchen window and saw Julie with her back to the kitchen door. Good. He could subdue her without any problems. He took out his gun and opened the kitchen door. Julie thumbed through the albums and looked at Tom as a high school student standing between Marsha and Phil.

"Hello, honey," the man said.

Startled, Julie turned and faced him. "My God… Daniel." The blood drained out of her face. "How did you find me?"

"You didn't really think that little trick of pretending to be dead would work, did you?" He asked with a sly grin on his face. "That was very clever of your police protectors, Miss Bishop, but it didn't work. You see, I bugged your house."

"Bugged my house?" She knew, but the thought this crazy man had been in her home turned her stomach. Violated was only one emotion that made her shiver.

"We have some unfinished business, you and I…" he said, skipping over explanations.

"What do you mean, unfinished business?"

Daniel's eyes, slightly glazed, were penetrating and crazy. He meant to harm her in a nasty, vicious manner.

"Let's call it a date with destiny. I'm a very thorough man, Miss Bishop. I always finish a job. But, this time, I think we'll have a little fun first."

Julie stood up and looked at the man.

Daniel walked slowly towards her, and Julie backed away from the table and towards the living room.

"That's right, honey, let's walk over to the living room and sit on the couch, shall we? Then we can have a nice chat. I love the way you chat," he said. "You turn a nice shade of white and grey when you plead… beg. I loved the way your face turned nice and blue this afternoon. Then red. It was so pretty. Just like your hair. The color of copper. You were very patriotic, red, white and blue. You think I'm crazy, don't you? Well, they say that makes me doubly dangerous. I've always been fond of redheads. My first wife was a redhead, and she was a pistol. You should have seen what I did to her." He smirked.

Julie backed up a step further, not looking where she was going or being familiar with the room. She backed into the wall.

"Good. I gotcha just where I want you." He stepped closer, looked her up and down, and licked his lips. She was now within his reach. He held the gun up to the level of her head.

"Come on, honey, play nice. Come to papa."

Julie thought frantically for the karate moves that she learned in high school. Fear prevented memories from coming to her aid. He pushed up against her, close enough for her to feel the heat from his foul breath and the metal from his gun stroking the side of her face. His hands pressed against her blouse, aiming for those buttons.

"Just a little fun before you slowly sink into oblivion. Have you ever been strangled before? Oh yes, I remember now." He giggled again, his right hand pressing the gun harder against her temple, his left hand unbuttoning her blouse. "You almost strangled this afternoon. Poor Julie." He caressed her face with the cold metal, playing with her buttons with his other hand. "No. There will be no Tom to protect you now. No one will come to your rescue. Just me." Another giggle emerged as his voice took on a sing-song effect. "And your date with destiny. You can never get away from… *me*." Furious with rage, Julie attempted to push him away. He was too strong.

"You push away from me one more time, you slut, and I'll have to enjoy you dead." He snorted. "I wonder what *dead* would feel like?"

Suddenly, coming from somewhere behind him, there came three throated growls. Daniel spun around, and Julie pushed him away. She ducked. Spinning toward the back porch, Daniel faced the barrel of a Sig P226 and three growling, gnarling Rottweilers with drool hanging from their ferocious mouths.

"What the…?" He stopped. The woman at the other end of the semi-automatic, with the dexterity and authority of an experienced marksman, blasted the gun directly into the arm that held the gun.

"Drop it," she said, "or you'll be inflicted by a bullet in your brain before these three nasty Rottweilers could tear your body limb from limb. I am more ferocious and bloodthirsty than even my husband, and he's a hardnosed cop."

The impact of the blast forced Daniel to drop the gun. He went down on his knees in pain.

"Julie," Marsha said, her eyes not leaving Daniel's face for one minute. "Get me the rope in the top drawer over there by the sink."

Julie did as she was told.

"Now," Marsha said, "You make as much as a teeny movement, and the second blast will render you useless from any further reproduction your rotten body may ever enjoy." Her dark eyes flashed, and the dogs approached him, teeth bared, barely under her control.

"Good boys, stay."

"Put that useless limb behind your back," she commanded.

"Oh my God… It *hurts*," he whimpered.

"Put it there. I hope it hurts you down to the jaws of Hell, you son of a bitch," Marsha said. He did as he was told, and when Julie tied his feet to his hands behind his back, he fainted from the pain.

"Good," she said. "Call Phil, Julie. He's probably back at the office. Tell him that your would-be killer is rendered useless and that, unless he gets over here quick, brains will be scattered all over his beautiful kitchen wall.

"How did you know?" Julie asked. "How did you know he was there?"

"Easy. It was Karl. He started to growl when we got into the truck. The others followed suit. I knew there was trouble. It was their *trouble* growl. I drove around the corner and then came back. These are police-trained dogs, Julie. Two are retired police dogs, and the younger one is learning. I'm training him. I forgot to tell you. I train dogs, too."

Julie sighed in relief as she picked up the phone. She had a profound admiration for Marsha Swanson.

CHAPTER 24

Pulling a matching twelve-horse slant trailer, a black and silver Dually maneuvered down a long, narrow, and winding driveway. Hauling any large rig was not an easy feat for even the most experienced in the horse transportation business. This seemed like a monumental task for Tom, who was used to driving the smaller two- and four-horse trailers. Now that he was getting the hang of moving the rig, he wondered what it would be like to have horses riding back there.

At the end of the driveway, an old man of nondescript age waited for him in front of a run-down barn, also ageless. Contrasting the shabby barn, a new blue pick-up truck perched on a huge, new concrete slab, the start of what appeared to be a new stabling facility. Modern white vinyl fences, new and expensive, enclosed a five-acre pasture.

"You Tom Carter?" The man, missing two front teeth, whistled as he talked,

"Yep." Tom got out and stretched his legs, checking out the Silver Star slant trailer that seemed to go on for miles.

"Name's Sonny Ubel. George told me you'd be pulling up about this time. It's the same trailer as your brother drove. Good. Any problems with it?"

Tom shook his head.

"Good, just like yer brother. He could handle anything." His accent was thick backwoods, hillbilly, and he was missing his front two teeth. Not only was he hard to understand, but Tom wondered how in the world he could eat.

"Yeah," Tom said.

"Too bad about him, though," Sonny continued. "We'll miss him. Come up to the house fer some coffee. We'll load the mares for you."

So, that was how it would be done. He would be lured into the house while they loaded whatever they would load. Shit, he thought, maybe it's nothing more than just horses. Maybe. The old man took him into the back of the barn, where a couple of horses were tied in small straight stalls. They looked as old and leathery as the man himself.

Sonny accompanied Tom to the house, where he was greeted by a tall, thin woman with a longish-hooked nose who looked frumpy and wore a torn house dress and apron.

"Set yourself down and have a sandwich with your coffee. Do you like ham and cheese?"

She reminded him of the Wicked Witch of the West from *The Wizard of Oz*, how her salt and pepper hair kept falling in her face, and how her voice cackled as she made small talk until it was time for Tom to leave. She did the talking. Tom did the eating. The woman scurried back and forth throughout her kitchen, laughing at her own jokes and rubbing her hands together as if to say, "I'll get you my pretty and yer little dog too." Tom thought it was good that he didn't have a little dog, too. He might be eating it for lunch.

Sandwiches were eaten, coffee was drunk, horses were loaded, papers were handed over to him to deliver to his uncle, and Tom was returning to I-57. The weight was noticeably heavier with the horses, but the live, shifting weight didn't seem unmanageable.

He thought about Julie. He hadn't seen her since Friday morning, and he missed her. The whole setup had backfired when they discovered that Julie's house had been bugged, something they had overlooked. It wasn't just the phone. Julie had been attacked again. Now, those bastards were in jail, and Julie and Marsha were somewhere in protective custody. Even Phil didn't know where they were this time. The only consolation was that Phil missed his wife as much as Tom missed Julie. This is stupid, he thought. I've known her, God, what… a week? Why do I feel like I've known her for a lifetime? Because, he thought, answering his own question, this week had been a lifetime.

He noticed a pickup truck following a short distance down the road. He couldn't be sure, but it looked like the truck in Sonny's driveway.

He checked Larry's itinerary and found that his next stop was a truck stop about five miles down the highway. Turning off the ramp into the parking area, a small blue Kia Sportage sat near the pumps with two men inside. He couldn't be sure, but he thought one might be Larry. Then, he saw the pickup truck following him into the station.

"Shit."

As the door to the Kia opened, Tom jumped out of his truck and flagged down the pickup.

"Sonny, I'm glad to see you," Tom said, grinning. "See, I left my logbook back at your house. You brought it to me?" he said, with a look of anticipation on his face.

The surprised man stammered back, "Uh, no. I just came here to get gas. I'll look for it when I get back. You need it?"

"Well, nah, I can stop there on the way back."

The Feds in the Kia closed the door and waited.

Tom filled his truck, and Sonny picked up the pump next to his. His eyes never left Tom or his rig. Tom waited, and so did the man. It was a standoff. As Tom went in to pay the bill, the man sauntered in behind him, following into a long line at the cashier's counter. Monday morning typically was not a busy time heading on the southbound lane, but today, there appeared to be a number of truckers all heading in the same direction at the same time. There was some commotion as a well-muscled man with tattoos on his arms, dressed in jeans and a tank top, tried to cut in front of Sonny. Tom recognized the man as one of the passengers from the Kia.

Tom paid his check, shot Sonny a look that said, "See ya when I get back," and walked out the entrance nearest the pumps. The ruckus continued. As Sonny tried to cut back to the head of the line, the trucker bumped into him, scattering change on the floor. Several irate customers got involved, and each was arguing with others standing in line. When he looked back, he chuckled. There, in the middle of the fight, was Larry Ortega.

By the time Sonny ran out, Tom had already pulled the rig down the ramp and was heading south on I-57. Sonny was no longer following him, but the Feds hadn't had a chance to check the van, either. It was going to be an exceedingly long journey.

Mile after mile passed as Tom went through Illinois and into Missouri. He finally passed off I-55 and started west on I-40 through Arkansas. It would be another two hours until he hit the I-440 belt around Little Rock before finding the motel, where someone would be waiting to recheck the van.

Thoughts of Julie crept into his head as he drove over the White River and saw signs that pointed toward Carlisle, Arkansas. Why did everything remind him of her? Did the two women talk about him? How much had Marsha told her? And, even more important, what had Julie told Marsha? He knew she would have a girl talk with Julie. It was what sisters did for their best brothers.

He used his cell phone to call home.

"Hello?"

"Paul… hi. Is everything all right?"

"Yes, fine. Where are you?"

"Just passing through Carlisle, Arkansas. Where's Brenda?"

"Down at the barn. Searching through some old records, I think."

"How did Brenda take the news?"

"Which part? The one when we told her that Julie was dead. Or the one when we told her that Julie wasn't dead, or the one when I told her that she had been attacked again and now was in hiding."

"Oh, jeez, poor Brenda. This has got to be hell on her."

"Yeah, it is. She's not feeling so hot. Touch of the flu or the strain of everything. She broke down this morning after you left."

"Poor kid."

"Yeah, then she did something else. She went riding."

"What's so strange about that? She loves to ride."

"She took out the black horse."

"What?"

"Yep. She was back before I knew that she was gone. She picked up some old horseshoe from the back pasture. She said that Julie wanted it for something."

"Julie called?"

"Yeah."

"She shouldn't have done that. Er… how's dad?"

"Fine. That's another thing."

"What's another thing?"

"That black horse…?"

"Yeah?"

"You remember when a horse was stolen from his farm?"

"Yeah… so?"

"It was his favorite. From his champion mare… she died when she foaled."

"Vaguely, Paul. He was heartbroken. I remember that."

"Tom, this is the same horse."

"Crap." Tom's mind reeled, and he nearly veered into the oncoming traffic before pulling himself and his rig together."

"How many horses are you hauling?" Paul asked, changing the subject.

"I've got two in here now. I'm stopping at a farm outside Little Rock to dump them off. Then I'll find a motel room. I'll pick up another five to bring the rest of the way." Tom maneuvered his way around the right-lane traffic and then continued.

"How's Phil doing?"

"Lonely without Marsha and the dogs. The girls took them for protection. After Friday night's performance, there isn't anyone else I'd rather have around." Paul chuckled.

"You talking about the dogs or Marsha?"

"Both. Annie is still here, though. She's keeping Brenda company."

"Paul, if you hear from Julie, tell her I love her. Okay? Paul, I can't stand being away from her for even another second. Suppose there's another attempt?"

"Hang on there, big brother. She's safe where she is… you can tell her you love her when you see her."

He hung up, annoyed that he couldn't talk to her and that they had gotten in so deep that their lives were up for grabs. What started to be an adventure was turning into a non-ending nightmare. He took the I-410 belt around Little Rock and noticed the terrain was prettier than before. He could see the Quachita Mountains in the distance as he pulled off the highway and onto the gravel road that led him to the Flying W. Ranch.

Grinding to a halt by the barns, two men came out as he exited the truck.

"Long trip?" asked one of the men, grinning at him. The man extended his hand to Tom.

"Hi," he said. "I'm Buzz Weaver. I own this ranch. You're a relative, I gather?"

"Yeah, I'm Tom Carter. George Carter is my uncle."

"I heard about your brother."

"Yeah."

"Pretty awful. But now, you're taking over for him. George told me you have plenty of experience with horses. Your brother ran the ranch up in Illinois, didn't he?"

"Matt and his wife, and Paul. I think that Brenda will stay there. At least, I hope she does. She's an excellent rider and trainer."

Buzz looked in surprise and said, "Oh? I thought Matt did all the training."

"Who told you that… Matt?" Tom looked at Buzz for confirmation. Buzz nodded.

"Actually, Brenda did most of it. Matt did some work, but most of the success was due to Brenda. Paul keeps the business side going, and he's good with horses, too. I hope he gets back in the saddle. He hasn't ridden in the past few years.

"How about you?"

"I left some time ago. I'm an actor in Chicago. I came home a week ago to watch the horse show and see old friends. Matt was killed the day after they got back from the show. Things have changed a lot since then. I've taken over hauling horses for Uncle George until, well, indefinitely, I guess. We'll see."

Buzz looked as though he was going to say something, then changed his mind. "You must be starved. Come on in and meet Emily and my boys. You'll stay for supper, of course. We arranged to have your horses stabled here for the night. I wouldn't dream of making you stay in a motel. You'll stay in our guest room overnight."

This was not in Tom's plans. He was supposed to stay at the Hidden Valley Motel about ten miles down the road. "I wouldn't want to put you to that much trouble. I have reservations at a motel, prepaid."

"Hell, cancel them. You can use the phone. We'll call George and say, 'Howdy.' You can tell him where you are."

"*Oh!* I'm not sure that George is back yet. He left Saturday afternoon but had some stops to make along the way."

"Hell, boy, let's try and call him, all right?"

Tom couldn't think of a way to reject the offer. He needed to call Larry and tell him about the change of plans, as their arrangements weren't going according to plan.

"Okay. I'll go out and get my stuff and check on the horses. I'll be back in a minute." He made his way back to the van and called.

"Just a minute, Mr. Carter," the receptionist said. She came back a few minutes later.

"I'm sorry. Mr. Ortega is not here just now."

"Damn! Give me his car phone number."

"We don't give out that car number, Mr. Carter, I'm sorry."

"Is this Bessie? Bessie, come on, it's Tom. It's an emergency. I've got to talk to him."

"Is there a number I can reach you at?"

"No. Look. I can't stay on. I gotta go. Tell him I called, and my plans have changed. Thanks." He hung up just as Buzz came up to the van.

"Son, you could've called from the house."

"Thanks," Tom said. "I wanted to call home and save the long-distance charge." Buzz smiled and walked him back into the house, carrying Tom's cell phone as he went.

Emily was a good-looking woman with a friendly manner and nice smile. Tom doubted she got involved with her husband's business of buying and selling horses and running the ranch. She kept house, keeping her domestic eye on their two boys.

Tom was starved and dug into fried chicken, green peas, mashed potatoes, and steaming rolls fresh out of the oven. Afterward, they sat on comfortable sofas and lounge chairs in the living room, eating peach cobblers with ice cream and talking horses. Dessert was cleared as if by magic and replaced with cordials, as the discussion of quarter horses and the future of the American Quarter Horse Association was explored, and judging tactics at a local horse show was examined. Buzz Weaver knew his horses.

"How long have you been doing business with my Uncle George?" Tom asked.

"As long as I can remember. He made it easy for me to make sales out of state. I can't keep running horses all over. I've known Matt since he was a teenager," Buzz said.

"You knew Tony Richardson?"

"Tony Richardson? No, I can't say that I know that name. I know a Greg Richardson from Kentucky… Eagle Ranch. That the same family?"

"Tony was Greg's brother. He died last year."

"Yeah, now I remember something about that. He'd been arrested for trafficking drugs. Yeah, Matt mentioned it to me when it happened."

"He did? You remember what he said?"

"Sure do. He was supposed to deliver some horses down here. He arrived later than expected because he had to go to a funeral. It was Good Friday, I remember, 'cause we always go to church on Good Friday."

One of the sons, Jeffrey, came in and announced, "Dad, the horses are bedded down for the night. I guess I'll go to bed. Night Tom. Night Dad."

Tom went to bed and was so tired he couldn't fall asleep. The contrast of his business stung when he looked around at the beautiful four-poster bed and the country wallpaper hung with oil paintings of old farmhouses and family portraits.

Tom thought that Buzz Weaver did quite well in his business.

CHAPTER 25

Tom dreamed about Julie that night. She wore a white silk nightgown, her long red hair flowing down her back, standing in the desert, beckoning toward him, and the more he came to her, the further away she traveled. She moved further and further until the desert ended at the edge of a cliff, Tom running after her in a panic. Just as he got to the edge of a cliff, Julie turned into Uncle George, who was floating in the air and laughing hysterically. Tom woke up with sweat pouring from his body. The sheets were wet. He thought he had a fever. He fell back to sleep, and Julie came into his dreams once more. This time, they were locked in an embrace, and as he started to kiss her, a door banged, and they fell apart, Julie floating away. As Tom reached out to catch her, he woke up again. This time, he realized that the noise was not part of the dream. It came from outside.

Tom got dressed as fast as he could in his dark bedroom. He steadied a ladder-back chair as he bumped his shins and stubbed his toe on the door jam. Rubbing his sore toe, he carried his shoes while tiptoeing down the landing past the other bedrooms. Moving down the staircase, he held his breath until he was out the back door. The moon was out, and the chill of the night caused him to shiver. He was sure he had a fever. He felt dizzy and giddy, alternating between hot and cold. In the distance, he thought he heard a car start, and he turned just as a hand touched his shoulder.

"Sssh," the owner of the hand, who turned out to be Larry, said.

"Damn, you scared me. What are you doing here at this time of night?"

"Come here and be quiet," another voice whispered.

They walked over to the back of the van, and the heavy-muscled man with tattoos from the gas station truck stop line opened the back door. He pointed to the floorboards, which had obviously been tampered with.

"That's where they're stashing the stuff."

Tom peered under the floorboards. Instead of seeing the white powder he expected, he saw money piled in neat little stacks.

"Is *that* what I'm hauling?"

"Yep." That's the exchange for the cocaine that you'll bring back with you."

"*Damn!*"

"Sssh!"

Tom whispered, "I tried to call you last night to tell you about the plans change. The receptionist couldn't reach you."

"I know. She called me. We'll meet you at your uncle's ranch. Probably beat you down there. Tom, be careful. George is a crafty guy, and he's on to you. He hasn't survived doing this by being stupid. Watch yourself."

Larry turned and walked back out into the shadows. Tom turned in his direction and heard a car door slam somewhere down the road. He closed the van door and walked into the barn where the horses were stabled for the night. Sitting on a hay bale, he stared into the darkness.

"Hey! Who's out there?" called a dark, sleepy voice with a tinge of alertness built in. Tom started and jumped up just as the light came on in the barn.

"Sorry! It's just me. I couldn't sleep. I thought I heard a noise, so I came down here."

"And did you?" Buzz asked with curiosity and a raised eyebrow. "Hear a noise?"

"No. I guess not. It's been a long day, just hearing things I guess."

Buzz stared at him. "Are you okay?" he asked. "You looked flushed like you got a fever. You feel sick?"

"No. I'm just tired. Probably from the long trip."

"Tomorrow, you sleep in. I'll call George and tell him you'll be behind schedule. Come on, Tom, let's go back to the house. Maybe tea with whiskey?"

Around ten o'clock the following day, Tom dragged himself downstairs and into the kitchen.

"Good morning, Tom," Emily said, with a warmth added to her tone. "How did you sleep after your little escapade last night?"

"You heard about that?" Tom grinned and stretched, thinking that he really did feel much better. "Thanks, fine. I kept hearing noises last night. I might have dreamed them. No one was outside when I got there." Tom smiled at her and ate bacon, eggs, and toast with real butter and marmalade. "Thanks. This smells great. I'm not used to driving that much. I still have another fourteen hours to my uncle's ranch."

"You sure you want to do this?"

"Do what?"

"Transport horses for a living. It can't be much fun. You're not like the other drivers that come through here."

Emily was making a statement. Tom was sure of what she was telling him. He pretended not to understand. "Well, I'm just filling in for now. My brother seemed to manage this quite well."

"Yes, he would. You're not like your brother, somehow," she said.

Tom started driving his van to Route 30, that would take him down to Texarkana and the Texas border. The weight of the extra horses made it more difficult for him to maneuver the van, and the extra cargo underneath the floorboards made it more difficult for him to maneuver his emotions. So far, Larry had been keeping up with him. His car phone rang.

"Tom? How are you doing?"

"This is your Uncle George. I just talked to Buzz. Says you weren't feeling too well last night. How you're doing now?"

"Much better, thanks. Nothing a good night's sleep and a large breakfast couldn't cure."

"Good, good. He said you and him got along just fine. It's just what I need. Good PR. Having any trouble with the van?"

"No. I had some difficulties adjusting to the rig's weight with the horses. So far, everything is going okay. I should be there in about 13 hours. I'll stop for lunch somewhere, then drive straight through."

"Good. If you get too tired, you stop. Hear? Oh, thanks, Tom. I needed your help. You came through for me. I'll make this worth your while."

Tom felt guilt hit his stomach as he passed the border into Texas.

Suppose they were wrong about George? Suppose he was just what he claimed to be, a very wealthy businessman with many fingers in many pies. They were family, and family was supposed to stick together and be loyal. Passing through the outskirts of Waco, he felt like a traitor going into his own country as a spy.

Tom continued south on I-35, so buried in his thoughts that he saw the signs for Austin before he knew he'd left Waco. I know I've been here before, he thought. When I was a kid. When he entered San Antonio, he nearly missed the entrance onto I-37 because he'd been driving next to a little yellow Sportscar. Driving was a young woman with fiery red hair flying out behind her. Finally, coming to US-59, he drove southwest and into Duval County. He was getting close.

Ominous thoughts of evil filled his mind as he neared where he remembered Devil's Waterhole stood. He, Paul, and Matt were taken there as kids by his parents when they visited their grandparents. It had been a long time—too long since he'd been here. He passed into his destination, Webb County.

"Dear God, I'm tired," he said, pulling his van over to the side of the road. He checked the van clock, which read midnight. I don't know how much more I can take."

He checked out his map and memorized the final roads. "Okay, Lord, keep talking to me. This shouldn't be too far away. Thank God the horses are quiet." He looked around him into the blackness of the desert. "Is there anything out there?"

He got out of the van and stared at the darkness of the desert and a black background sprinkled with bright, flickering lights of stars strewn around in well-formulated patterns. The stillness was occasionally assaulted with coyote howls, first reverberating from one side of the landscape, then echoing back from the other. The cool night air felt good, contrasting the terrible heat of the day, and he thought about Julie. He wished to hell she were here. Thoughts of camping out in the desert with a tent and a sleeping bag made for two filled his head. He wondered what she was doing and where she was doing it. Then, he thought about his apartment in Chicago and suddenly knew where he wanted to be—where he belonged—back at the ranch. No, not only that, "I wish I were sleeping in my bed with my arms around her." He said it out loud to the desert—for posterity to record and destiny to implement. With that last wish, he got back into the van.

He started on the last leg of his journey, onto the road that would take him to Uncle George's ranch. It loomed up ahead, and even in the dark, the brightness of the fencing and the archway leading into the driveway was visible. Tom pulled up to a massive white mansion with Southern-style white columns surrounding a vast porch. He didn't need to make his presence known. An elderly man came out and helped him out of the van.

"Hello, Master Tom. Your Uncle's expecting you. We've been waiting up. Someone will be up to take your truck down to the stable. You just come with me."

Tom followed the white-haired old man, who shuffled along as he walked up the porch stair, through the porch, and into a large hall with a winding staircase leading upstairs.

In a red dressing gown over his jeans and cowboy boots, Uncle George looked like a cross between a cowboy and the English gentry. His hand held a glass of whiskey and a Cuban cigar.

"Well, you finally made it. Good… good. I'll have old Jerry make a drink for you here, son. You remember Jerry, don't you?"

"Yes, of course," Tom remembered Jerry. He'd been with his Uncle George since he could remember, dating back to his early childhood. He'd played piggyback rides on Jerry's back all over the house. Not this house, though, he thought. In those days, it was a small ranch house that he loved. The old man didn't move to greet Tom, he just smiled and waited for instructions. He'd always been like that—the perfect butler.

"What'll it be?"

"What do you have?"

"We'll fix you up. Jerry, make Tom a Whiskey Sour. It's his specialty. And Tom, come into my study. We can talk there."

The door to the study was to the right of the great staircase. As Tom walked through, he saw walls lined with bookcases filled with what appeared to be first editions. The bookcases also framed original oil paintings of famous horses, going back in time to the renowned quarter horse, Leo. Tom noted the paintings were done by artists who commanded six figures for each painting they sold. The highly polished Rosewood desk, filled with papers, made an L for the computer desk in the room's left corner. An oval southwestern-style rug lay in the center of the room, framing a glass coffee table, and appeared hand-woven. The leather sofa where Tom started to sit lined the right wall, which overlooked a fireplace on the opposite wall.

"No, Tom, not there. Come. Sit here by the desk." Uncle George ushered Tom over to his desk, where Tom sat by the fireplace on a soft, plush office chair that rocked back. Tom felt as though he could fall asleep in this chair by the air conditioner.

"Great room, isn't it? Everything I've always wanted in a room is in here. I've got first-edition books, first-class paintings of first-class horses, a fireplace, oak furniture, a leather sofa, and a well-stocked bar. The window overlooks the gardens in the back. It's beautiful this time of year. Tomorrow, I'll give you a tour. You can see how well your old Uncle George has done for himself."

Tom smiled at his uncle. This was fantastic. He'd never seen such luxury. How much of this had Uncle George acquired on his own… from his horses? He'd heard stories about how his uncle had swindled land out from under the neighboring ranchers. He'd started with a small spread, then expanded slowly but with devastating efficiency. His uncle was shrewd. What exactly went on down here at his ranch? Then, he realized something. He now believed that Uncle George was the driving force behind this drug operation and that all the little lieutenants, sergeants, and children drug runners, ultimately, all worked for Uncle George. It took a bit of swallowing as Jerry came in and handed him a whiskey sour.

Swallowing, Tom said, "This is fantastic. Beautiful."

"So how was the trip?" his uncle asked, smiling—broadly.

Tom could almost see fang-like teeth and eyes turning into slits.

Tom told him. He talked for fifteen minutes about his two stops and his visits with Sonny Ubel and Buzz Weaver. He decided the best way to handle his uncle was to tell the truth or the near truth. So, he talked about Julie's near escape from her first attack and how she was followed and attacked again. Then he talked about Matt's death and how little more they knew now than they had before.

"You and Julie shouldn't have gotten involved. Phil should know better. He showed poor judgment to let you two get in over your head like that. I'm sorry about Julie. She's a nice girl. I hope she'll be all right."

"I hope so, too," Tom thought. She will if you leave her alone.

He took a long sip of his drink. It was good.

"Do the police have any suspects?"

"No. Not that I know of. I've dropped out of the investigating business."

"I'm glad to hear that. You could tell me this, though," he looked intensely at Tom. "I understand that they suspect Matt of running the drugs?"

"That's what they tell me. I don't know what connections he had, and I don't know what else they're up to. Matt had a lot of enemies. I think they're looking at his girlfriend."

"Girlfriend?"

"Yeah. He was fooling around with one of the girls at the barn. She wanted him to divorce Brenda, but Matt wouldn't do it. She was mad."

"Mad enough to kill him? I suppose that's possible. What about Brenda? Could she have killed him?"

"Don't know. I don't think she's capable of killing anyone. You know, Uncle George, if there's a link between Matt's death and Eddie and Tony's, that would put Brenda and his girlfriend out of the picture. If they had killed him, it would have been more personal."

Uncle George frowned. "No, I don't suppose so. You think they're all related?"

"Yes, somehow. I'll be darned if I know how."

Tom went to bed after finishing the Whiskey Sour to beat all Whiskey Sours. He followed Jerry up to one of the guest rooms, which overlooked the back pastures and barns. He fell asleep and didn't dream about anybody.

CHAPTER 26

Miguel left home that morning around the time Tom was getting into bed. His wife was up, as usual, making him breakfast and waking the children so they could see their papa off to work. Juan, the eldest, had already been helping on one of his papa's runs. Already, he was playing 'plane,' pretending that he was the pilot making runs to the big country to the north. Someday, he would be a pilot, too. Miguel hugged his kids, each in turn, ruffling their hair. Then, he kissed his wife, long and hard, partly to say goodbye and partly for her part in their passionate night. She giggled, and a new diamond ring he'd bought from the spoils of last week's assignment turned on her ring finger as she ruffled up his hair.

He sniffed the mountain air as he walked from the makeshift parking lot down the dirt path to the waiting plane. It was still dark, and the stars were still bright in the heavens, but Miguel could see the first sign of dawn pushing its way through the gaps in the mountains.

It averaged about once a week now that Miguel flew to the United States and the ranch near Laredo. He'd been hearing stories. One of his friends had been flying over the Rio Grande the other day when a Cessna came out of nowhere and nearly collided, forcing his friend to return to Mexico. He'd almost run out of fuel after using an alternative flight plan and finally landing on a deserted island off the coast of Florida.

Hopping into the small plane, his friends were already loading fuel drums. Life had become much easier since they loaded the fuel into the plane. He didn't have to make any stops to refuel and bribe airport officials.

Once again, Miguel took off over the Andes toward Columbia. Once again, he made a skilled and rather spectacular landing on a private airfield. Once again, he waited while his leaves were unloaded and the finished product was packed into the plane's shell. Then, Miguel started off flying low into Mexico under radar detection.

As he approached the Rio Grande, he noticed a small jet taking off from the airport in the distance. It seemed to approach his airspace, then it turned and disappeared. "Maybe a business flight," he told himself.

The small private landing strip lights lay ahead as the sun tried to come up. Storm clouds blocked its view as the sunlight filtered through the puffy dark grey and white, blustery vapors looming on the horizon. Miguel was glad he would be landing soon because those clouds looked like bad news to him. Texas storms were notorious, and he didn't want to get caught in one. He saw the strip and went for it. His gifted and capable hands gently helped the plane glide onto the runway, and he slid to a stop.

Tom arose that morning to hear the crack of thunder in the distance and the sound of a small plane beginning to descend. He shook himself out of his stupor and managed to find the bathroom adjoining his bedroom.

Uncle George provides all the amenities. The shower was perfect, with just enough pressure to massage his sore back. He let the streams fall on his neck and back muscles, and he kept thinking about how much he would enjoy Julie giving him a back rub, especially in the shower.

Tom didn't waste time. He dressed and found a back staircase at the end of the hall. It led to the kitchen, where breakfast was waiting for him.

"Looks like rain, Jerry," he said to the old butler laying out a table for him. "Where's my good Uncle George?" He looked around. Except for Jerry, the place was deserted.

"Your uncle said to tell you he'd send someone to pick you up and take you to the back barns. They should be here soon, sir. Eat your breakfast."

"You're a strange one, Jerry. You talk to me like I employ you, then you talk to me like my father. Which is it?"

"Both, sir," Jerry said, ambling out of the kitchen. Tom looked after him and laughed. We could use him to take care of us, he thought.

He marveled at the huge kitchen with big butcher block tables in the middle and the massive counters that ran the entire length of the kitchen. Modern conveniences were everywhere; natural lighting came in from huge French windows. The garden in the back of the kitchen paralleled George's study, and two doors led out onto a large patio. After breakfast, he walked onto the back deck and looked over the gardens. This was quite an accomplishment. It was like being in another world. Unreal was the word that came to mind. He was looking up at the vast trees and rows of every color rosebush—a horn honk.

"Hey, Tom," the voice in the pickup truck yelled. "Over here… get in. We're going down to the south side of the ranch. Your uncle's waiting for you."

Tom walked over to the truck and hopped in the back. He looked over at a blond man of about thirty-five, tallish and thin, wearing old blue jeans and a blue cotton work shirt. Although it looked like it had been put on clean, tell-tale signs of brushed-off hay were everywhere. His brown cowboy boots were well worn, looking like they'd served their wearer for a long time. The man was rugged looking, with a well-tanned and leathery face. He looked like he'd been around the block once or twice.

They passed miles of pastureland. The sky was darkening, and the sun gave up trying to come out. Another clap of thunder crashed like the clash of symbols in Beethoven's Ninth. He'd sung in the chorus once, right behind the drums. The rain started to fall.

"Looks like we're in for it, but we're almost there," a man named Bob, who remained silent throughout the ride, said. "None too soon. Looks like a bad one."

"You get a lot like this?" Tom asked.

"Yeah, some much worse. This is a tornado alley out here. You know about them, being from the Midwest."

They approached the small airstrip, and Tom noticed a plane parked near the barns. "You guys fly planes around here?"

"Sure. It's a big place. We do crop dusting here."

"What crops?" Tom asked.

"Get out," Bob said.

They ran for the barn and got in just in time as a wall of rain plunged onto the earth. Uncle George and three other tough-looking cowboys, dressed in working jeans, dirty shirts, and boots, met them at the door as they raced in to avoid getting soaked.

The pole barn had stalls on each side and an open arena in the middle. In the front of the barn was a glassed-in office where activities could be observed and closely monitored. Tom looked around and whistled. Piled in the center was a stack of white packets that Tom could only surmise was a mountain of cocaine. By its side was the horse van Tom had driven down from Illinois. And, instead of horses, cases of ether occupied the stalls.

"Holy shit," was all he could say.

"Sit down, boy," Uncle George said, ushering him into his office. "Don't try to go anywhere. We're friendly here, but we're not stupid. Each man has a gun and is trained to use it. They're all perfect marksmen."

"Wow… why?" Tom was afraid he knew the answer.

"Look, no one, not even family, is going to screw up my business for me. Do you take me for a fool? I know you're working for the Feds. I know you're trying to bust this place wide open. You want to know who's in charge of this empire? Well, I am. If it weren't for the blundering of that fool nephew of mine, none of this would have happened."

"Wait a minute. Did you have Matthew killed?" One of George's men focused a gun on Tom's stomach, and he felt a little sick. There was no turning back now, no getting out of this gracefully. Uncle George was admitting things Tom knew might be a death sentence.

"Hell no. Matthew was like a son to me." Uncle George put his feet up on his desk and smirked. "Actually, seeing how we're laying the cards on the table…"

You're laying the cards on the table, Tom thought.

"Matthew *was* my son, Tom. He was your half-brother. I'm not even positive that my brother knows. At least, I don't think he does."

Tom stood up. "No! I don't believe you. That's not possible."

The cowboy with the gun shoved him down again.

"That's okay, Joe. Sit down, son. You may as well know the truth. Your ma dated me long before she hitched with your dad." Tom wanted to throw himself over the desk and strangle the living daylights out of Uncle George. He wasn't sure how that could be accomplished, so he waited.

Uncle George continued, "Matt's been muleing for me for a long time. It's worked perfectly until now. You're not coming down here and ruining my business. I can't let a billion-dollar industry go bust just because of a relative. Loyalty is a two-way street, boy, and right now, I'd say that street is one way. You're a dead end."

Of course, his uncle knew he was working for Phil. That was never a secret. This was part of their strategy. This is what Larry planned all along. But where were the Feds? Were they taken care of as well? Where was Larry? He needed to stall.

"How did you manage all this? How could you build such an empire with no one catching on?"

"Oh, they've suspected. That's why Larry put on that stupid charade at your barn. They're spinning their wheels and can't prove anything. I raise horses and work on business deals on the side. I do some chemical sales, as you can see in my stalls."

"What's the ether for?" he said, nodding toward the stalls. "How does any of this work?"

"I'd like to think you're not stupid, son, just naive." He sat back on his chair and folded his hands like an employer might when interviewing a potential employee. "We're one of the major employers of the world, Tom. A lot of extremely poor people have made a very good living because of me. When the mines in Peru dried up, these people had to eat somehow. So, they raised a crop that grows abundantly in Peru, the cocoa leaf. The peasants grow and harvest the crops; the leaves are soaked in kerosene or bleach to form a paste. The paste is imported to labs which refine it into what you know as a cocaine powder with ether."

"Ether. Doesn't Brenda's father deal in the chemical manufacturing of ether?"

"Good. I'm glad to see you catch on quickly. Yep. Why do you think I wanted Matt to marry Brenda? It's nicely tied up right in the family. I have a finger in every area of this business. I employ thousands of families. The Bolivian Mafias need me for their laboratories. Most of the exports come through Florida by boat, but a great deal of it comes in here by the kind of planes you see out there."

"Why did you want to kill Larry Ortega?" The words shot out of Tom. For the first time, the realization hit that Uncle George maneuvered that scheme.

"Oh, Larry. He really thought he could pull one over on us. Yeah, he was the smartest of all the boys… pretty well had it figured out, just like you. Matt was dumb about Larry, but he knew something about training horses. He trained that horse right under Brenda's nose, and she didn't even notice. Dumb on her part. He knew what he was doing. When Larry asked to buy a horse, we figured out what he was planning."

"So," Tom said quietly, "You sent that black horse up to Illinois."

"Yep, it was me. The funny thing about that…" He chuckled, almost talking to himself, "Was that…" He chuckled again, "I stole that horse from your dad. It was his prize futurity winner. I saw him show it in Oklahoma. Fabulous horse. He had a lot of talent for jumping. It was an even exchange. Couldn't do enough for—to my brother after he stole my girl. Anyway, I still got a son out of her, and… and the horse."

"How did my mom die?"

"What do you mean?"

"I mean, why? You know that wasn't a riding accident, Uncle George. My Mom was too careful with her equipment, and that horse was too gentle. She wouldn't have gone out with a saddle with a broken strap. And that horse never spooked at anything."

Uncle George sat back on his office chair, crossed his legs, and took out a bottle of whiskey.

"Take a shot of this, boy. You're going to need it." He poured a round of drinks for both. He continued, "I don't know, but I'd look at that saddle strap. Maybe it was cut. Maybe it was replaced with a bad strap. Did she saddle her own horse that day?" He drank his shot of whiskey and poured himself another. "Probably wasn't an accident. Matt didn't take well to being lied to. When I told him that he was my son, he went ballistic. I was glad that I was on the phone and not in person. Whew! That boy had a temper. Takes after his old man."

"Matt? Killed mom?" Tom's mind returned for only an instant until Uncle George set him back into the present.

"I have a temper, too. I like to have my revenge."

"What exactly do you mean by that?" Tom asked.

"I mean, son, an accident, I think. You left here with five witnesses to say it was so. You never made it out of Texas. Too bad I could've used the van, but it's replaceable. So," he said with emphasis, "are you. We could just take you out and shoot you, but I don't want anyone to know that you didn't die on your own."

Uncle George was enjoying this thought as Tom stared at his uncle. The man was crazy, and Tom knew he was in big trouble. What the hell? Did a bunch of psychopaths run this billion-dollar empire? Matt, his uncle, and certainly the Smiths were all candidates for a state mental hospital. Tom decided to pump for more information.

"So, you're going to kill me like you killed Eddie and maybe Tony, too? Did they know too much about your business?"

"I didn't kill them. Eddie came down and worked for me for a while. He was on the run after his boss got nabbed, and Matt asked me to give him a job. So, I did. It only lasted about a year. He was way too hare-brained. I sent him up to Daniel to help there."

Uncle George poured himself another shot of whiskey, and it looked like he was calculating what else he would say. As he looked at the expression on his uncle, he thought that whatever might come next, it probably wouldn't be the truth. Why? He wondered. They were going to kill him anyway. What difference did it make?

"As far as Richardson is concerned, he was dealing drugs on his own or with someone else. I don't even care. Tony was just plain stupid. He got caught and killed himself. That's not my problem. What is my business? Who killed my son? If it was Brenda or that bitch he was fooling around with, I'll kill them myself."

Tom shook his head and finally took a swig from the shot glass.

"Aren't you at least interested in how all three deaths are linked? You're telling me you didn't have anything to do with them?"

His uncle just smiled. "Nope. I've done my share in my time, I must admit. But I can't claim those to my credit. You. You're my problem. You, boy, are a *big* problem."

The crash of the thunderstorm outside filled the barn and made everyone jump. Joe interrupted, "George, we gotta get that ether out of here. If lightning strikes this barn, we'll all blow sky-high, as will the powder."

"Okay," Uncle George said to Tom, "*you* stay here." His focus darted to the barn door he'd made into hanger size. He was planning to leave. Then, he turned to Bob, "Tie him up." He flung some twine from a hay bale at Bob, who stood quietly listening to George and Tom. Uncle George and Joe walked to the doors and opened them.

Bob tied Tom's hands behind him and whispered, "Ssh! You can break away, but not yet. Just play along with what's happening until I signal you. Say okay."

"Okay."

Tom glanced at Bob in surprise and realized he must be one of the undercover agents working with Larry. How could he have gotten into such a trusted position here? Tom sat with his hand tied loosely behind his back and waited.

He heard the commotion outside the barn as four men charged the door. George and his cowboys got out their guns and jumped behind the van as the men broke their way through the door. Tom slipped out of the twine and raced into the barn as one of the Feds yelled, "Federal Agents, you're under arrest." He pulled out his badge, ducking as he was met with gunfire. Bob ended the standoff nearly as soon as it started. Lunging at Joe, he wrestled the gun from his hand and banged his head against a stall door. As the others turned in disbelief, Tom jumped a burly-looking cowboy and caught him off balance. The guy went down, and one of the agents grabbed him. Bob grinned at Tom and said, "It's the element of surprise that gets 'em every time."

Tom noticed Uncle George racing out the door as everyone's attention was focused on the barn. "Miguel, get me the hell out of here," yelled Uncle George, dragging the arm of the surprised Miguel hiding in one of the stalls. The two raced to the plane and jumped inside.

Tom darted out the door after them but wasn't quick enough, as the motor of the plane started racing and the plane shot down the runway. Just as the plane became airborne, the agents ran after them in time to stand with Tom and see the plane leave the ground. As it did, a shot of lightning crashed into it sideways, causing an earth-shattering explosion that sent the plane and its crew back down to earth. As the men approached, all that was left were the metal pieces of airplanes and the charred remnants of Uncle George and Miguel.

CHAPTER 27

Julie sat with Brenda in the office, sorting and stacking old records by names, dates, and events and culling out those they felt might be useful. Even though Brenda had not been officially charged, they thought it might just be a matter of time.

Tom's trip to Texas had been a success from the standpoint that Uncle George's empire was shattered, and Tom was still alive. But they seemed no closer to solving Matt's murder. Julie was sure of what happened, but she needed proof.

"Brenda, are you sure that Matt delivered those horses on Good Friday last year?"

"Yes. Positive. I remember because I wanted him to put it off until after Easter so we could all go to church together. He refused."

"When did he leave?"

"I don't remember, Thursday night, I think. He was supposed to stay somewhere in Arkansas Friday night. I guess he did."

"Brenda, did Matt go to a funeral that day?"

"A funeral, Friday? No, not that I know of, why?"

"Just curious."

They heard a commotion from the barn and saw Lynette standing in the doorway, carrying her saddle.

"I'll bet you're glad that I'm leaving," she said. "Both of you."

"You can leave anytime you want. Your board's paid up. We don't need anyone who's going to cause trouble here, Lynette. You're not happy, so it's better you go." Brenda went back to clearing out a file drawer.

"Can I speak to you for a minute?" Julie asked, suddenly getting up and walking over to Lynette. The woman eyed Julie suspiciously, with one hand on her hip. Lynette was dressing more conservatively, less provocatively than before. She wore a black T-shirt under a lightweight jean jacket, her hair was pulled back in a ponytail, and she wore no makeup.

"Were you dating Matt when Tony died? Please, it's important. It's not going to hurt anyone's feelings anymore."

"Yes, I was. Why?"

"Matt delivered some horses that day, down south, for his uncle. Did you go with him?"

"No. I didn't travel with him. He stayed with me Thursday night, though."

"You sure?"

"Yeah, because he talked about almost nothing else other than Tony's being arrested."

"Oh,"

"Anyway, he left Friday morning. He told Brenda that he left for Texas that night. He stayed with me and left the next morning."

"Did he go to a funeral that morning?"

"No. Not that I know of, why?"

"I don't know why. I don't." Julie sighed. She didn't know what else she could find out from Lynette.

"Was Matt with you last Thursday night before the horse show?"

"Yeah, part of the night. He left early in the morning to get back in time to get the horses down to the show."

"Do you remember what time that was?"

"I'm not sure exactly… but… I know it was before two, though."

"Thanks, Lynette. I have one other question that's been puzzling me. Did you make a phone call from your car phone on the afternoon of the funeral?" Julie didn't know what she had to gain from asking that. It was important to her to know if Lynette had made the phone call to Tom. She hoped she would say yes.

"Uh… no, no, I didn't. Is that all?"

Julie looked into her face and saw the hesitation. Yes, she was sure of it. Lynette was lying.

"Thanks a lot. We'll contact you if we have any more questions."

"Questions? What for? What do you mean by 'we?'" Lynette stood gaping as Julie walked back into the office.

"Brenda, who's picking Tom up at the airport?"

"I think Paul will; you can go too if you want."

"No. No, I don't."

"Julie, what's wrong?"

Julie didn't know what was wrong, except that she was afraid—afraid after this was all over, she and Tom wouldn't have anything in common or that he wouldn't love her anymore. She remembered the night she lay with him, the passion in his eyes, the aching for him running down her body. She tried to focus back on Brenda.

"Nothing. At least, I don't think there's anything wrong."

"Julie, it would be better if Jonathan and his sons were alone together for a while. This isn't very good, Julie… Uncle George running a drug empire. You know my father was arrested this morning. His chemicals were provided in the manufacturing of cocaine. Maybe they won't be able to prove he knew what they were being used for. My father made a great deal of money from his association with Uncle George. I guess that was why it was so important for me to marry Matt." She looked at Julie, still pouring through the books.

"Poor Julie, this isn't exactly turning out to be the summer of your dreams, is it?"

"Well, there's some positive results."

"You mean Tom, don't you? Julie…"

Brenda hesitated before asking Julie's dreaded question. "If Tom asks you, would you marry him?"

"Brenda, I've only known him a short time." She put the accounts book down and sighed. "But, if he asks me, I'd go anywhere with him. I don't think I'd even ask where we were going."

Marsha and Julie sat at the kitchen table recounting their adventures while in protective custody.

"I'm jealous as hell," Brenda said. "Nothing neat ever happens to me!"

"You've got to be kidding," Marsha said.

"I think I hear a car door," Julie said, nearly jumping out of her skin. She suddenly needed to comb her hair and brush off hay and dust in her tank top.

Three men charged into the kitchen—Jonathan, Tom, and Paul. Tom stopped when he saw Julie standing by the window.

"Hi," he said.

"Hi." At first, Julie felt nervous, and her face flushed. Her heart pounded so hard that she feared the whole room would hear. Please, don't let me hyperventilate, she thought. It wasn't until she fully focused on Tom that she realized Tom was as nervous as she was. His eyes shifted back and forth with questions that asked for, no, demanded answers. She relaxed.

"Hello all," bellowed a voice stomping up the porch steps. The screen door slammed, and Phil walked into the kitchen.

"Hi, Phil," said almost everyone at once.

"Hi, honey," Marsha said. "Glad to see you."

"Nice to see you home, at last. You're a hero, Tom, terrific." He went over to the kitchen table and kissed his wife with a tenderness that lasted throughout their married life and reflected how much he'd missed her.

"Look, Tom, can I speak with you outside? You too, Julie."

Julie put her thoughts about hyperventilating aside and followed Tom and Phil to the porch.

"Look, I'm sorry to have to tell you this, but I have a warrant to arrest Brenda for the murder of her husband. I was hoping that something would come up when you were in Texas—that maybe George knew who did it. But it keeps coming back to this over and over. She had motive, opportunity, and the means to carry it out."

"No," Julie said.

"I'm sorry."

"She didn't do it." Julie was nearly shouting now.

Phil politely entered the house as Julie grabbed Tom's hand for support. She couldn't stand any more of this.

"Tom, I'm not going to let this happen," she said, dragging Tom into the house.

Phil was already making his official statement, including Brenda's Miranda rights, as Julie and Tom entered the kitchen. Brenda stood with her back plastered against the kitchen cabinets, looking like a caged animal with wide, frightened eyes.

"That is," Marsha said, "the most asinine thing you have *ever* come up with, Philip Swanson. You know damn well she couldn't kill her husband."

"I'm sorry. Brenda had more than enough motives for killing Matt, and Brenda, you had the chance to do it, and you're strong enough to carry it out."

"Marsha's right," Julie said. "That is the most stupid reason for arresting someone. Everyone who knew Matt had a motive for killing him, and if you delve down deep enough, they probably had the means and the opportunity."

"Brenda didn't do it," Paul said. They all looked at him.

"No, Paul." Brenda's voice cracked with emotion. "Don't… please."

"I have to. This has gone far enough. Brenda did not kill Matt, and I will stand up as a witness if it ever comes to trial."

"You? Why?" Phil frowned.

"Because Brenda was with me when Matt was killed."

"That was somewhere around five o'clock in the morning. You were asleep."

"With *me*. She was in bed with me at the time. It's time that everyone knew the truth, Brenda. I'm not going to let anyone accuse you of murder. I swear that. Brenda and I have been lovers for almost a year."

"Can you prove it?" Phil turned his back on them and stared out the window.

"Can you prove otherwise?" Paul's voice rose to the occasion.

"Brenda can prove it, can't you?" Julie said.

"How did you know?" Brenda started to cry.

"I just guessed.

"Know what?" Phil turned back. "What?"

"I'm going to tell them unless you do," Paul said, wrapping his arm around Brenda and whispering, "Honey, it will be all right."

Julie nodded, went over, and stood next to Paul and Brenda.

"You knew?" Brenda looked at Julie. "How?"

"Little things, but go on, tell them. I think it's great, but I'm not interested in what anyone else thinks.

"Okay… Julie. I will." She sighed, sat at the table, and looked at her father-in-law. She looked down at her hands. "Dad, I'm pregnant. I'm going to have a baby. I found out the day before the horse show."

Everyone sat in stunned silence, with Julie holding on to Brenda.

Jonathan glanced at his daughter-in-law. "But I thought you and Matt weren't getting along."

Paul cut him short. "I'm the father."

"Oh." Jonathan was so flustered that he wasn't sure how to proceed. He didn't have to worry. Julie took over.

"Here's what I think happened if anyone wants to know. I think I know who killed Tony, Eddie, and then Matt. Are you interested?"

Jonathan sighed and relaxed. "Hell, yes, Julie. You know who did it?"

"I think so. You've got to understand this is pure conjecture by putting pieces together. I don't believe any of this can be officially proven. But it should be enough for you to stay off Brenda. God knows, she had reason enough to hate him.

"This is so difficult to tell, and it's pathetic. There's a lot of background here. Believe it or not, it doesn't have anything to do with drugs, although they were used as the scapegoat. It was diabolical."

"Get on with it," Tom said.

"Okay. It has everything to do with Brenda."

"Me! Julie, please…"

"No, I don't mean you're the killer. You are, however, the reason for the killings. Matt was a very possessive and jealous man. And he had another quality about him that I didn't recognize until Daniel Smith attacked me. It was in those eyes—insanity. Matt was used to getting his way and usually found a way to get what he wanted. He once wanted to use a research paper from his college advisor. Bruce Warner wouldn't let him have it, so he came back and stole it. It was a paper on how to train a horse to kill someone… using a horse as a weapon." She paused.

"Oh, *God!*" Jonathan said.

"Well, I'd like to hear that story myself," Larry said.

Larry Ortega came in from the outside, grunted another greeting, poured himself some coffee, and sat in an empty chair by the table.

Julie continued, "Matt was introduced to Brenda through Uncle George and her father. They thought it would be a good match because of her father's involvement with Uncle George's drug business and her ability with horses. They needed a respectable cover and someone to help Matt with his business. Jonathan fell in love with her as well. Why not? Who wouldn't? She was an excellent choice for a daughter-in-law. Matt might have loved her, who knows? Anyway, the pressure was on, and the marriage was arranged.

"This was an arranged marriage. Her parents pressured… no, forced her to marry him. She broke up with Tony, whom she loved, and married Matt, whom she didn't. Last year, she and Tony started getting back together again. Right?" Brenda nodded. Julie looked at Brenda and said, "Brenda, correct me if I'm wrong. You wanted to divorce Matt and marry Tony, right?"

Brenda nodded her head, unable to speak.

Another presence was noticed in the room. Lynette had entered and stood with her mouth open, quietly listening to Julie.

"Whoops!" She said, "I didn't realize you were having a family gathering here. Oh, hi, Phil. You come to arrest Brenda?"

Paul was about ready to throw Lynette out on her ear, when Julie stopped him and said, "Lynette, you might be interested in hearing this."

Paul raised his eyebrows, and Tom looked at her curiously.

"Matt got jealous. The first thing he did was to try to make Brenda jealous. He started seeing Lynette. It didn't work on Brenda because she didn't care. So, Matt tried another tactic. Matt was running drugs for Uncle George and decided to play a lone hand, I suspect, without his uncle's knowledge or approval. He set up a business transaction where Tony sold two of Matt's horses to a client out of state. He got Eddie to plant cocaine in the floorboards of the trailer, and then he called Phil with the anonymous tip. The Feds stopped Eddie and brought him back. Eddie played his part, denying any knowledge of the drugs and implicated Tony as the trailer's owner. The next day, they arrested Tony.

"I think what happened next was that Matt waited for Tony to get back, then followed him into the house and killed him with Tony's own pistol. He knew the layout of Tony's house and could have gotten hold of his gun easily. Then, he typed the message on the computer and left."

"But wait," Brenda said. "Matt was delivering horses that day."

"Later that day, he did. But he spent Thursday night with Lynette. She told me so yesterday. Tom told me over the phone that Buzz Weaver told him Matt was late delivering the horses because he had to attend Tony's funeral. Tony had just been killed that day. Matt never attended anyone's funeral."

"She's right," Tom piped. Everyone turned in his direction. "When I talked to Buzz, he said that Matt called, saying he would be late because he had a funeral to attend. He didn't mention that he was *causing* someone's funeral." He became silent, and everyone turned back to Julie.

"Why, though? Why kill Tony? He never did anything to anyone," Brenda said.

"He was set up, Brenda, because of you. It wasn't enough that he wouldn't give you a divorce and that he had another woman. He had to kill what you loved. Tony was a threat to his home life and his ego."

"Oh, Lord," Paul said.

"Oh no… Tony."

"Anyway, Eddie disappeared. He went down to Texas to work for Uncle George. Matt swore him to secrecy about the Richardson affair, and I suspect that even Uncle George didn't know. He worked for him for a while, but Uncle George didn't like Eddie. So, Eddie was sent back up to Illinois to stay with Millie and Daniel. Yes, he was there. It was interesting that when Eddie came back here, barns in the area started being robbed. He was becoming a liability to everyone, but especially for Matt. Everyone thought Tony had committed suicide except for Eddie, who was sure Matt had pulled the trigger. He set up a meeting with Matt and tried to blackmail him. With Matt's money, he could be set up for life. Matt came up with the idea of meeting him in Greg Richardson's trailer so he could implicate Greg when he killed Eddie… to look like revenge and, once again, another Richardson would be set up."

"You think Matt was responsible for the death of two people?" Jonathan asked.

"I think he was responsible for the death of three people."

"Three?" Phil asked, puzzled. "But wait a minute, who killed Matt? You mean there were two murderers?"

"Yes."

Everyone turned their heads toward Brenda.

"Oh, no. No, I didn't. I didn't kill my husband." She stood up and went over to the window, staring out over the arena at the black horse pawing at the dust and kicking up his heels. "Don't think I didn't want to. I hated him. He was a mean, evil man, and he deserved to have his head bashed in. But *I* didn't do it."

"No. For God's sake, people, Brenda did not kill Matt." Julie almost screamed at Phil. "Matt went down to the barn the morning after the horse show to feed the horses for another reason. My guess is Matt was planning on doing something to hype him up. He was already trained to injure or even kill someone seriously, but Matt wasn't taking any chances. He was putting the fear of the Lord into that horse to make him scared to death. That was a stupid move because if the horse appeared crazy,

Larry wouldn't be so fooled to get on his back. I suspect that Matt's back was against the wall after that conversation that I overheard in the trailer. Well, it didn't happen the way Matt planned. Matt went to get the horse, but the horse panicked. You all know he was afraid of loud noises. There was a crash of thunder about that time. I think we all heard it. It was very close. I think it hit a generator downtown.

"Anyway, the horse reared up and caught Matt by surprise. He swung around and got kicked in the head as the horse's heels swung into the grating of the stall. He was killed instantly, as the coroner's report states. The iron bar jimmied loose and toppled on Matt as he fell, picking up blood and some matted hair in the process. Panicking, the horse ran out of the stall and out the back door. His instincts and jumping ability propelled him over the gate and into the forest preserve, where he remained until Brenda and I found him."

CHAPTER 28

They all stared at her, unable to speak. Finally, Tom broke the silence. "You mean Matt was killed by that horse? There is a God."

"And Matt was using him to harm Larry because he was getting too close," Julie said.

"I was planning on riding that horse," Larry said with numbness in his voice. "Why didn't he just shoot me?" He shook his head. "Don't tell me. I think I know the answer."

"Matt was always rough with horses. But this went far beyond rough. Matt scared him when he went into the stall, but the crash of thunder was what sent the horse over the edge."

Jonathan began to talk softly at first, so Julie could hardly hear him. "I knew that horse."

"You did?" Phil said. "But I didn't think he came from your ranch."

"He didn't. About two years ago, he was stolen from my ranch. He was a great horse, beautiful… with all the best qualities of both sire and dam. I showed him in a couple of yearling futurities, and he won each time. I hand-raised him when his mother died. We had a special…"

Jonathan's voice started cracking, and Julie's heart went out to him. She noticed that Tom's eyes were red.

"Bond," Jonathan continued, chuckling through his tears. "He always had an instinct for self-preservation. It's good for him." He regained control, and his eyes looked around at his family, resting on Phil.

"My son, a killer. I don't… is it possible? My brother always was a bad lot… into serious stuff, but my son…"

"Mr. Carter," said Julie gently as she could, "Is it possible that Matt might not have been your son? Could he have been your Uncle George's real son?" Julie waited for an explosion of anger, but it didn't come.

Tom said, "How did you know?"

"How did you know?" Jonathan whispered in a hoarse voice. "And," he said, glancing at Tom, "how did *you* know?"

"I knew because Uncle George told me just before he was going to kill me… but…"

"How did you know?" They both asked Julie at the same time.

Julie looked over at Marsha, and Marsha gave her a nod and a go-ahead. Julie forged ahead with her story. "It was only a guess at first. Everything started to fit together. When I saw your Uncle George for the first time, he looked like you, Mr. Carter, except for one thing. I couldn't place the look in those eyes. Then, I remembered Matt. All your boys looked like each other and resembled you, Mr. Carter, except for Matt. He resembled Uncle George. Then, Marsha told me a story her mother told her about a young woman who came into the shelter. She had been raped and brutally beaten."

Jonathan took over the story. "Ethel was a beautiful young woman when I became engaged to her. We were young, and we were in love. George was jealous, just like Matthew. He and Ethel went together before Ethel broke it off. George was furious.

"He took the opportunity to come up for a visit. When I left town on business, he beat her up and raped her. God help me. I should never have left him alone with her. She never got over it… but we just pretended it didn't happen. She delivered Matthew about ten months after we were married. I thought that I could… well, I just put my head in the sand and pretended he was mine. There was always that chance. I loved your mother, and it broke my heart when she died. An accomplished horsewoman on her own horse, I couldn't believe it."

It was Phil who spoke up this time. "Maybe the horse had some help." They all stared at Phil. "Julie, you said Matt was responsible for three murders?" Julie nodded her head and knew where Phil was taking the conversation.

"I've often wondered about that accident. Did Matt know he wasn't Jonathan's son?"

Tom said, "Uncle George told him. Matt went down to Uncle George's ranch every chance he could. He would have relished the opportunity to engulf Matt further into his empire. The close bond of father and son would have sealed Matt's position. Matt was down there about a week before the accident. He was in a bad mood that whole week and would hardly say a civil word to anyone. I didn't think much of it because Matt did that periodically about almost anything." He sighed.

"Mom was sitting at the kitchen table eating breakfast with me when Matt came down. Out of the clear blue she started to shake. She said, 'Someone's walking on my grave.' It was a premonition. She knew something was going to happen.

"I really don't know for sure what happened. Paul, Matt, and I were out riding. Her horse blew up and reared, scared to death of something. She was caught unawares and fell, her head hitting some rocks. Dad and I had a violent fight afterward, and I left home."

"Tom said that he thought it wasn't an accident. Somehow, it was a deliberate murder. He wanted me to look into it and have it investigated. I flew in anger at him. Everything, every emotion I possessed, landed in Tom's lap that day," Jonathan said, wiping a tear from the bottom of his eye.

"We don't know that it was deliberate, though," Phil said.

"No, not really. But we all thought that Tony killed himself, and we've been on the wrong track in just about every way. Ethel's horse was as gentle as they came. He never hurt anyone and hasn't since."

Larry Ortega cleared his throat, and everyone looked at him. He had the floor.

"Julie, I don't know how you managed to do it, but everything you've said so far is true."

"How do you know this?"

"How?" He chuckled. "We grilled the butler. Tom, your uncle lied to you when he said that he didn't know about Eddie or Tony's death. Matt told George everything he did. Jerry, the butler, had a habit of listening in on conversations. It was his form of entertainment. After a brief but all too intense interview, he broke down and told us everything. It was your uncle's idea to bring Eddie down to his ranch after Tony was killed. He would have bailed Matt out of any situation, even though Matt was becoming increasingly a liability to him.

"When Matt killed Eddie, he called your uncle. Jerry heard the whole conversation. Matt even told him about the riding accident with Ethel. They had been on a long trail ride with saddle bags for the lunches and pop. Matt saddled the horses that day. He changed the girth on his mother's saddle, using one hanging by a thread, and carried her new girth in his saddle bag. When attention was focused elsewhere, Matt stuck the horse in the rear with a hypo. Ethel's horse blew up, and the girth broke; Ethel was thrown and killed. While Paul went to get help, Tom attended to Ethel, and Matt took care of the horses. He quietly switched girths, putting the broken girth in his saddle bag."

A cuckoo clock on the wall suddenly let out its hourly call, breaking the silence that permeated the room.

"Frankly, Phil, if Brenda had killed Matt, I would have arranged to get her the Congressional Medal of Honor for a job well done," Larry said, still looking at Julie with awe. "You—are you a mystery writer? Or are you up for detective of the year?"

Julie laughed and shook her head.

"So, then we've cleared up four deaths?" Phil asked.

Julie took over. "If you believe my theory, I can't prove… Oh, wait, yes, I can." Julie went over to the refrigerator and reached for two nails and a broken horseshoe lying on top. "I found these nails in the horse's stall. I don't know why. I thought it was important, so I hung on to them. Later, when I was in protective custody and couldn't do it myself, I asked Brenda to scout around in the back pasture for this. It turned up outside of the back-pasture gate. When we found the horse, he was missing a shoe, and his hoof was cracked and mangled. I think he jumped the gate and caught his already loose shoe as he went over. It tore up his hoof and came off. Here's your proof."

"So, a horse killed Matt?" Lynette asked.

Everyone turned to her in surprise. In the intensity, she was forgotten. "Can I leave?"

"Just a minute," Julie said. "There's still one thing that I want to clear up. This concerns Tom and me. This afternoon, I asked if you had made a phone call on the day of Matt's funeral, and you said no. Larry tells me he saw you in your car on your cellphone."

Larry looked at Julie in surprise for an instant, then deadpan turned and nodded to Lynette.

Julie was grateful.

"Oh."

"Why, Lynette? Why did you call saying that Ellie was engaged to Tom? You knew that I would pick up the phone. Why would you do something like that?"

"Damn it! Okay. Because… because I was mad as hell at you. You all made me feel so cheap. When you said that Matt would never marry me, I swore I would get even. Did it ever occur to you that I had feelings, too?"

"You nearly got Julie killed," Tom said, his voice rising in anger.

"How did you get the idea to do that?" Phil asked.

"Well, the woman called when we were sitting in here. Your Uncle George suggested I could pay Julie back by telling her that she was Tom's fiancée and wanted him to come home. I thought that it was a rather good idea." She looked at Julie belligerently. So, Lynette was in George's confidence. Another mystery solved.

"Did you call here to say that there was an emergency at her house?" Phil asked.

"No. I only made one phone call."

"I believe Millie Smith pulled that one off," Julie said. "Poor Lynette. You were used in this also."

"You could go to jail for conspiracy to commit murder," Phil said.

"Oh my God… I swear I didn't know anything like that was happening."

"No, I don't think you did. Anyway…" Julie said to the rest of the group, "That's my theory about the whole impossible mess. I delved into your whole history, Mr. Carter. I hope you don't mind too much. I love your family."

"I know you do," Jonathan said. "You're really part of us, you know." He looked at Tom. Tom flushed and looked away.

Oh, dear God. He's embarrassed. Please, Mr. Carter. Please don't say anymore.

Phil interrupted, "I guess we'll never be able to prove anything else, not that I'd want to. I'll make some calls, check your records, and look at that horse of yours again if that's okay. Julie, you're a marvel. Both of you are." He said, complimenting Tom, who glowed from the approval. "Have you ever thought of becoming a detective?"

"Well, yeah. I guess I'm going to play one in a couple of months. I certainly did enough research."

Julie laughed and broke the tension. Then she turned to Brenda.

"Wow, you and Paul. What a team you would be… or are."

"Yeah, we like each other," Paul said.

"I think it goes a bit deeper," Julie said.

"I've been in love with Paul since Tony was killed. He saved my life. He was the only one I could talk to. I could never have gotten through all that without him. I think, looking back, that I was in love with him from the moment I met him. We had some bad clashes at first. We figured out it was because we were so attracted to each other."

Jonathan had been staring out into space. "I was just thinking how lucky you were to get out of this in one piece. What a monster. I'm truly sorry about Tony, Brenda. God help me for any part I might have had in that."

"If you did, it was entirely unknown to you. You can't be responsible for what Matt did. It certainly wasn't the way you brought him up. Look at how Tom and Paul turned out. They're great men, and I love Paul."

"Yes, I can tell you do. And I'm going to be a grandfather." He almost smiled. "By the way…" Everyone looked intently at Jonathan. "That black horse has a name. I'm sick of him being referred to as 'the black horse.'"

"What is it?" Brenda asked.

"Aladdin's Black Avenger, commonly called Lucky, after his survival when his mama died."

"How appropriate," Julie said.

Jonathan looked at Tom and then at Julie. She knew he was going to meddle one more time.

"Tom, if you married Julie, maybe you could all live together and run the ranch as a team. There's plenty of room here. Then Julie could become a part of this family."

Julie thought, dear God, don't say anything more, Mr. Carter. You'll drive Tom away, and I couldn't stand that. Julie felt her face flush and looked at Tom, who stood sullen and withdrawn. Neither spoke. Jonathan lapsed back into an embarrassed silence. Suddenly, Julie couldn't stand it any longer. She had to get away.

"I'm going down to the barn for a little while."

"I'll go with you." Brenda stood.

"No, I want to be alone." She walked past Lynette, who was standing beside Phil.

"Let's go, Lynette," Phil said, nodding from Lynette to the door.

"Go? Where?"

"To my office. We're going to have a very… very long talk."

"Darling," Marsha said sweetly, eyeing Lynette, "I'm coming with you."

After Phil and Marsha left with Lynette, Tom went to where his dad was still silent, looking very old.

"Dad," Tom put his hand on his dad's shoulder. "Your heart's in the right place, but there are just some things that a man has to do alone. I've only known Julie since before the horse show. I'm in love with her, yes. I'm going to ask her to marry me someday… soon. But I must do it alone and not because my family wants her to be part of the family. We have to get to know each other, you know?"

"Give your old man a break, will you, Tom? I can't promise I won't interfere; it's my nature, but I'll allow you to tell me to mind my own business, okay?"

Tom grinned, nodded, and hugged his father.

"Wait..." Jonathan took out his wallet and fumbled into its inner pockets. He pulled out a very old and very beautiful diamond ring.

"Tom, I only dated your mother a brief time before I asked her to marry me. Granted, we knew each other at school and then when she dated George. But still... here. This was the ring I gave to Ethel. She never took it off 'til the day she died. I want you to have it. Go, give it to her."

Tom sat stunned, holding his mother's ring.

"Tom, I'm proud as hell of you... proud of your character, proud of your courage, and proud as hell of the man you've become. You always thought Matt was my favorite. That wasn't true. I was always a little afraid of him... always knew deep down... how it was. I probably overcompensated. Tried to make him into something good. It just couldn't happen."

"Dad," Tom said softly, "none of this is your fault. Thank you for this ring. You have no idea how much it means to me."

"Yeah, I think I do," replied his father. "Now, boy, go rope that filly."

CHAPTER 29

Julie stood close to Socks in his stall, rubbing his glistening grey neck and crying softly. The heartbreak and tension of the past hour had taken its toll on her senses, and she broke down in uncontrollable sobbing.

Vivid images of Matt standing over Tony, firing a pistol at him repeatedly, and other images of Uncle George's plane crashing over the Texas countryside came sharply into her mind. The memory of Matt slapping Brenda at the horse show and then visions of him abusing that black horse slashed into her mind like so many demons. Those thoughts were replaced with the equally disturbing terror of Daniel Smith's attacks. She remembered the pictures of Ethel—lovely Ethel, murdered by her own son. Haunting frames of Matt again surfaced, now with him shooting Eddie and framing Greg. Greg—thank God he was home again in Kentucky. She wondered when his wedding would be. Then, fantasies of Tom came to her. Tom picking her up and carrying her into the bedroom—the romance that had nearly been but never quite happened. The scent of his body and the gentleness of the touch of his hand as he caressed her breast

Tom was such a handsome man with a winning personality. He could get any woman he wanted. He probably had many women he could turn to—women who were better lovers than she could ever hope to be. She cried softly into Socks's neck, wetting his soft hair, until suddenly, it was all too much, and she fell on her knees and cried into the soft sawdust that covered the stall.

"Julie?" Even though the voice was soft, it still made her jump.

"Julie, what's wrong?"

"Oh… Tom, I didn't hear you come in. I wanted to be alone for a while."

"Julie, come on. Please tell me. What's wrong?"

"I'd rather…" she stumbled on her words, "rather not."

"Come on," he said and picked her up, gently leading her out of the stall and over to the hay bales. He sat with her.

"I feel so stupid."

"Okay, that's a start," He grinned. "How in the hell can you feel stupid? You just turned the police force upside down. How in the world can you feel stupid?" He wiped her face with his hands, which smeared her mascara, and kissed her forehead.

"Is it something I've done… or said? Because I had an insane brother?"

"It has nothing to do with any of that."

"Oh? Then just what does it have to do with?"

"Everything." She sighed. "I'm crying for life. I'm crying for Ethel and Tony and for Brenda and for that beautiful, abused black horse. I'm crying for Jonathan and lost relationships and for new ones, and I'm crying for you."

"Me?"

"I don't know if I can talk about this now."

"If not now, Julie… when? When is a better time? Next week? Next month? When we're a hundred years old and can't have kids anymore?"

"Kids?"

"Oh look, I know we've only known each other for a couple of weeks, but I've got to say, after what we've been through together, I feel like I've known you a lot longer. Please believe me, Julie, when I tell you I'm hopelessly in love with you. I'd die if you didn't say that you loved me and didn't want to spend the rest of your life with me."

"You do?" Her sobs were starting to turn into hiccups.

"Look, I've not been such an angel. I haven't had a lot of experiences with women. Some, not many."

"You haven't? Why not?" Her breathing became more rhythmical now.

"Well, mainly because I haven't been serious about anyone since high school."

Julie nodded her head, tears subsiding. She was fascinated by Tom's intensity and finally opened up about his past life for the first time. She needed and wanted to know everything about him.

"I adored Marsha, and she was in love with Phil. But I got over that long ago, and they are my closest friends, outside my family… and you."

Tom pulled Julie close and gently dried her tears with his hands. Then, wrapping his arms around her, he kissed her—lightly at first, but which turned into a fierce longing and intense passion. Tom pulled away first and then got down on one knee.

"Julie, I want to do this properly. Will you, please… please, give me the greatest honor of…"

"Tom, you don't have to do all that."

"Ssh, stop. I want to do this right. Be quiet for a minute."

"Okay." She started to smile.

"Will you give me the great honor of becoming my wife, my mistress, the mother of my children, and my best friend?"

Surprised, Julie sank to where Tom knelt and held onto him while she whispered in his ear. "No kidding? Of course, I will."

"Er… if you want some proper dating time, uh… want to go out Saturday… or something, first… what did you say?"

"Yes. I'd like to be the mother of your children," Julie said. "Besides, I don't like to date."

"You don't? Damn," he said, fumbling into his pocket, "I almost forgot. This was my mother's ring. My dad gave this to me—to give to you."

Julie was speechless as Tom put the ring on her finger. It fit perfectly.

"So, Brenda, let's clean up this black horse of ours, shall we?" came a booming voice from outside the barn, followed by the clip-clop of hooves.

"Damn," Julie and Tom said almost simultaneously.

"Look," Tom whispered, "do you think we could make it out through the office back to the house and up to my room without anyone seeing us?"

"We could sure try."

Julie and Tom made a run for it.

ABOUT PATRICIA A. GUTHRIE

Patricia A. Guthrie is the author of romantic suspense, paranormal, mystery novels and short stories. Her current published novels *IN THE ARMS OF THE ENEMY, WATERLILIES OVER MY GRAVE,* and *LEGACY OF DANGER,* and her short story *WILLED ACCI-DENTS HAPPEN* are available in online bookstores such as Amazon. com. She also has short stories published on Amazon, *Skyline Magazine* and *Affaire Du Coeur* and non-fiction articles in the *Collie Cassette* and the online *Nature Journal.*

Guthrie is an accomplished musician: opera singer, church soloist and music teacher. After leaving the opera, Guthrie became a music therapist in a school for children with special needs and then went on to teach music in the Chicago Public School system. She resides in the Chicago area with her cats, Archie and Kitzy Kitty, and her horse, Dixie, who help her write every chance they get. Pat's an avid animal lover and advocate.

ACKNOWLEDGEMENTS

want to thank all the horse people I have known who contributed to this book through their life experiences, horses, dogs, and kindness in sharing them with me.

Here are only some of them:

Gary "Stephen" Geez and Beem Weeks, my publishers who wouldn't let me—let my novel go.

Bruce and Mary Berg, great friends and "family" who shared my love of dogs and dog showing with me. They played a key role in a major clue in Matt's Murder.

My animals who appear in this novel: Socks, my great and talented grey quarter horse who Julie owns and shows in this story. Annie, my beloved sable and white collie, and my favorite dog, who is Julie's constant companion.

Carol Craig: I patterned the Carter's ranch after Carol's stable.

Dottie Smith: My former riding instructor and excellent horsewoman. Helpful in relating her experiences.

Kathy Fitzpatrick, who owns the barn where I board my horse, Dixie.

All the horse people I've known throughout the years who contributed to the making of this story.

Fresh Ink Group
Independent Multi-media Publisher

Fresh Ink Group / Push Pull Press
Voice of Indie / GeezWriter

❦

Hardcovers
Softcovers
All Ebook Platforms
Audiobooks
Worldwide Distribution

❦

Indie Author Services
Book Development, Editing, Proofing
Graphic/Cover Design
Video/Trailer Production
Website Creation
Social Media Management
Writing Contests
Writers' Blogs
Podcasts

❦

Authors
Editors
Artists
Experts
Professionals

❦

FreshInkGroup.com
info@FreshInkGroup.com
X: @FreshInkGroup
Facebook.com/FreshInkGroup
LinkedIn: Fresh Ink Group
Instagram: @FreshInkGroup and @FIGPublishing

Psychologist Annabelle O'Brien flees from her psychotic ex-husband in New York City, only to find he is stalking her across the country with deadly intentions. She takes a job in the resort town of Lake Nager. When a series of attacks place her in ever greater danger, Annabelle turns to hostile burnout of a detective Mark Driscoll, who is assigned to protect her. Then two women who resemble her are murdered, and the town is gripped with fear. Mark and Annabelle must work together to catch the killer before he catches them. Waterlilies Over My Grave is a novel of psychological suspense about one woman searching for a new life even as she is threatened by her old one.

Lucifer loses his day job, so he starts his own gig. A little girl's tantrum destroys her toys, but will they lash out in revenge? Can a miserable housewife find a new life for herself in a tear-stained old painting? Stories include a snake deciding the fate of the world, a slot machine choosing life's winners and losers, a malevolent fairy dancing men to their deaths, a couple desperate to escape a train station, the dog-show judge facing death, and more. Patricia A. Guthrie offers a cauldron of eerie delights that will please, delight, and yet terrify you!

Elena Dkany inherits her family's castle in Romania, a land dipped in myths, folklore, and the legendary walking dead. The local proverb serves as warning: "Do not speak badly of the Devil, because you cannot know to whom you will belong." When she's attacked by an international assassin, only her deceased husband and her ex-boyfriend's live presence can protect her on her journey to the mountainous region of Transylvania.

But that's not the only problem troubling Elena. Who is that boy invading her dreams? And what really happened to a priceless gem-crusted silver cross buried by an earthquake in the fifteenth century? Who's stalking Elena? Who wants her dead and why?

Hardcover, Softcover, Ebooks

Fresh Ink Group
FreshInkGroup.com